PRAISE FOR WILL

NOVELS

"*Judge and Jury is* a fast-paced, well-crafted story that challenges each major character to adapt to escalating attacks that threaten the very existence of their unique law firm."

— RICK LUDWIG, AUTHOR OF *PELE'S FIRE*

"I could not put *Trial by Blood* down. The plot is riveting —with a surprise after the ending, when I thought it was all over....This book is special."

— NIKKI HANNA, AUTHOR OF *CAPTURE LIFE*

"*Court of Killers* is a wonderful second book in the Daniel Pike legal thriller series....[A] top-notch, suspenseful crime thriller."

— TIMOTHY HOOVER

"Once started, it is hard to let [*The Last Chance Lawyer*] go, since the characters are inviting, engaging and complicated....You will enjoy it."

— *CHICAGO DAILY LAW BULLETIN*

"Bernhardt is the undisputed master of the courtroom drama."

— *LIBRARY JOURNAL*

JUDGE AND JURY

JUDGE AND JURY

A Daniel Pike Novel

WILLIAM BERNHARDT

BABYLON
BOOKS

For my son Ralph,
Photographer, filmmaker, storyteller, and much more
I am so proud of you.

"'I'll be judge, I'll be jury,' Said cunning old Fury: 'I'll try the whole cause, and condemn you to death.'"

— LEWIS CARROLL, "THE MOUSE'S TALE,"
ALICE'S ADVENTURES IN WONDERLAND

"The past is never dead. It's not even past."

— WILLIAM FAULKNER, *REQUIUM FOR A NUN*

CUNNING OLD FURY

CHAPTER ONE

DAN WATCHED AS THE 500-TEU CONTAINER SHIP SLOWLY EASED into port, knowing full well that every member of its crew would kill him on sight—if they knew who he was. But he put that thought out of his head. Because he had to meet them. He had no choice.

His father was counting on him. Even though his father had been dead for more than twenty years.

The cargo boat was surprisingly maneuverable. It didn't need a tug. The wind was low and the waves were negligible, so it had no trouble easing into the dock. Its crew was experienced. The boat had already passed through the port authorities and delivered the official cargo listed in its bill of lading about three miles north. But he was convinced there was more on board. He'd spent the last four months collecting information and it had all brought him here. He was certain he was right.

He had to be right.

A few minutes later a middle-aged Hispanic man emerged on the bottom deck and lowered the gangplank. Huge beard. Tattoo of a heart squeezing a dagger. Solid black clothes. This was the man Dan knew they called The Captain. He'd been supervising smuggling operations for a South American cartel for more than a decade. Which was far too long.

Three other men appeared behind The Captain. Large men, burly, tough. Protection, no doubt. Men who had flouted the law so long they only recognized one authority—profit. They made their own law. They killed without thinking about it. They knew how unlikely it was that they would be arrested, and even if they were, they'd be bailed out instantly. Once free, they would disappear, never to appear at trial.

Given that Dan had spent his entire adult life in service to the law, this was a hard reality for him to acknowledge. These men were beyond the law's grasp. And he wanted information from them.

The Captain strolled down the gangplank, maintaining a watchful eye. He found a midpoint on the dock and stopped. The three men positioned themselves around him, forming a vague semicircle. Dan could tell they carried handguns, probably Sig Sauers, beneath their jackets.

He drew in his breath. Now or never. All the chips on the table.

The Captain was waiting.

He emerged from behind one of several small shacks used as offices during operating hours. "You The Captain?"

Even the smile had a swagger. "You the Bank?"

"I am." He nodded toward the black metal briefcase he held, indicating that it contained money, which it did. Damn it—were his knees shaking? He couldn't afford a tell, not now. He needed to look like a cool experienced professional. The Captain would be flattered to know how badly he terrified others, but Dan wasn't interested in delivering that kind of ego-boost.

The Captain strolled closer, his entourage close at hand. He spoke with a thick Spanish accent. "A few questions. Are you a cop?"

"Do I look like a cop?" He wore a black shirt and jeans, with a ballcap pulled down low, several days' stubble, and a pair of eyeglasses he didn't need. He didn't flatter himself that he was world-famous, but it was just possible someone might recognize him. A few months before, he had put a witness on the stand who was smuggled into the country by a human-trafficking cartel, and The Captain had been in charge of that operation too.

"You will please to answer the question."

"I am absolutely not a police officer."

"Are you wearing a wire? Any kind of recording device?"

"I am not."

"Do you have the money?"

"I do."

"Show it to me."

Dan laid the briefcase flat across both arms. He didn't like how that immobilized his arms, made it impossible to defend himself. But he suspected there was not much he could do against these brutes anyway. He was in good shape, exercised regularly, but that was not the same as being an experienced, cold-blooded killer.

He popped open the briefcase. The bound bills fluttered a bit in the breeze. "It's all there."

"Very good. I will take it now."

Dan took a step back. "After you've shown me the goods."

The Captain smirked. "Do you not trust me?"

He did not answer the question. "After you've shown me the goods."

The Captain waved his hand vaguely and pivoted, returning the way he had come. Dan assumed he thought that was sufficient to indicate that he should follow. One of The Captain's bodyguards hung back to make sure he followed. When he didn't walk fast enough, the man, who was at least a foot taller, gave him a shove. "Move."

"Keep your filthy hands off me."

The man's fists clenched.

"Stay cool, Frankenstein. Your boss doesn't want this deal to go sour."

The man growled—actually growled—like a rabid dog. Probably not smart to provoke a monster. But then again, he was playing the role of a professional black-market organ dealer, and he suspected you wouldn't get far in that business if you allowed yourself to be pushed around.

He followed The Captain up the gangplank—but the bodyguard slapped him hard on the back of the head as he passed. Just to make sure he understood the man had his eyes on him.

As if he didn't know that already. They all had their eyes on him. And they were all ready to take him out at the first sign of trouble.

They stepped inside the lower cabin and took a flight of stairs to the fore balcony railing. Why? He didn't see anything here. No carriers, no cases.

The Captain cleared his throat. "Invoice."

One of his associates handed him a crumpled piece of paper. "For delivery upon receipt of payment: sixteen kidneys, eight livers, sixteen corneas and numerous unfertilized eggs. Correct?" He handed the paper to Dan.

He barely glanced at it. "Correct. I want to see the merchandise. I assume you've used a hypothermic solution. How have you stored it? Dry ice? Liquid nitrogen?"

"We use a different kind of container," The Captain said. He pressed what appeared to be a silver bolt on the side of the railing. Dan heard a clicking sound. The hull of the boat vibrated a bit.

A secret hold. He wasn't surprised. This was a smuggling boat, after all. It probably had a dozen hidden nooks and crannies.

The Captain placed his fingers on the edge of a compartment door. It was dark inside—but he heard movement.

"As you can see, a different kind of container. The original container." One of his men shone a flashlight inside the compartment.

Dan's lips parted.

Eight young women were bound and gagged inside what appeared to be a refrigerated box. They were chained to the walls, barely dressed, wrapped in blankets, sitting in filth. Their eyes were wide and frightened. Terrified. They looked as if they hadn't eaten for days.

Dan rubbed his sweaty hands on the sides of his jeans. *Keep your head together*, he told himself. *Bottle it up.* Even though his heart was pounding so hard it threatened to explode, he couldn't let that show. If he revealed his feelings, they'd know he was not the real buyer.

"You will have to develop your own means to remove the organs from their containers," The Captain said, chuckling. "But I'm sure you will think of something. A scalpel, perhaps."

"This was not our arrangement," Dan said, clenching his teeth.

"It was necessary. We could not be certain when we would make port and did not have the resources for long-term storage. We leave the extraction to you."

"This—was not—our arrangement."

The Captain shrugged. "I will make it easier for you. We will kill them now. Then your people can take all the organs you want. Everything on the invoice and more. I understand there is a market for every part imaginable these days. Even for the bones." He glanced toward the largest of his three bodyguards, the one who had hassled Dan. "Kill them."

Dan drew in his breath, crouched, and whispered. "Move. Now."

Four men appeared against the skyline, silhouetted on the rooftops of the onshore office buildings. They were dressed in black but clearly armed. Someone spoke through a bullhorn.

"This is Jacob Kakazu of the SPPD. You are all under arrest. Drop your weapons and prepare to be boarded."

The three bodyguards pulled their guns out and started firing at the shadows. Dan did a drop and roll, then took off down the side of the boat. Gunfire erupted all around him, thudding into the boat and ricocheting off metal railings. One whizzed past his head, far too close. He had to get out of here—

Something grabbed his ankle, yanking him to the floor. He fell with a clatter, banging his chin.

The Captain had him. "You lied to me."

"About being a cop? No. About wearing a wire? Yes." He kicked hard, pushing his captor back.

The Captain lunged. He threw himself on top of Dan, wrestling him down to prevent him from escaping. Behind them, the goons kept firing and dodging, but that wouldn't last forever. They were massively outnumbered.

He needed to do something fast. He wasn't much of a match for The Captain. He certainly wasn't a match for all four of them.

He heard someone running down on the dock below. If he could just stay alive another minute or two...

The Captain grabbed him by the throat. "You think you can cheat me? You think you can steal from me?"

Dan grabbed his wrist, trying to yank the arm away. "You—kidnap women and sell them for parts."

"Worthless whores. If they save a life, it will be their greatest achievement." His fingers tightened. "Killing you will be mine."

"I—don't—think so." He managed to bring a knee up, right between The Captain's legs. The man winced and loosened his grip. Dan seized the opportunity. He threw The Captain off and scrambled to his feet.

Another bullet whizzed by. The bodyguard who had harassed him appeared at his boss's side. "There are too many of them," he reported.

"Have they called the Coast Guard?" The Captain asked.

"The waters are clear."

"Then we must go. I'll start the engines."

"What about him?" He jerked a thumb toward Dan.

The Captain opened a door to the control cabin. He paused only briefly. "Cut him up. Slowly. Then feed him to the sharks." He slammed the door behind him. Barely a second later, Dan heard the engines engaging.

The bodyguard pressed his gun toward Dan's head.

Dan raised his hands. "You're going to be caught. The FBI, ICE, and the local police are already here."

"Still time to kill you."

"Why? So you can do time for kidnapping *and* murder?"

"Because it will give me pleasure."

Three dark-clad FBI agents emerged from the stairwell. "Freeze."

The bodyguard fired anyway, but Dan had already moved out of the way. An officer tackled the guard amidst a hail of bullets.

"There are two others," Dan said.

The man in the lead disagreed. "They're already down."

"The Captain is inside. He's started the engines."

"He's not going anywhere." The door flew open. The Captain was shoved out the door—by Jake Kakazu, senior detective for the St. Petersburg police department.

Dan collapsed, leaning against the bulkhead. "Jake, this may be the first time I've actually been glad to see you."

"I won't take that personally." He pulled The Captain's wrists back and snapped cuffs on them. "Thank you for your help. That was a gutsy move."

"You promised you'd let me talk to him."

Jake glanced at the frowning FBI agent in charge. "We will honor our agreement. You have one minute."

One minute? Well, he wasn't going to waste it. Dan crouched down and rolled The Captain over. "Do you know who I am?"

"A liar. A weasel. And soon, a dead man."

"No. I'm Daniel Pike. My father was Ethan Pike."

A slow smile spread across The Captain's face. "I have heard of you."

"And I bet you know Conrad Sweeney too."

The Captain didn't take the bait. "I could tell you much about your father."

"Like what?"

"I want a deal. Immunity."

The FBI agent made a snorting sound. "For giving this lawyer info about his dead dad? I don't think so. Now if you give us information about the cartel-—"

"That will never happen." He turned back to Dan. "But I could help you. There are many important details you do not know."

"Like who framed my father? Who really committed the murder?"

The Captain only smiled.

The FBI agent glanced at his watch. "Okay. Minute's up."

"But I'm not done. I—"

Two more agents hauled The Captain to his feet. "You're under arrest."

"I will be out before sunset."

"I don't think so." They hauled him toward the stairwell, but he turned and gave Dan one last look. "It seems I need a lawyer. Can you help me?"

Dan's answer was succinct. "Never."

"There is much I could tell you. But you must give me something in return."

"Never."

"Come talk to me later. Perhaps we can reach an...accommodation."

Dan hoped they could get some information out of this man, but it wasn't going to happen tonight. "Someone should release the women. They must be terrified. And get this scumbag out of my sight."

The agents tugged on The Captain's arm, but he remained in place, staring straight into Dan's eyes. "Let me give you a taste of how much I know that you do not, Mr. Pike." He smiled, but it looked more like he was baring his teeth. "You have a sister."

CHAPTER TWO

DAN STOOD IN THE TINY BATHROOM ON THE BOAT HE LIVED IN, *The Defender*, and stared at himself in the mirror. Technically, he was making sure his tie was straight. But his eyes kept drifting toward the eyes staring back at him.

Who are you? he asked himself, not for the first time. Where did you come from?

And who else might be in the family circle?

He spent the largest part of his adult life ignoring those questions, or at the least not talking out loud about them. His father, a police officer, had been convicted of murdering another police officer. He was sentenced to life and died in prison when Dan was fourteen. Dan grew up alone, isolated from a mother who lost her ability to function and soon would lose much more. He became a lawyer, doing his damnedest to make sure no one else got railroaded the way his father had. He didn't care what the charge was or what kind of person the client was. If they didn't do the crime, Dan made sure they didn't do the time.

He had no proof that his father was innocent. He had a little boy's absolute belief that it was true—but no evidence. Another police officer, Bradley Ellison, testified against his father, and that convinced the jury. But recent events had caused him to question Ellison's honesty—especially his alliance with Conrad Sweeney, St. Pete's leading mover-and-shaker, tech magnate, and philanthropist, who Dan knew was crooked to the core.

He'd taken a few months off to investigate, but he'd made no real progress. Everywhere he went he hit a dead end. No one wanted to talk. Sweeney was calling in favors and dishing out the dough, making sure Dan didn't get anywhere. He knew Sweeney was involved with the cartel, so he investigated it and eventually got the intel that led to the bust at the dock. But so far, no one had told him anything useful.

What did Sweeney know? And how could Dan get past this rigorous and highly compensated code of silence?

He still remembered seeing his father dragged out of the house by the police. He remembered the painful, prolonged, high-profile trial. He remembered each and every visit to his father behind bars. Never once did his father complain. Never once was he angry. And every visit ended the same way.

His father smiled at him, a big, goofy, lopsided grin, and said, "Keep the faith, kid."

Everything Dan had learned during the past few years suggested that Sweeney was involved with a South American cartel specializing in human trafficking, organ smuggling, and virtually every other hideous evil known to man. His wealth supposedly came from his tech enterprises, but Dan thought that was a respectable veneer laundering the big bucks. His investigation of the cartel led to his discovery that this organ shipment was due. The local police and the FBI knew too, as he learned when he reported it to Jake Kakazu. They needed a front. Jake believed they had a mole. He wanted someone outside the force to lure the smugglers out. Dan had agreed to take the risky job—which was why he had been there when The Captain dropped his bombshell.

Did he really have a sister? Why would The Captain say that if it weren't true? Why did The Captain even know who he was?

He glanced at the tiny table beside his bed. He only had a few photographs of his father, but they were all there. He picked one up and brought it close.

Dan was usually good at reading people, at noticing what others didn't, at making small observations that later led to larger conclusions. But he wasn't sure what he saw in this photo.

He studied the expression on his father's face. Thoughtful, reflective, perhaps even a little sad. Intelligent. Gentle.

That man killed a fellow police officer in cold blood?

He just didn't believe it.

He slipped the photo into his jacket pocket, strapped on his Air Jordans, grabbed his backpack, and headed for the courthouse.

THE INSTANT DAN STEPPED THROUGH THE TALL THICK WOOD-paneled doors, he felt a comforting surge course through his body.

Home.

He had only been away from the courtroom for about five months, but it seemed like an eternity. This was where he did his best work, where he did the most good, where he did what he thought he was supposed to be doing.

Since the arrest, The Captain's bodyguards had been released on bail. They disappeared instantly. The Captain remained in custody, but that was only because the judge refused to set bail. That decision would be appealed of course. He didn't know why any appeal court would want to interfere, but when powerful forces with ungodly amounts of money infiltrated the system, nothing was predictable. One bribe was all it would take to set The Captain free.

Which was why this preliminary hearing was being held today, as quickly as possible. Once The Captain was formally bound over for trial, Dan would sleep much better.

He heard a voice behind him. "Why am I not surprised to see you here?"

He turned and saw his friend, Jazlyn Prentice, now officially the City District Attorney. Peace sign lapel pin. Flats. Hair in an up-do. She was a fine attorney, an honest prosecutor, and best of all, despite the fact that they were typically on opposite sides of a case, they were good friends.

"Because you know I'm a model citizen?"

"Because I know you couldn't possibly stay out of trouble for long. Sounds like the sting got hairy."

"Oh, you know. Three guys shooting at me at once, one trying to strangle me. Just a typical day in the life of a defense lawyer."

"Pretty sure they never covered anything like that in law school."

"Thank goodness. Everyone would quit. And then the world would have no lawyers."

"Horrors." She reached out and adjusted the lie of his tie. "Nice suit."

"Thanks. Zegna."

"Of course." She paused. "I don't want to get your hopes up, but...The Captain is wavering. He might talk."

"Worried about not getting bail?"

"Or that someone will take him out behind bars. Hard to know."

"Can't you figure out his real name? I hate calling him The Captain, like he's in some official military service. The rank 'Captain' should be reserved for important people. Like Captain Hornblower. Or Captain Kirk."

"This guy's more like Captain Hook."

"Well, a few more days of interrogation by you and he'll be Cap'n Crunch."

She laughed. "Seriously, assuming the judge binds him over—"

"How could she not? We caught him red-handed."

"Assuming he's bound over, we might get him to talk. But I have to say…his immunity will be contingent upon giving us information about the cartel. Not your father."

"I understand. But it's still possible—"

"Yes. It's possible. I just don't want you to be disappointed."

"I appreciate that." He changed the subject. "Am I imaging it, or is that a new outfit you're wearing?"

"What, this old thing? Give the credit to Esperanza. She's been livening up my wardrobe. She says I dress like a grandmother."

"She's ten. She doesn't know how lawyers are expected to dress."

"True. But a woman in her mid-thirties still doesn't want to hear that she dresses like a granny. So I'm changing it up."

"Points for the ten-year-old." Dan had been instrumental in preventing Esperanza, an orphan, from being deported, and subsequently persuaded Jazlyn to adopt her. Jazlyn told him it was the smartest thing she had ever done. He could see that she was a much happier person since Esperanza entered her life.

Jazlyn's gaze travelled a bit. "Did you notice who else is in the courtroom?"

He had. "Prudence Hancock. Sweeney's right-hand…whatever the hell she is."

"Anything Sweeney wants her to be, I suspect. But why is she at this hearing?"

"Because Sweeney wants her to be." Prudence sat on the back row of the gallery, poised to make a hasty exit. She was a tall, muscular woman with red hair and an expression that defied you to mess with her. "Which tells me he's interested in the outcome."

"But why? He's smart enough to know this scumbag will be bound over for trial."

"Then there must be something more going on. Something we don't know about."

Jazlyn glanced over his head to the rear of the courtroom. "Looks like it's almost showtime. Let's catch up soon."

"Game night?"

"Do I have to play Gloomhaven?"

"No. That's more of a team thing."

"Thank God. That game takes forever. And I thought Risk was bad."

DAN SLID INTO THE FIRST ROW ON THE PROSECUTION SIDE. FELT weird to be sitting behind the rail, but he would have to adjust. There was a remote chance the prosecution would call him to testify, but he doubted it would happen. The feds in particular tended to trust their own, and there were more than enough FBI witnesses on the scene to establish sufficient grounds to bind the witness over.

Jake Kakazu was the first to take the stand. Dan was mildly surprised, since Jake was local, not federal, and the FBI was running this show. On the other hand, Jake was extremely intelligent, Oxford-educated, and had a tony British accent that made him sound smart. The judge couldn't help but be impressed.

Jake explained how they learned about the organ smugglers, how they detained the usual buyer and replaced him with Dan. How surprised they were to learn that the organs had not been extracted from the dead but were still in use by the living. Presumably some women kidnapped for sex trafficking were diverted to fill a gap. He described all they knew about The Captain and his long smuggling history. Much of what Jake said was technically hearsay, in a few cases double and even triple hearsay, but at a preliminary hearing he could get away with that.

The court-appointed attorney representing The Captain did not cross-examine. There was no reason to. He knew his client would be bound over. Asking questions would just preview their defense to the prosecution without benefitting his client.

After Jake testified, two other officers took the stand to describe the shootout and arrest, the collection of evidence, and to sponsor the exhibits—the video recording, the weapons taken from the goons, the photos taken at the scene. They described the young women trapped in the secret storage compartment, who were taken to the hospital for counseling and treatment.

The prosecutor announced that he was finished. He undoubtedly could've gone on for days, but why? He'd done enough. Like the defense attorney, he might as well save the rest for trial.

"Very well," Judge Harris said, bouncing a stack of papers on her desk. "If we're finished, the court will—"

The defense attorney rose. "Your honor, if I may."

The judge's forehead creased. "Yes?"

"We would like to present our case now."

The judge was as surprised as everyone else in the courtroom. "You would?"

"Yes, your honor. I call my client, Xavier Reynaldo, aka The Captain, to the stand."

The judge blinked. "You're putting your client on the stand? Now?"

"Yes, your honor." He almost shrugged. "It's...his idea. He insists. He wants to be heard."

The judge's confusion was evident. It would be unusual to

put this defendant on the witness stand during the trial. It was unheard of, and truly pointless, at a preliminary hearing. The prosecution could not compel the defendant to speak or to preview his case. Usually, they heard the defense theory for the first time at trial.

The judge cleared her throat. "Mr...uh, Reynaldo, I feel I must advise you, as I'm sure your lawyer has already done, that you cannot be compelled to testify—"

"I wish it," The Captain said, rising to his feet. "I wish to tell my story."

The judge appeared completely gobsmacked. After several seconds, she tilted her head and shrugged. "Very well. Take the stand."

The courtroom was not half-full, but there was still an audible buzz as The Captain approached the stand.

Dan threw a glance toward Jazlyn. He could see she was just as confused as he was.

The Captain settled into the large wooden chair.

"Would you please state your name?" his lawyer asked.

"Xavier Reynaldo."

"And why are you testifying today?"

He raised his chin. "The prosecution has made me a most generous offer, in the event that I answer certain questions. I have decided to accept their offer. But I wish to do it in public, on the record, with no chance of trickery or reneging later."

The judge leaned in. "Sir, if the prosecutor has made an offer, I can guarantee they will honor it. And the court will accept any reas—"

"Is there a rule against doing it here? On the record?"

The judge still looked as if she were presiding over a Wonderland court and expected someone to shout "Off with his head!" She took a deep breath. "As you wish. Proceed."

The Captain stared straight ahead, as if he were speaking to an invisible camera. "I wish to state that everything I am about to say is true, and although I have made an arrangement with the prosecutors, I am speaking now because I wish to cleanse my soul. For years I have engaged in..."

If Dan had not been seated on the front row, he would have missed it altogether. Like everyone else in the courtroom, he was mesmerized by the witness. But some subliminal alarm system exploded in the back of his brain when his peripheral vision noticed the courtroom deputy advancing.

The Captain continued in a virtual monologue. "...was forced to do what I did by a cartel headed by two men, one controlling the El Salvadorian end and other controlling the American end of this disgusting human pipeline. These two men..."

The deputy flipped the holster strap with his thumb, removed his weapon and pointed it at the witness.

Dan saw what was happening but reacted too slowly. He shouted, "No!" and tore down the aisle toward the deputy.

The gun fired. The Captain stopped talking.

Pandemonium erupted. The screaming hit a fever pitch. The judge ducked behind her bench. Everyone scrambled.

Dan tackled the deputy and brought him to the ground. The deputy tried to push him away, but Dan slammed his head down on the floor hard.

"Why would you do that?" Dan screamed. "Why?"

The deputy punched him in the gut, then tossed him off, struggling back to his feet.

Jake and some of the other officers surrounded them, but Dan knew they probably weren't armed.

The deputy lifted his gun.

Dan slowly rose, his hands held way above his head. "There are security officers all over this building. You can't possibly escape."

The deputy's lips curled. "They're coming for you, Pike."

"Who? Why would they come for me?"

Another deputy burst through the doors, gun raised. "Drop the gun."

The deputy did not respond.

"I said, drop the gun. Drop the gun or I will fire!"

The deputy turned slightly, smiling. "Don't bother."

"Drop the weapon!"

The deputy pointed the gun at his own head and pulled the trigger.

CHAPTER THREE

DAN PEERED THROUGH THE PEEKABOO WINDOW OF THE KITCHEN oven, trying to determine whether it was time to open the door.

Timing was everything in gourmet cooking, and particularly important for flatbread dishes. You didn't want to undercook and serve chewy flatbread. You didn't want to overcook and serve crackers. But when you opened the door, you lost temperature consistency and wouldn't get it back for at least two minutes, by which time the flatbread would almost certainly be less than optimal.

Cooking was challenging—but in a good way. And a welcome respite from the traumas of the past few days. Focusing on something else, even for a brief moment, was soothing to his soul.

Maria entered the kitchen. Long thick black hair. Trim figure, apparent even in baggy casual clothes. Beautiful. She stood close, but not too close. Closer than she did before they shared that first kiss on the back patio, but she didn't throw her arms around him or anything. She stood tentatively, as if she weren't quite sure what to do with herself. "Smells wonderful."

"Let's hope." He knew she was trying to feel her way around

this new...whatever it was. Not pushing. But perhaps persistently reminding.

"Nice to have you around, Dan. We missed you. I mean, you know. All of us."

He smiled. "I missed you, too."

"Kitchen hasn't smelled this good since you took off on your...vision quest. Or whatever. Jimmy tries to cook occasionally...but...it's not the same."

"He gets all his recipes from the DC Heroes Cookbook. Which was written for eight-year-olds. Super-Hot Dogs and Bat-Nachos."

"What are you making?"

"You're about to see. Stand back, please." He opened the oven door and a rush of hot air blew upward. Wearing his oven mitts, he removed the oversize sheet pan and placed it on a trivet. Eight pieces of flatbread adorned with zucchini and tomatoes sizzled. "Perfect timing."

Maria peered at the pan. "Have we had this before?"

"No. This is my super-special Flatbread Not-Pizza. Ricotta and lemon-based spread, adorned with sautéed veggies." He paused. "It's for special occasions. And special people."

That aroused her interest. "It is?"

He removed his mitts. While it cooled, he would add the chili flakes, fresh basil, lemon zest, and honey drizzle. But that could wait a moment. "Maria, I appreciate how...understanding you've been."

She inched closer. "You mean about you taking a powder just when it looked like we were starting something?"

"Precisely."

"You asked if we could put this...whatever on hold till you worked out your personal issues."

"I need to get my life in order. I have to learn the truth about what happened to my father."

"I get it. We don't have to rush." She paused a moment, and

when he didn't say anything, she added, "Because this is going to be something, right?"

He started adding the dressings. "You did notice that I'm making my special Flatbread Not-Pizza, right?"

"Yes…"

"It's a Relationship Dish."

"It is? Like, that's a thing?"

"Of course. Only for people who are in a relationship. Yet to be defined." He turned to her, reaching out slightly. "That okay with you?"

"Well…sure."

Their heads moved closer…and of course at that moment Jimmy came bounding down the stairs. Red cardigan, bottom button undone. Bit too much hair oil. Loafers. Jimmy was an invaluable member of the team. He handled the legal writing, and he had connections with virtually every useful person in town. "What's going on down here?"

They both straightened. "Maria is helping me cook."

"Uh-huh." He walked past them and took a whiff of dinner. "Oh my gosh. That smells heavenly. We've missed you, Dan. And not just your cooking."

"Thanks."

"But mostly your cooking. Got any more plans for the day?"

"Just lunch with my posse. Thought I might get in a little kitesurfing later. Then back to—"

Garrett entered wearing a Rays t-shirt and carrying his laptop. He was a former prosecutor and easily the most conservative member of the team, but it didn't show in his attire. "Do I smell lunch?"

"You do. Everyone grab a plate."

Dan had almost forgotten how much he adored his team—his law firm, technically. The mysterious Mr. K, who only appeared to them via voice-only Skype, was the leader, but the four of them worked together on almost everything. Mr. K had

remodeled a Snell Isle mansion into their office space—
complete with a gourmet-grade kitchen. He would stay with
this firm even if they met in a shack—but the mansion was
better.

Breaking with tradition, they each took a bar stool around
the kitchen bar. Close quarters, perfect for catching up.

"Judging from what I read online this morning," Garrett said,
"you've gotten yourself into a hell of a mess, Dan. Why am I not
surprised?"

"Because that's the story of his life," Jimmy sniffed.

"I understood when you wanted to learn more about your
past. How did that turn into a sting operation with
international organ smugglers? Or a courtroom execution? I
don't think these associations are beneficial for the firm."

"I'm not entirely sure how this happened myself. Did you
have any idea how pervasive organ smuggling has become? It's a
billion-dollar business. Some authorities believe there are more
black-market organ sales than legal ones."

"Hideous."

"And the cargo we uncovered was living human beings.
Intended to be harvested for their organs."

"Like something out of a horror movie. But I'm not sure how
it relates to your father. Or how it's beneficial for this firm."

"If you prevented those girls from being dissected for parts,
that's good enough for me," Jimmy said. "Hank has told me
about those Salvadorian butchers that claim to be surgeons,
even though they have no real training." Hank was Jimmy's
husband, also African-American, an ER doc at a local hospital.
"Sounds horrific."

"Organ smuggling has become a worldwide problem," Dan
continued. "These organ cartels exist all over the world—Russia,
China, even some European countries. The largest near us was
Los Caballeros Templarios."

Maria jumped in. "The Knights Templar Cartel."

"Exactly. A quasi-religious crime syndicate. How you combine Catholicism with kidnapping humans to harvest for organs is beyond me. But that cartel recently suffered some law enforcement problems and diversified into other operations—like mining, logging, and extortion. It's believed that created an opening for this cartel that was already sex trafficking into St. Petersburg."

Jimmy winced. "Isn't there anything we can do about this?"

"The only real solution is to increase the number of legally available organs. They're in short supply. We should have a global policy of presumed consent. That would increase the number of organs available by something like 25-30%. But only the US, Brazil, and a few European countries have done it."

"Far as I'm concerned, what Dan did makes him a superhero." Jimmy beamed. "He's our Aquaman. As I may have mentioned."

"Once or twice," Maria said, muffling a grin.

"I think you're both missing the point," Garrett said. "Dan is putting the firm at risk—and for what? His own private thirst for knowledge? A vendetta?"

"That's not fair," Jimmy said.

"I hear what you're saying," Dan replied. "But we've hurt the cartel. Seriously. We've dinged it and nicked it before, but this time we've truly done some damage. If we can bring it down for good, we'll have done an immeasurable service to this community. To the world. Thousands of people will be safer. Maybe millions."

"This is a law firm, not the Justice League."

"My father used to talk about keeping the faith. With your family, your community, the people you work with, and the people you love. I think he walked the walk—"

"And paid a huge price for it."

Dan drew in his breath. "He kept the faith. I'm going to do the same."

Maria cut in. She was often the peacemaker between him and Garrett. "We understand completely, Dan. But we still miss you. When are you coming back to work?"

"I'm really no closer than I was before to learning what happened to my father, how the most decorated member of the St. Pete police force ended up behind bars for a murder he didn't commit." He paused. "I just wanted to stop in and see you guys. I kinda missed...all of you."

He saw Jimmy's eyes dart, first to him, then to Maria. "Uh-huh. All of us."

"Yeah. Even you."

Jimmy pressed his hands against his cardigan. "Wait a minute. Is this Flatbread Not-Pizza?"

"Yeah..."

"This is a Relationship Dish, isn't it? That's why we've never had it before."

"Relationship Dish?" Dan said, blank-faced. "Is that a thing?"

"Don't play coy with me. Something is going on here. I can smell it."

He forced himself not to look at Maria. "I don't know what you're talking about."

A pinging sound emerged from Garrett's laptop. "It's Mr. K. Apparently he wants to talk."

"I didn't know we were having a meeting."

"Neither did I." Garrett pushed a few buttons and turned up the sound. "Hello, Mr. K. Can you hear me?"

A familiar voice emerged from the speakers. "Loud and clear. Hello, team. Am I interrupting?"

"Nah. We're just eating lunch. Go ahead."

"Thanks. I wanted to chat with you all while Dan was in the office. Glad to have you back, Dan."

"Thanks." How did K know he was here? How did he know they were all together? K always seemed to know everything about everybody's everything.

"What's for lunch?" K asked. "I'll bet Dan made something wonderful."

"We're having Flatbread Not-Pizza."

"Really?" K sounded intrigued. "Isn't that a Relationship Dish?"

"Ok, now I'm smelling a rat." Dan glanced at Maria, who had her phone in her hand. "Have you been texting people?"

"Perish the thought."

"It would explain a great deal."

"Dan," K said, "I heard about what happened at the dock. And that horror show in the courtroom. How's everyone taking it?"

"The courthouse is closed and likely to stay that way for at least a week. They're scrubbing it down and hiring extra security. Anyone wants to file anything, they have to do it electronically."

"Any idea why the deputy did that?"

"It appeared he did not want The Captain to talk."

"But why?"

"I'm baffled. I've known Dick Ennis for years. Didn't know him personally, but he seemed like a good guy. We assume someone got to him, one way or another."

"Money won't help him when he's dead."

"It might help his family. His wife seems to have disappeared."

"Kidnapped? Blackmail?"

"That's what everyone is assuming. But unless they find her, we'll never know for sure."

"Then we'll never know. What about the girls locked in the hold of that cargo ship?"

"They've all survived the ordeal, thank goodness. Most were seriously malnourished. But they're coming around. ICE is involved, and the FBI. They're trying to return the abductees to the families. If they have families."

"Most won't. Smugglers target vulnerable girls without strong family connections. People who won't be missed."

"I know."

"You might...think about handling some immigration cases again, Dan. See if you can help those women find a place in the world."

"Happy to do it, K, but—just to be clear, I'm not coming back to work yet."

"Sorry to hear that. We've been shorthanded for too long. Still investigating your father's case?"

"Yeah. Everywhere I go I run into closed doors and brick walls. No one will talk."

"To a persuasive guy like you?"

"I think Sweeney has gotten to them. Threatened them. Bribed them. To be honest...this is getting more than a little frustrating."

"I can understand that."

"But it seems futile to investigate. Every lead is a dead end."

The kitchen fell silent for a moment. He heard the faint crackle of static on the Skype line. Finally K spoke. "I know one way to get people to talk. Even Conrad Sweeney."

"And that is?"

"A court order."

"Like a subpoena?" Maria asked. "You can't get a subpoena unless—" Her voice dropped off. "Oh."

"Precisely."

Dan tilted his head. "K, are you suggesting...?"

"I read that Sweeney is opening another one of those women's shelters this afternoon. Supposed to give a little talk and hold a press conference afterward. He'll be taking questions."

A small smile played on Dan's lips. "So...anything could happen."

"But Dan—be careful. You're playing with fire."

"I know Sweeney's dangerous."

"You're right, but it's not just him. You interfered with a South American cartel. If they can get to a courtroom deputy, they can get to anyone. No one is safe. No one."

CHAPTER FOUR

DAN HAD TO PARK THE COMPANY CAR—THE JAG F-PACE SVR—
three blocks away, but eventually he found an empty space.
Downtown St. Pete was usually crowded—but not this crowded.
His destination was near the Dunedin area filled with restaurants and boutiques and quirky places to pass an afternoon. But
he would never have imagined you could attract a throng this
size with a ribbon-cutting ceremony.

"Isn't this the seventh shelter Sweeney's opened in a few
years?" Dan asked. "Why is it such a draw?"

"Slow news day," Maria responded. "Sweeney knows how to
generate publicity. I think he likes to be on camera. The center
of attention."

"Like all egomaniacs. He should run for president."

She shook her head. "Too much scrutiny. Not enough profit."

He slid out of the car and walked to the front lawn of the
new shelter where the ceremony would be held. These shelters
were built with a combination of taxpayer funds and private
contributions, and Sweeney was taking credit for soliciting
most of the contributions. The city had owned this prime

stretch of unoccupied land for many years, so Sweeney scooped it up for his initiative.

As they approached the brick building, the front lawn was already covered with reporters, cameras, and dignitaries, but also many people in casual dress, people who appeared to be there just because they wanted to be there.

"On the bright side," Maria said, "we do want these shelters. Abused women need a safe place to escape. A place to take their children."

"Abused men and women," he corrected.

"Right, right. But abused men are a small minority of the cases and you know it."

"Don't we have a duty to protect minorities?"

"Of course, but—"

"Not when they're white males?"

"Ok, stop mansplaining domestic abuse to me."

"I'm not. I think every woman should feel safe, free to speak out, and every accusation should be taken seriously. But we can't forget that not all abusers are male, and not all men are sexual predators."

"Point taken. Slight though it may be." They filtered through the crowd and found a comfortable spot near the front. "Are we allowed to stand next to one another?"

He pulled a face. "We are in the same law firm."

"But I know you want to keep our...personal relationship on the downlow."

"Just for now. Until I get this business with my father worked out. Till I can be fully present for you."

"You sound like a character in a CW show."

"I want to be the best me for you I can possibly be."

"If you say, 'It's not you, it's me,' I'm gonna slap you."

He smiled. "We can stand next to one another."

"But no handholding?"

"That would seem a bit unprofessional."

"Tickling? Smooching? Jumping into your arms and wrapping my legs around you?"

He tilted his head to one side. "I wouldn't stop you."

He noticed some activity behind the dais. Looked like the show was about to start. He steeled himself—then noticed a familiar female face making a beeline toward him.

Prudence Hancock. Sweeney's assistant. The woman he'd spotted in the courtroom the day The Captain was killed. "Leave, Pike. Now."

She was dressed more conservatively than usual, in a black pantsuit that looked stifling in the Florida heat. "I thought this was open to the public."

"Not to known troublemakers. It's a charitable event."

"I'm a big fan of charity."

She shifted her attention to Maria. "I know he's a stubborn, pompous ass. But can't you talk some sense into him?"

"I don't know," she replied. "Can you convince Sweeney to confess that he's involved in South American cartels?"

Prudence snorted, a derisive, almost pitying sound. "You have no idea what you're messing with. The response you're virtually demanding."

"All I want are some straight answers."

"All you're going to get is a death sentence." Prudence stopped, obviously making sure her words had their intended impact. "You've escaped—just barely—too many times, Pike. Your enemies are done trying to scare you. Now they just want you out of the way."

"I saw you in the courthouse, Prudence. How'd you get the deputy to turn?"

"That deputy was having serious emotional problems. His wife left him."

"Or was abducted."

"His son was arrested on drug charges. He was looking at ten years, minimum."

"But the charges were dropped after the complaining witness disappeared."

"I don't know anything about that."

He stepped closer. "I don't believe you."

"Believe what you like." Prudence drew in her breath. "Despite what you think, Pike, I don't dislike you. In fact, I think you're rather hot. I don't want to see you wasted before I have a chance to find out if you're as tasty as you look."

Maria pointed her finger into her mouth and made a gagging sound.

"But if you continue on this path," Prudence said, "not even I will be able to save you."

"The show is starting," Dan said, not breaking eye contact. "Shouldn't you be up there massaging Sweeney's feet or changing his diaper or whatever it is you do?"

Prudence gave Maria one last look. "I want you to remember this. I want you to remember that I tried to help him. But he refused to listen."

She pivoted on one heel and marched away.

"Brrrr," Dan said. "Is it just me, or is every visit with her like the sudden onset of a killer frost?"

"Sweeney needs someone to be nasty. So he doesn't have to."

"In public."

"But you know, Dan…she's not wrong. You've been attacked twice. Framed for murder. What's next?"

He didn't answer. He didn't have an answer. And thinking about it sent chills down his spine.

The first speaker on the program was not Sweeney but the current mayor of the city, former Deputy Mayor Denton, who took over after Camila Pérez—Dan's former flame—tendered her resignation—and pled guilty to conspiracy charges.

"Thank you all for joining us today. It warms my heart to see so many of you here. St Pete has always had an amazing level of community involvement. We've been through some traumatic events of late. Gang warfare. COVID-19. Political turmoil. But we are good people, strong people, and we will persevere."

A small cry rose from the rear. Planted cheering section? Probably.

"And today we celebrate another great step forward for the community, for securing safety and peace of mind for all our citizens, another Sweeney House for those needing a short-term safe venue. Ladies and gentlemen, let me introduce the man who has made this possible, whose endless largesse has done so much for us—Conrad Sweeney."

Sweeney moved with considerable grace despite his enormous girth. He was three hundred if he was a pound, though he masked some of that with his immaculately tailored white suit. He was completely bald, flashed French cuffs, and wore Italian shoes that probably cost a thousand bucks. Which Dan recognized because he had a similar pair. That he had never worn.

Sweeney beamed, spreading his arms wide as if he were about to embrace the entire audience. "My friends. Thank you for joining me here today. Our city is improving every day, and there can be no surer sign of that than our spectacular new mayor. It's no secret that I had some...objections to prior administrations, and I think my instincts there proved to have merit. But now we have the leader we need, and with his guidance, St Pete could go anywhere. Anywhere!"

Another cheer rose, from the same people as before, unless Dan was mistaken. He and Maria exchanged a glance. Despite her flaws, Camila at least had a vision for the city. The new guy was a sycophant. Sweeney was elated because they had replaced a leader he couldn't control with a leader he could control without trying hard.

"The purpose of the Sweeney shelters is to ensure that every citizen has a safe place to live, to grow, to flourish, and to explore new horizons. In recent years we have become increasingly aware of the threats to our society, threats eating it away from the inside. We must end domestic abuse. We should have a zero-tolerance policy for anyone who strikes another with physical violence. And we must stand firm against other threats, threats to the American way of life, people who don't understand what it means to be a real American."

Dan scrutinized Sweeney carefully as he spoke. Sweeney was hard to read. It was almost as if he knew Dan was watching and made a conscious effort to eliminate all tells.

Maria whispered, "A *real* American? What does that mean?"

"A rich white male, probably."

"Is he reading this off a teleprompter?"

"He doesn't have to. He's smart."

Maria made a harrumphing sound. "Probably has talking points written on his hand."

"But this is just the beginning," Sweeney continued. "We have plans for much more than just the Sweeney shelters. We've been in conversations with the designer of The Gathering Place, our magnificent park network, about Sweeney Afterschool Centers, places where children of working parents can engage in wholesome activities, not just staring at screens. Where they can learn valuable life skills. We are acquiring land for the Sweeney Rehabs, to help people struggling with addiction get the help they need. And much much more. One day soon St. Pete will be America's model city. But I can only do this with your help. Will you join with me to make this city a better place?"

This time the cheering was not limited to the cluster in the rear. He even had some of the reporters applauding.

"You know, Dan," Maria murmured, "if you go through with this, you're about to become the most reviled person in the city."

"I'm a defense attorney," he muttered. "I'm used to it."

As the applause died, Sweeney stepped away from the podium. "I'm afraid my schedule is quite full, but I think I have time for a brief dialogue." Off to the side, he could see Prudence subtly shaking her head no, but Sweeney either didn't see or didn't care. "Are there any questions?"

An ocean of hands flew up—including Dan's. Unsurprisingly, he was not chosen.

An attractive blonde reporter near the front jumped when his finger pointed to her. "Mr. Sweeney, all these plans sound wonderful, but expensive. How will we pay for them?"

"Through the enormous generosity of the successful entrepreneurs of this city. My hope is that we can proceed without taxpayer dollars, using private donations from people like Albert Kazan and Richard Brookings, and of course, myself."

The reporter followed up fast. "But sir, there are reports that you're experiencing some financial setbacks. Will this impact your plans?"

Sweeney waved his hand dismissively. "Simply temporary cash-flow issues. It happens to every business. This world has been through some tremendous economic setbacks recently. But we'll bounce back. SweeTech is as strong as ever."

Sweeney pointed to a reporter on the far left, but Dan cut in before the man had a chance to speak. "Mr. Sweeney, isn't it true that the vast majority of your wealth comes from illegal smuggling activities? And has for decades?"

The crowd appeared stunned. What?

Sweeney drew in his breath. His eyes flared for only an instant. Then the calm settled back in. "I called on Mr. Smith from the *Tampa Bay Times*."

"Yes," Dan shouted, "but I'd like an answer to my question. When are you going to come clean? We don't need rehabs financed by sex trafficking and black-market organ sales."

In the corner of his eye, he saw Prudence point to two security officers. He didn't have much time.

"Many people believe you were behind the courtroom execution of the man known as The Captain who was involved with a South American smuggling cartel."

"These are lies," Sweeney said, his jaw locking. "Filthy lies. Don't we have security here?"

A tumult arose. In the distance Dan could see officers making their way through the crowd toward him. "They aren't lies, Sweeney. I have proof. And soon I'll have more."

"Just for the record," Sweeney said, "the arrogant young man speaking is Daniel Pike, a criminal lawyer who has put dozens of drug dealers and murderers back on the street, including the man responsible for the horrendous Trademark Massacre."

"That's not even—"

"The Pike family has been a blight on this city for generations." Sweeney's face flushed. Dan had finally managed to crack his calm-and-collected veneer, at least a little. "His father was a dirty cop and a convicted murderer. And what a coincidence—the son has been accused of murder as well. I guess what they say about the murder gene is true. The apple doesn't fall far from the tree."

"That's a slanderous lie!"

"That's a matter of public record."

"My father was a hero."

"Only to the underworld. He was a crook who, like you, had significant ties to organized crime. What a coincidence—whenever a new story breaks involving this smuggling cartel, you're always involved."

The security officers arrived. He noticed that the TV cameras were no longer focused on Sweeney. They were focused on him.

"Come with us, sir," the lead officer said.

Dan shrugged them off. "Leave me alone. I haven't committed a crime. I have a right to be here."

"Don't make me use force, sir."

"Isn't this still a free country, Sweeney? Are you using Gestapo troops to silence dissent? Using military force to suppress public protest?"

Sweeney rolled his eyes. Prudence inched behind him and whispered in his ear. Sweeney nodded. "Perhaps I should just end the conference. I don't want a riot. I invite any legitimate members of the press to email me questions."

"You can silence this conference," Dan said, "but you can't silence me. We'll continue this conversation later."

Sweeney shook his head. "As God is my witness, Mr. Pike, I will never speak to you again in my life."

"I think you will." He gave Sweeney a small salute. "See you in court."

CHAPTER FIVE

"Has it arrived yet?"

Sweeney sat at his antique mahogany desk in the enormous penthouse office of his downtown headquarters, surrounded by a floor-to-ceiling window on the east side, Louis XIV furniture, magnificent artwork, and two people. Standing at his side was Prudence Hancock. Seated in the chair on the opposite side of the desk was Bradley Ellison, the man who in many ways was directly responsible for the problem that now confronted him.

Sweeney leaned back in his leather chair and folded his hands in his lap, the position he had assumed on so many previous occasions, a visual reflection of his inner calm and confidence. And power.

But not today. Today it was a pose he was assuming to present the façade of inner calm and confidence, a calm he did not possess and a confidence that was eroding by inches.

Pike set a trap and he fell into it. Bad enough that Pike had hurt his business enterprises, again and again. Bad enough that Pike had thwarted his carefully laid schemes and presented a serious threat.

But Pike had played him. Played on his vanity, knowing he

would get a predictable response. Sweeney was accustomed to playing others for fools. Not being one.

What he wanted to do was slam his fists down on the desk, bellow like a madman, and bash a Van Gogh over someone's head. But instead, he smiled slightly and spoke in level, measured tones.

"Let me ask again. Has it arrived yet?"

Prudence stood at attention, not quite looking at her boss. "No. But we know it's on its way. Shawna tells me Pike has already filed."

"So we can expect a visitor."

"I assume the process server will arrive any minute. Want me to give him the runaround?"

"And have the press report that I'm ducking service? No. By the way, how is our friend in the court clerk's office?"

"Worried. Not liking this at all."

"Is she a threat?"

"No." Prudence thought a moment, then corrected herself. "I mean, I don't think so. You could destroy her life if she talked. And her nephew's life. But she wants out."

"She's in too deep."

"And she knows too much. I told her to cowboy up and stop whining."

"Monitor the situation. If she needs to be eliminated, let me know. At least see if you can do that right."

Prudence looked wounded. "Sir, I hope you're not blaming me—"

"You knew Pike was there."

"I told you Pike was there."

"You did not tell me he intended to cause a disruption."

"Did you think he was there to throw bouquets?"

They stared at each other, eyes wide. That was as close as Prudence had come to insubordination in fourteen years of working for him.

It would sting more if he didn't know she was right. He should've foreseen what arose. But he let his confidence get the best of him. And now there would be hell to pay.

He changed the subject. "What are the allegations?"

"Just as you expected. Defamation. Slander, specifically. Damages to business and character. He's asking for ten million dollars."

Sweeney snorted. "If I just give it to him, would he go away?"

"I don't know. But I know you won't give it to him."

"True." And the sad, utterly humiliating truth was, he couldn't. Not right now. After his investment in the Coleman bio-quantum computing system turned into a giant sinkhole, the sex-trafficking network fell apart, and the organ-smuggling operation was disrupted, he was having financial problems unlike anything he'd seen since he was a young millionaire of twenty. "That is not currently an option."

"Pardon me for reminding you of this, sir." Prudence hesitated. "I don't wish to anger you. But you could eliminate any possible cash flow issues by selling a few of the many works of art adorning this floor."

"Out of the question."

"You would still have enough to float a museum. Probably several museums."

"Never going to happen."

"Dr. Sweeney—"

"Prudence, would you sell your children?"

"Well...no."

"And neither shall I. We will be forced to fight."

"You'll win. I know you will. You always win."

He ignored the last part, so obviously not in keeping with recent events. "This isn't about winning the lawsuit. Pike couldn't care less about the money. He already has more than enough for a small-minded insect like him. What he's done is create an environment in which he can compel people to talk. A civil lawsuit. Subpoena power. The right to take depositions."

"He can't make people tell the truth."

"Does he want to? He can get more mileage out of catching someone telling a lie."

"You can plead the fifth."

"Only by suggesting an answer might incriminate me."

"You have the best lawyers in town. They can spin Pike in circles, file motions, demand discovery, delay, delay, delay."

"Perhaps. But Pike is an experienced attorney. He knows the tricks. And he will make sure any evasion is dutifully reported in the press. 'Why won't Sweeney talk? What is he hiding?' I can't bear it."

Ellison had been silent so far. As a retired police officer, he had undoubtedly learned that he gained more knowledge from listening than from talking. "I have some friends at the *Times*. I can talk to them if you like. Make sure this is reported as a waste of taxpayer money. An act of vengeance by a crooked attorney. That sort of thing."

"Good. Do it. Get it on the internet, too."

"I also have many contacts on the force. I can get the word out. No one will talk."

"Then they'll be held in contempt of court."

"Okay, let me rephrase that. No one will tell Pike anything useful. Nothing he wants to hear. Cops stick together."

"Pike's father was a cop. Police solidarity didn't help him much."

Ellison pursed his lips. "That was a special case. I only reported what happened."

"Part of what happened."

Ellison was getting visibly heated. "I testified about what I saw with my own eyes. I saw Pike's father fire the gun. I saw his victim fall down and die."

"You've been telling that story so long I wonder if you know what really happened. Memory is a fragile thing."

"Not mine. I remember every damn second."

"Let's hope so. I'm counting on you."

"You have my complete support."

Sweeney leaned closer, knowing full well that the overhead lighting would cast his face in shadow, masking his eyes. "You know, in a very real way, you're responsible for this problem that now besets me."

"I—don't follow."

"You created Pike. When you arranged for his father to be convicted of murder." His voice crept louder. "You created this self-righteous crusader for justice. But for you and your imbecilic accomplices, I wouldn't be facing this crisis." He pointed a finger. "I blame you."

Ellison's neck stiffened. "Blame Pike, not me."

"I blame you both. And I expect you to do something about it."

Prudence lifted her chin. "Then perhaps it's time to take off the kid gloves."

"What are you suggesting?"

She didn't quite make eye contact. "The final solution."

"And by that you mean…?"

"You know exactly what I mean."

"I'd like to hear it from your lips."

"I am simply suggesting that if you believe this man, this lawsuit, is so dangerous…then maybe it's time to remove him from the equation."

"You're suggesting I should kill him? Or have him killed?"

"It would reduce the threat level considerably. If the plaintiff dies, the lawsuit is probably dismissed."

"But what would be the fun of that?" He pivoted, casting his eyes upon the Old Master painting hanging directly behind his desk. "Do you know what I love most about this work of art, Prudence?"

"It's a Vermeer?"

"More than that."

"It's a Vermeer worth millions?"

"Keep trying."

"It's a painting most people don't even know exists?"

"No. I love it because it is a work of genius created by an artist in his prime. And do you know how he did it?"

"Umm...oil on canvas?"

"Planning. Elaborate, painstaking planning. That's the secret of all genius. Not DNA. Not talent. Planning. That's what makes a man great. And that is why I will emerge from this situation victorious."

"Because you have a plan."

Sweeney leaned back in his chair. "We'll go along with the suit. At least for now. We will present the public image of compliance...while making sure Pike gets nothing. Let him be exposed as the arrogant ass that he is." His hand clenched into a tight fist. "Then we destroy him."

CHAPTER SIX

DAN LOVED BEING IN THE COURTROOM. EVEN WHEN THE STAKES were enormous, even when he was worried to death about the outcome, a part of him loved being here. It was his home away from home—in a real sense, the only home he'd had since he was fourteen and his entire life fell apart in a single day.

Of course, he was normally here on criminal cases, which most people thought were more interesting, more exciting. Civil courts were just people suing each other, arguing over money. But in criminal courts, lives were on the line. Futures. Freedom.

That might be the conventional wisdom, but today, even though no one was accused of murder, the stakes were sky high.

Maria tugged him toward the plaintiff's table. "Just in case you've forgotten since last time, let me remind you of the courtroom protocol. I'm the lawyer. You're the client. I talk. You sit quietly with a pleasant expression on your face."

"I'm having a strong feeling of déjà vu," he grumbled.

"Did it work last time? Did we win?"

"Technically, the charges were dropped."

"That's a win." She pulled two chairs out and they both took their seats.

"You know," Dan said, "I agreed that it was crazy to represent myself in a criminal case. But in civil court? Not the same."

"You're the plaintiff. You have no semblance of impartiality."

"You're not impartial."

"It's different. Judges and juries expect lawyers to say or do whatever is necessary to help their clients. That's doing the job. When clients act that way on their own behalf, they look like they're buttering their own bread."

"But we're members of the same law firm. We know each other personally."

"The court doesn't know you've been lusting after me since the first moment you laid eyes on me."

He gave her a look. "What I meant was, we work together. We share financial interests."

"No one cares about that. Sex, sure, that's interesting. Money is boring. Law firms are even more boring."

"I think our law firm is anything but boring. But..." Out the corner of his eye, he saw the back doors open. "Some are."

Two lawyers strode up the middle aisle, brandishing briefcases like they were cudgels. Dan knew them both—because he had worked with them in his previous life at Friedman & Collins, one of the largest firms in the city. Fancy offices, corporate clients, big egos. They were Linda Caldwell and Richard Drake, both senior partners, the kind of big shots who rarely made personal appearances in the courtroom, especially for preliminary docket calls. Of course, Sweeney's ego demanded that he have the most expensive lawyers in town.

Dan nodded cordially. "Linda. Richard. Good to see you."

Caldwell did not smile, but neither did she frown. Her affect was so completely flat and emotionless that he sometimes suspected she was an android. Small blue earrings. Smudge on the right side of her neck. Tag out at the back of her blouse.

"Daniel. It's been several months since we saw you last. In this same courtroom, if I recall correctly."

"Apparently Judge Fernandez gets all the best cases."

"You do realize that you have no chance of success, right?"

Dan didn't take it personally. It would be like arguing with Siri. "As a matter of fact, I do not realize that."

"I understand that you want to generate favorable publicity for yourself. I don't blame you. If I'd been accused of murder, associating with a South American cartel, and sleeping with a murderer, I'd probably want to rehabilitate my reputation as well." She paused. "Not that I would ever allow any of those things to happen to me. We don't go in for that sort of thing at Friedman & Collins."

"I don't care about publicity," Dan said. "All I care about is the truth."

Drake inched closer. Skinny. Protruding Adam's apple. Expensive but ill-fitting suit. Like he had tons of money but didn't know what to do with it. "Truth, huh?" He smirked. Apparently he was the member of the team responsible for having a personality, repellent though it was. "Don't forget justice and the American Way."

"I won't."

"Newsflash, Dan. Courtrooms have nothing to do with truth. Especially in the civil arena. They're a way of resolving disputes. Better than, say, trial by combat. Or holding accused witches underwater to see if they drown. But they have nothing to do with truth."

"That speech explains why Sweeney hired you. Where is the big guy, anyway?"

"I saw no reason for him to attend this. He's a busy man."

"He'll have to appear eventually."

More smirk. "Not if we get the case dismissed today."

"Not possible."

"That remark explains why you're no longer at Friedman & Collins."

"Leaving your firm was the best move I ever made."

"Translation: After being kicked out on your ass, you managed a decent rebound. But you're messing with criminals and lowlifes, while we're representing the finest members of the community."

"Is Sweeney an example of these model citizens you represent?"

"Biggest philanthropist in the city. Has done more good for St. Pete than anyone else on earth."

"It's a cover. He's scum."

"Says you. I spoke with Dr. Sweeney this morning. You've gotten away with a great deal in the past, but the line must be drawn somewhere, and he's drawing it right here, in this courtroom. You're going to be sorry you filed this action. And you're going to pay the price for your folly." Drake glanced at Maria. "You and everyone associated with you."

Without another word, Drake and Caldwell crossed to their table.

Maria gave Dan an arched eyebrow. "Classy bunch you worked with."

"You can see why I didn't fit in."

"Because you have a soul?"

He couldn't stifle the laugh. "Something like that."

JUDGE FERNANDEZ ENTERED THE COURTROOM WITH THE USUAL fanfare. He was an elderly gentleman of mixed Hawaiian and Hispanic descent. Reasonably fair, though with a decidedly conservative, pro-business bent. Dan had last appeared before him when he represented Ossie Coleman's quest to establish his identity as an heir to a fortune.

Fernandez raced through the preliminaries associated with a case's first appearance on the docket. His clerk set deadlines for the completion of discovery and a date for a pretrial hearing— which was considerably sooner than Dan had expected, but Fernandez had a reputation for running a tight ship.

"And we already have a motion before the court." Fernandez stared at the briefs as if he had never seen them before. "A motion to dismiss. Before discovery has been completed. Or even initiated. I assume you have a legal basis, counsel?"

Caldwell rose. Apparently she was taking the lead. "Yes, your honor. Failure to state a claim."

"You don't feel any of the statements alleged in the Petition are actionable?"

"Certainly not, your honor. Truth is a defense. You can't run around suing people for stating facts just because you don't like them. The plaintiff's father was convicted of murder. He received a life sentence and died behind bars. Sad, and no doubt hard on a teenage boy. But hardly slanderous."

Fernandez nodded, then turned to the other table. "And responding to this motion we have..."

"Maria Morales." She stood.

"I assume you have a few words to say. Remembering that we are not here to argue the facts. Only the law."

"Your honor, I believe Ms. Caldwell is well aware that our case is not based solely upon allegations pertaining to my client's father. He is sadly deceased, so a tort claim on his behalf would have no chance of success. This case is based upon the false and defamatory statements made about my client."

Fernandez nodded. "Which are?"

"The defendant, Conrad Sweeney, who is not in the court-room today, suggested that my client is a criminal and that he has affiliations with organized crime."

Fernandez pulled down his readers, scanning the documents. "Now that's a serious accusation."

"And as far from the truth as it's possible to be. My client is a defense attorney. His associations with criminals, if you want to call it that, have arisen from his constitutionally protected duty as a member of the bar to provide a reasonable defense to the accused."

"That is how the system works."

"There's more to it than that," Caldwell said, cutting in. "Dr. Sweeney was referring to the fact that time and again the plaintiff has been associated with smugglers and sex traffickers."

"Again," Maria said, "this is so not true it hurts to hear it. In fact, my client recently worked with the local police and the FBI on a sting operation to apprehend four men involved in an organ-smuggling ring. My client was present in the courtroom when one of them was executed."

"I did hear about that, of course," Fernandez said. "Horrible thing."

"Agreed," Maria continued. "But the point is, my client has always worked on the side of the angels. Sweeney tried to turn him into a devil. That's slander. Worse, it's an act of defamation that has had a direct impact on my client's ability to earn a living."

"It's my understanding," Caldwell said, "that her client has not worked as a lawyer for months."

"Which is not relevant in the least."

"We also understand that he receives a salary from the head of his law firm which has not been interrupted."

"Also irrelevant."

"I disagree. If he's still getting a salary, he's suffered no damage."

"Your honor, courts can take into account future damages. He can't keep his job forever if he doesn't have clients. That much is clear."

"What's clear," Caldwell said, "is that this whole case is

trumped-up nonsense conceived for the purpose of giving an egomaniac a public forum to vent his spleen."

Fernandez raised a hand. "What's clear is that there are many factual issues that need to be explored. Dismissal at this time would be premature. The motion is denied."

"Your honor," Caldwell said, "if I may—"

Fernandez gave her a stern look. "I've ruled, counsel. That means you stop talking."

Caldwell drew in her breath. "Yes, your honor."

"Discovery will proceed. After it has been completed, counsel, if you see fit to file a motion for summary judgment because the plaintiff cannot possibly prevail, I will entertain the motion. Is there anything else?"

Maria reached for a folder on the table. "Yes, your honor. Since you raised the issue of discovery, I've prepared a list of witnesses we want to depose. I'd like to present it to defendant's counsel at this time. I also will submit a copy to the court."

The judge nodded. "Of course."

Maria crossed to the other side of the courtroom. "We will also be sending written interrogatories and document requests. We believe the defendant has many written materials pertaining to this matter that are not in the public record."

Caldwell grabbed the list and almost made a facial expression. "Your honor, this is more than twenty people."

"And there may be twenty more after that."

"We will not comply."

The judge intervened. "Counsel, I hope you're not suggesting you're planning a lot of discovery disputes. Nothing on earth I hate more than discovery disputes. I take a liberal approach to—"

"We will comply with all reasonable requests, your honor. Not unreasonable ones."

Judge Fernandez drew in his breath. "Counsel...did you just interrupt the court?"

Caldwell tucked in her chin. "I—knew what you were going to say."

He drummed his fingers on the bench. "So there was no reason to let me say it?"

"Just trying to move things along, sir."

Drake stood. "Your honor, we're aware that opposing counsel has a history of courtroom tricks. Theatrics. Dragging things out. Abusing the process."

"Excuse me?" Maria said. "I'm not the big-firm lawyer billing four hundred bucks an hour. I'm just trying to expose the slander. Which you are clearly trying to cover up by refusing to produce witnesses for deposition."

Drake started to speak again, but the judge raised his hands. "Stop. Both of you. Right now. I will not have this. Ms. Caldwell, if you have a specific objection or a need for discovery protection, you may file a motion. But failing that, I expect you to comply with standard procedures and to produce witnesses upon request. If you can't manage this voluntarily, the court will issue subpoenas. Either way, your witnesses will have to talk. Don't cause unnecessary problems. Be a professional and show opposing counsel the collegiality she deserves."

Caldwell lowered her head. "Understood, your honor."

The judge glanced at his watch. He was obviously ready for this to be over. "Is there anything else?"

"Yes." If Caldwell felt at all chastened by what had happened before, she didn't let it show. "We would like to give notice to the court and opposing counsel that we will be filing counterclaims on behalf of our client. Significant counterclaims."

"I'm sure we all saw that coming. Another defamation claim?"

"Yes, your honor." Caldwell drew in her breath. "Plus tortious interference with business relations."

"Tortious interference? Are you familiar with the law of the State of Florida, counsel?"

"Of course, your honor. We know this is a rare claim—"

"Rarely successful."

"But these are extreme circumstances. Our client, Conrad Sweeney, typically grosses more than a billion dollars a year. A great deal of that goes to charitable enterprises. Nonetheless, the plaintiff sought him out and intentionally staged a public scene for the sole purpose of humiliating him, which inevitably will cause people to be reluctant to enter into business or charitable activities with him in the future. The damages here could be in the tens of millions. Perhaps even billions."

"And who exactly will you be suing?"

"The plaintiff, of course. Daniel Pike. And every member of his firm. Ms. Morales. Mr. Armstrong. Mr. Wainwright." She paused. "And the leader of the firm, whose name is not known to us. We will identify him as a John Doe, but through discovery, we hope to learn his true identity. We believe he is the deep pocket who has financed these tortious activities and therefore it's only proper that he should be held responsible for them."

Maria spoke. "Judge, surely you can see that this is just blackmail. The defendant is trying to get us to back off by threatening to use his economic power to destroy our business."

The judge's eyebrows creased. "That may or may not be true, but they have a right to assert counterclaims, just as you have a right to oppose them. And if there's nothing more, we are finished here. I will see you all next time you're on the docket." He rose, smoothing his robe. "Though I can't say that I'm looking forward to it."

CHAPTER SEVEN

FABIAN FUENTES SAT IN THE DARKEST CORNER OF BEACHCOMBERS nursing his Captain Morgan and waiting for his associates to report. Perhaps drinking a booze brand that used a pirate logo was a bit on-the-nose, but he couldn't help it. He loved the stuff. And he suspected he was going to need a calming influence if he was going to get through this conversation. The drink was not a way of handling stress. It was a way of containing his temper.

Two men entered the bar, scanned the room, spotted him. The bar was not that crowded. Even after the social distancing requirements brought by the COVID-19 lockdown faded, people still seemed to space themselves in public places. He wasn't sure if that was good or bad. He didn't want anyone near him. But the isolation made him easier to spot, more likely to attract notice.

His associates took seats on the opposite side of the booth. They were dressed like Americans, blue jeans and T-shirts, nothing that stood out. The instant they opened their mouths, it would be clear that they were not Florida natives. They needed to keep their voices low.

"Report," Fuentes said succinctly.

The man on the left, the bulkier one, took the lead. Roberto was his favorite and by far the more competent of the two. His cohort, Jose, might be somewhat smarter, but that was of little consequence. This was not a business in which intellectual contemplation often produced benefits.

"How much do you know already?" Roberto asked.

"Assume I know nothing."

Roberto shrugged. "The Captain is dead."

"Not merely wounded?"

"The bullet struck him in the forehead. He died at the hospital."

"The deputy?"

"Also dead."

"Release his wife. Make an anonymous donation for the care of his family."

"Generous?"

"Sufficient. Warn her not to talk or do anything suspicious."

A waitress approached, a tiny woman with blonde pigtails. Fuentes couldn't believe she was old enough to drink in this establishment, much less to serve drinks. But he suspected she received excellent tips. Americans seemed to disfavor real women, women who looked like women, instead favoring non-threatening dollies like this one who looked and behaved like children.

"Would you boys like—"

He cut her off. "They will have the same as me. And I will have another."

"As you wish. Be right back with that." She winked, swiveled, swung her rear a little and bounced away.

Americans. Mother of God, how did they ever become the leaders of the free world? "Tell me about the other men. The three who were arrested at the dock."

"All three were released on bail. And smuggled out of the country. They should be in El Salvador by now."

"Make sure that they are."

"I will."

"And the whores? The cargo?"

"Three are still in the hospital. The others have been placed in a shelter. The authorities are discussing what to do with them."

"Given the current political climate, I assume they will be deported."

"Possibly not. There is much sympathy for them. Sweet young children almost dissected for their choice bits. You know."

"Americans."

"Exactly. They might be adopted."

"They are too old to be adopted."

"Sponsored, then. Helped to assimilate."

Fuentes took a long drink of his whiskey, unable to mask his contempt. "How much do they know?"

"About our operation? Nothing."

"They must have seen something."

"Not enough to hurt us."

"Or seen someone."

"The Captain. His three associates. But they no longer pose any threat."

"They know how we work. How we recruit. How the operation functions."

"They were kept in a dark hold for days. They saw almost nothing."

Fabian wiped his mouth. "I will be happier when all threats are eliminated. As will our leader."

The two men exchanged a wordless glance. After a moment, Roberto spoke. "I'll explore the possibilities and report back to you."

"See that you do. Now let's discuss more important matters. Conrad Sweeney. And Daniel Pike."

"Sweeney is scared."

That was the most disheartening piece of information he had received yet. Sweeney had been the bedrock of the US end of the cartel's smuggling operations for longer than he had been involved. Sweeney was the one they could always count on, the one who got things done, who could produce a miracle under the worst of circumstances. "Why do you say this?"

"He has taken some severe blows."

"Haven't we all? Does he think he is the only one who has seen a loss of income?"

"Of course not. But he may be the only one he cares about."

"These stupid federal agents have cost us millions. Maybe tens of millions, long-term."

"That's the problem. Sweeney can't afford a financial setback right now."

"Who can?" Fuentes's neck stiffened so severely veins popped out. "This is the worst reversal we have suffered in the last twenty years. Not since the days of the Sandinistas and filthy American meddling have we seen such problems. But not because of the federales. Because of Pike. First he removes our operative at ICE. Then he interferes with the sex trafficking. Now he goes after the organ trafficking. Soon we will have nothing left."

"This is just a temporary annoyance. We are still strong. We are family."

The waitress glided back to their table balancing a tray with three drinks. "Here you go, boys. Do you wanna run a tab?"

"No." Fuentes pulled a hundred-dollar bill out of his pocket without looking at it and put it on her tray. "That is for you."

The waitress's eyes widened. "Oh my goodness. Thank you so much."

Fuentes did not even look at her. "I will see you in the alley behind this building." He glanced at his watch. "Twenty minutes from now. Midnight. You will be alone."

"Oh, we don't go into the alley anymore. Not since that guy got whacked and—"

"You will be there in twenty minutes. It will not take long."

"Gee, mister, I don't—"

He pulled another bill out of his pocket and placed it on her tray. "I will see you in twenty minutes. Now go."

The waitress skittered away, lips parted, apparently deep in thought.

Fuentes returned his attention to his associates. "The worst part of this is not the blow to our income, though that is significant. It is the blow to our reputation. Our business partners are unhappy, and they have every right to be."

"What do you suggest?"

"We must regroup. Reorganize. Develop new networks, new connections. We must eliminate those who would defy us."

Roberto's head tilted slightly. "You want Pike out of the way."

"One way or the other." He picked up his drink and finished it in a single swallow. "Our leader's grandfather started this business. I will not be the one who sees it fail. Certainly not because of some damn American lawyer."

CHAPTER EIGHT

DAN AND THE REST OF THE TEAM SAT IN THE LIVING ROOM OF their Snell Isle office. He had called them together for an organizational meeting. Everyone was gathered on the semi-circular sofa, but he sensed he was forgetting something.

Jimmy was pouting.

"Something wrong?" Dan asked.

Jimmy seemed hesitant to respond. "I...uh...thought we were having a team meeting."

"We are."

"Then...aren't we missing a key element?"

Mr. K? A Kandan board? What was he talking about? "What's missing?"

Jimmy tucked in his chin. "Well, normally at these things... there's a little..."

"Food," Garrett said. "Let me supply the last word, just to speed things along. He's looking for the food."

Dan's eyelids fluttered. "Jimmy, I just got back from the courthouse. I haven't had time to cook."

"I would be willing to wait."

"I called the meeting now."

"We could reconvene in an hour...."

"Jimmy." He tried to put on his serious face. "While this is flattering, I don't have time at the moment."

Jimmy raised his hands. "Fine, fine. I'll survive. I just, you know, think it's important that we maintain these traditions..."

This sort of thing never happened at Friedman & Collins. Was he dealing with a lawyer or a twelve-year-old? Well, a twelve-year-old who was the best brief-writer in Pinellas County. And a hell of a lot more interesting than those big-firm stuffed shirts. "I'm swamped at the moment, Jimmy." Pause. "But I was thinking I might whip up some homemade ice cream later."

Jimmy's eyes widened. "The one with chocolate ganache?"

"And almond brittle."

"OMG. That's my favorite."

"Done." He widened his gaze. "I assume everyone has heard what happened in the courtroom this morning."

"Sweeney threatened to destroy us," Garrett said succinctly.

"That's about the size of it."

"And that should have surprised no one. I did warn you—"

"I know what you said. And to some extent...you were right."

"But it is what it is," Maria replied. "We have to deal with it. We need to take this civil suit seriously. Stop acting as if this isn't as important as our criminal work. This may be the most important case we ever handle."

"Agreed," Jimmy said. "I like working here. I don't want to go back to shabby offices and keeping time records. That's so boring. And there's no chocolate ganache."

"Maria is going to take point on the depositions. There will be a lot of them. I could help, but she feels strongly that I should stay out of the way."

"And I'm right," Maria replied.

"I could still—"

"She's right, Dan," Jimmy interjected.

"What he said," Garrett added.

Dan frowned. "I am not feeling the love…"

"More like your ego is getting bruised. But you know Maria's right. She can handle the depositions."

He grudgingly agreed. "That would leave me free to pursue other lines of inquiry."

"Like?"

"There may be people who would be more willing to open up in a private setting."

"I'll start investigating online," Garrett said. "See what I can turn up. If it leads to anything, I'll let you know."

"I'll do the same with my contacts around town," Jimmy said. "I know lots of old people. Someone must know something. A cop on trial for murder had to attract attention. Even in the pre-internet days."

"Jimmy." Dan raised a cautionary finger. "If you can possibly avoid it—don't tell Shawna anything."

"Gonna be tough to comb the courthouse records without her knowing about it."

"True. But I'm increasingly convinced that she's feeding info to Sweeney."

"He's gonna find out anyway," Garrett commented. "If you find anything useful. You can't use it at trial without his knowledge."

"But I'd like to keep my edge as long as possible. What's the first deposition?"

Maria glanced at her notes. "Ellison, of course. His testimony put your father behind bars. Then we do Sweeney. Cut off the head and the snake dies."

"That won't happen. Sweeney's too smart. You'll have to fight for every answer to every question."

"Then I will."

"He has massive resources and a massive advantage."

"I have a few advantages too."

"Like what?"

"He underestimates me," Maria replied. "Because I'm stunningly attractive."

"Sounds like we're all ready to get on this. If you have any questions—"

"Dan, there's one other matter we need to discuss."

Garrett. Why was it always Garrett? "And that is?"

"We could talk in private if you prefer."

That sounded ominous. "Anything you can say to me, you can say to everyone."

"Very well. I read the police report online. Apparently the slimeball they called The Captain made some remarks before he died. Including, apparently, implying that you have a sister."

Maria's head whipped around.

Dan tried to maintain an even composure. "I do not have a sister. Never have. I'm an only child."

Garrett didn't flinch. "Then why would he say that?"

"He was trying to get me. Trying to suggest he had a bargaining chip. Something he could trade for immunity."

Garrett pursed his lips. "I think there's more to it. There has to be."

Dan tried to control his voice, but once again, Garrett was getting on his nerves. "Don't you think I'd know if I had a sister?"

Garrett shook his head. "I don't know, Dan. I just don't know."

CHAPTER NINE

DAN ALMOST TIPTOED AS HE ENTERED THE DISTRICT ATTORNEY'S office. Most prosecutors saw defense attorneys as the enemy. The DAs were the tenuous barricade separating civilization from chaos—while defense attorneys were the chaos. Some of that rep was deserved. The prosecution had law enforcement on their side, which gave them a huge advantage at trial. So defense attorneys used every trick they knew to undermine police credibility. Undesirable, but necessary.

Dan preferred to be respectful to police officers—and then once he had them off guard, drop the hammer.

Jazlyn was seated behind the biggest desk he had ever seen in his life, stacked with the tallest piles of paper he had ever seen in his life. The scene was less reminiscent of a law office and more like the last scene in *Raiders of the Lost Ark*.

On a window shelf behind the desk, he spotted snaps of Jazlyn and Esperanza. Some were posed but all made it perfectly evident how much the two adored one another. What surprised him was the photo in the rear, a solo of Jazlyn in jodhpurs—on a horse.

"You're an equestrian," he said, eyes wide. "An equestrianess. Whatever the term is."

"Just go with—I ride horses."

"How long has this been going on?"

"All my life."

"How many horses do you have?"

"Two. I've had Buttermilk for years, but I just bought a pony. You know, for Esperanza. I'm teaching her to ride."

"You've never mentioned this."

"Oh, I have many dark secrets."

"Really? Spill."

"Not a chance." She glanced at the photo. "I don't get out to the stable as often as I'd like. You remember what Ronald Reagan said, about the outside of a horse being good for the inside of a person? I used to write that off as homespun scripted balderdash. But actually—he was right. It's my favorite spare-time activity."

"I taught you to kitesurf."

"Yeah…lots of splashing around. Not really my thing."

"How do you like being in charge of the office? No boss. No one controlling your hours. Lots of time to…ride horses."

"Almost everything you just said is wrong. I don't like being in charge of everything. I have no control over my schedule, and I have precious little time to do anything fun. I can't even try cases anymore. I have to assign everything out so I can deal with paperwork."

"That sounds nightmarish."

"It is. But you didn't come to hear me whine. What's up?"

"You've heard about my lawsuit against Sweeney?"

"Do I live in a cave?"

"We're going to depose Bradley Ellison tomorrow. He's the guy who testified that my father was the shooter."

"Sounds like a good place to start."

"Know anything about him?"

"Not really. He retired before I got out of law school."

"Any chance he was dirty?"

"That's not what the SPPD says. They still consult with him on cases. No, the one they say was dirty was...you know. Your dad."

"They just say that because he was convicted."

"Who was your dad's partner?"

"Don't know."

"You should find out. And talk to him. He might say things in a one-on-one convo that he wouldn't say in a deposition with a court reporter and a bunch of guys in suits listening."

"Makes sense." He paced around the perimeter of the office, drinking in the diplomas, the awards, and photographs of Jazlyn with two different governors. "I need more information about what happened."

"Aren't all the files and transcripts public record now?"

"The court records, yes. But they don't tell much. Bradley Ellison claimed he saw my father shoot a fellow officer, my dad didn't take the stand, and the jury put him away. What I want are the police records."

"Have you asked the police?"

"Yeah. That got me nothing. I filed forms, they made excuses."

"Freedom of Information of Act?"

"Might get me docs in federal possession, but what I want are the files in the bowels of the SPPD."

"They might not exist anymore. You should file a subpoena."

"Already done. Opposed by the other side. They say what happened twenty-odd years ago isn't relevant to the defamation." He paused. "Which is why I came to you."

Jazlyn flopped down in her chair. "You want me to lean on the cops. To help a defense attorney."

"I probably wouldn't put it exactly that way..."

"You realize I have no authority there at all. You should be talking to the chief of police."

"That's a brick wall and we both know it. You decide whether the cases they investigate go to trial. They want you on their side."

"How would I explain why I'm helping a defense attorney? Worse, helping an attorney trying to exonerate a guy accused of killing one of their own? I wouldn't even know where to start."

He looked her straight in the eye. "Jazlyn—if you're going to sit in the big chair, you have to make the tough choices."

"So now you're a motivational speaker?"

"You know it's true."

She let out a huge sigh. A moment later, she swiveled her chair and gazed out the window onto a busy downtown street. "I'll see what I can do."

"Meaning?"

"I'll talk to the records officer. But only because you're a good friend, and I know if I needed anything, you'd do it for me in a heartbeat."

"True dat."

She hesitated. "And I kinda like you."

"Uh...you..."

"After all, it's only because of you that I got the biggest source of joy I've ever had in my entire life."

He smiled. "You mean Esperanza."

"I do. Biggest source of worry, insecurity, and stress I've ever had, too. But she has made my life so much better. She puts a smile on my face each and every day." She grabbed the phone. "No promises. But I'll make the call."

CHAPTER TEN

Dan had not set foot in the offices of Friedman & Collins since the day they booted him out. He had no desire to return. Just glancing at the long carpeted hallways lined with private offices and glass dividers made him feel nauseated. When he worked here, he thought he was on the top of the world, cock of the walk. He'd made it.

Now he realized he hadn't made a damn thing, except a ton of money, and more of that went to the senior partners than to him. With the Last Chance Lawyers, he felt like he was part of a team, people working together to accomplish some good in the world. These stiffs in their identical suits were more antagonists than teammates, and their only goal was the perpetuation of a system that allowed them to buy those expensive suits.

Or so it seemed to him this morning. Maybe the fact that he was about to be confronted with the man whose testimony put his father behind bars might have something to do with his negative attitude.

"Remember," Maria said, as the receptionist escorted them to a corner conference room, "your job today is to be pleasant and not speak aloud. To anyone."

"They will speak to me," he replied.

"Ok, you can say, 'Hello,' 'Thank you,' and 'Good to see you.' That's it."

He nodded. "I understand that you're taking the deposition. Not me."

"Good. You have a right to be here, but you do not have the right to ask questions, harass, threaten, growl, intimidate, or even display a cross expression."

"That seems a bit restrictive..."

"These big-firm lawyers are experts in delay. They almost always represent defendants and they know time is on their side. The longer they can delay judgment, the longer their clients hold onto their money. I guarantee that if you misbehave, they'll terminate the deposition and we'll all be in court arguing about it, which will make Judge Fernandez angry and will slow down the case. Discovery is important, but I assume that at some point you'd like to get to the actual trial."

"True."

"So keep your mouth shut."

The receptionist opened the door to the conference room. He was not surprised to find Caldwell was already there, comfortably situated on the far side of the table. Drake sat beside her. The court reporter was on the other end of the table with her stenotype.

And between them, Bradley Ellison. The man whose testimony put his father behind bars. Tall. Aging well. Still fit. Immaculate nails, like he'd had a manicure. Buzzcut. Gray looked good on him.

Exactly how he imagined his own father would look today. If he hadn't died in prison.

Dan had interviewed Ellison once before about the Ossie Coleman inheritance, but the entire time they discussed that case, his father was the elephant in the room. Dan only recalled two things Ellison said. "I always liked your daddy" and "I told the truth."

Today, they would put both of those statements to the test.

The conference room was designed for larger gatherings, but Dan knew this was the most impressive meeting place F&C had, which was probably why it had been chosen. Artwork by notable local talents lined the walls. A refrigerator bar in one corner contained every kind of non-alcoholic drink imaginable. The chairs were plush and the table shone like a polished diamond.

Caldwell stood. "Good morning. Would you like coffee? Something to drink?" As always, her tone was flat, devoid of emotion. Like an AI bot that had learned it was traditional to offer beverages to visitors.

"I'd kill for some coffee," Maria said.

"That will not be necessary. Mr. Pike?"

"I'm good, thanks."

Caldwell walked to the corner and poured. The cup and saucer were Royal Albert bone china. Lady Carlyle, if he recalled correctly.

Maria drank the entire cup in a single swallow. "Oh, that's good. Pike Place?"

Drake grinned. "You have a discerning palate."

"For coffee. Other than that, I'm a simple girl."

"Ha. I've seen how you dress. I've seen you function in court. You're far from simple." Drake glanced at Dan, then back at her. "You would fit in here at F&C very nicely."

Dan tried not to choke. Was this man flirting with her? Tempting her?

Maria looked surprised and flattered. "Me? In this marbleized mausoleum?"

"We need more experienced litigators."

"Is that it? I thought maybe you needed to increase your diversity portfolio."

"It wouldn't hurt."

"Thanks for the offer, but I'm happy where I am. I assume this is the witness." She nodded in Ellison's direction.

"Bradley Ellison." He leaned forward and extended his hand. He looked uncomfortable, stuffed in a suit. It was much easier to imagine him in a police uniform, or perhaps since he was retired, in Bermuda shorts. "Mr. Pike and I have met."

Maria shook his hand. Dan did not.

"And you must be our court reporter. I don't think we've met." Which was not unusual, since they handled far more criminal cases than civil, and depositions didn't exist in the criminal world. In the courtroom, judges kept their own reporters.

"I'm Marjorie McKnight," the woman replied. She appeared to be in her early thirties. Small tattoo on the inside of her left wrist. Hoop earrings. Designer shoes, more expensive than the ones he was wearing. "I'm new to St. Petersburg. Moved a few weeks ago from Manhattan."

"Why Florida?"

"My boyfriend wanted to go someplace warmer. We both decided we had to get out of New York. I love the city, the theater, the fact that you can walk everywhere. But after the COVID-19 panic—it wasn't the same place. White semis filled with bodies trolling down the street with a police escort. So many people in our church sick or dead. I used to think all the city noise was annoying, but after the lockdown, every night was eerily quiet. Even after the situation improved, it didn't feel the same. I had to get out of there to stay sane."

"We had the lockdown here too, and it was bad—but I think New York had it worse than anyone."

"We're starting over, and so far, everything has gone well. I've had to learn to drive—but there are worse things than being able to go to the beach every day."

"No doubt."

Caldwell cleared her throat. "If everyone is ready to begin, let's go on the record."

Marjorie sat up straight and poised her fingers above her stenotype. "This is the deposition of Bradley Ellison." She recited the date, location, and parties present.

Caldwell nodded. "The usual stipulations?"

Maria had almost answered "Yes" when Dan cut in. "What are the usual stipulations?"

Caldwell peered at him for a moment. "In civil depositions, it's traditional—"

"I've taken lots of depositions. But we should specify exactly what the stipulations are going to be."

If it was possible to discombobulate an android, he had managed it. "The...most important stipulation is that we reserve objections till the time of trial."

"We won't agree to that."

Maria turned to look at him. No psychic powers were necessary to detect her annoyance. "It would certainly speed things along, Dan. I can still make a motion to strike—"

"I know these people. It's a bad idea."

Caldwell appeared perplexed. "This is standard procedure, and it benefits all parties equally. May I ask the nature of your objection?"

"Give you people any rope, and you'll find a way to turn it into a noose."

"And when you say, 'you people,' you mean..."

Dan tried to suppress his sneer. "The kind of people who would represent him." His head jerked toward Ellison.

"Actually, we don't represent Mr. Ellison. We represent the defendant, Conrad Sweeney."

"Even worse." Out the corner of his eye, he saw Maria glaring at him. He knew why. He was behaving with an appalling lack of professional courtesy, letting his feelings interfere with his common sense. And he had no excuse for it.

No strategic ulterior motive. He was just not thinking straight.

He was doing everything Garrett accused him of.

Maria launched into the deposition. Ellison's answers were short and precise. He always answered the question, but he added nothing extraneous. No rambling. No attempts to defend himself or win over the questioner. He answered like a police officer on the witness stand, which was not surprising. That was how he had been trained.

"We received a call about a disturbance on the Southside, near where the International Imports offices are today," he explained.

"What was the nature of the call?"

"Someone reported hearing gunfire. As it turned out, there was a shootout in progress. A gang war. Blacks versus Hispanics."

"Who started it?"

"I don't know." Attorneys typically cautioned deposition witnesses that if they weren't sure about the answer or couldn't remember, simply say so. Don't be bullied into giving an answer you might regret later. Depositions were not taken just to obtain information. They were also taken to make a record. If a witness's testimony at trial differed from what they said at a deposition, the transcript could be read to the jury to impeach the witness. "This was more than twenty years ago, after all."

"You must have some recollection of what was going on and why."

"I was simply following orders. I was a young lieutenant at the time, still in uniform, still patrolling a regular beat. I did what I was told."

"Who else went to the shootout?"

"Every available officer."

"Do you recall any specific names?"

Ellison glanced at Drake. He nodded slightly. "I knew everybody there, but the two most relevant to this case were Ethan Pike—the plaintiff's father. And Jack Fisher—the man he murdered."

"Move to strike," Dan said, a heartbeat later.

Maria drew in her breath. "What he said. But we'll get back to that in a minute. Let's hear this story in chronological order. You and the other officers went out to investigate the shooting. What happened next?"

"I can't agree to the word 'investigate,'" Ellison said. "There was nothing to investigate. By the time we arrived, the shootout was in progress. Two gangs were holed up on opposite sides of a basketball court. Some failed attempt at urban renewal, to give kids a safe place to go after school. Now it was a war zone. One gang was holed up behind a stone dugout. A storage shed for sports equipment. The other gang holed up behind a couple of trash bins. And we drove right into the middle of it."

"What happened then?"

"Exactly what you would expect. Both sides started shooting at the cops."

"What did you do next?"

"Four squad cars arrived at almost the same time. I drove one. Ethan drove one. Jack drove another. We came in with sirens wailing, but it didn't scare anyone off. A bullet hit my windshield before I had even stopped the car."

This sounded intense. A tiny voice inside Dan told him he should be feeling some sympathy. But he didn't.

"What did you do next?"

"I slid out, crouching behind the car door for cover. Almost immediately I felt bullets impact the door. Fortunately, they are reinforced. They will stop bullets, at least up to a point. Since I arrived first, I got out my bullhorn, identified myself, and told them to stand down." He paused. "No one did."

"Were you following standard procedures?"

Ellison made a disgusted sound. "There is no standard

procedure for a situation like this. None of us had ever experienced anything like it. I served overseas. I was a Navy Seal. But this was the worst scrape I've ever been in. I still have nightmares about it."

Maria glanced at Dan. He could be wrong, but he had the feeling she was asking for permission to go easier on him, given the circumstances. Permission was not granted.

"What did you do next?"

"The only thing I could do. I started firing back. This was an absolute nightmare. You can't imagine. Bullets flying in every possible direction. It became clear quickly that they were much better equipped and armed than we were. They were never going to run out of ammunition—at least not until long after we did. We were sitting ducks."

"But you returned fire."

"I wasn't trying to hit anyone. Frankly, I couldn't see well enough to hit anyone. I was laying down cover, trying to blanket a wide area, hoping to defuse a bad situation."

"Anything else?"

"I called for reinforcements. Told them we were desperate and they needed to send more officers. Even if they had to bring them from another jurisdiction. Or county. Even if it was the National Guard. We needed backup in the worst possible way."

"Did they comply?"

"The Chief said he'd see what he could do. You can imagine how much better that made me feel."

"Did help arrive?"

"Eventually. But we were on our own for twenty-three minutes, and let me tell you, that was the longest twenty-three minutes of my life. Before or since."

"How did you stay alive?"

"I kept firing, but judiciously. And I stayed behind the door. Ethan and Jack raced behind their vehicles to cover our rear flank, make sure no one came up on us from behind."

"You were wounded at one point, correct?"

"Damn straight." Ellison suddenly looked embarrassed. "Uh, pardon my language, ma'am."

"It's quite all right."

"Leaned out too far, trying to lay down some cover for my fellow officers. Took one right here." He rubbed his left shoulder. "Healed up, but I still have an impingement. Shoulder blade cuts into the tendon when I extend my arm too far."

"How do you deal with that?"

He grinned slightly. "I don't stretch my arm out too far."

"Could you see what the other officers were doing?"

"Sometimes. We could communicate by radio."

"I believe one of your fellow officers went down."

Caldwell cut in. "Is that a question?"

"Pardon me. Were any of your fellow officers hurt?"

"Yeah. And I still blame myself for that."

Caldwell cut in again. "I will caution the witness against making any statements that could be misunderstood as self-incriminating. You have the right to assert your Fifth Amendment privileges at any time. Including during a deposition."

"It's ok. I did what I did."

Maria tried to recover the thread. "Was anyone hurt?"

"Yeah. Jack. Killed dead."

"I would imagine that in the midst of this chaos, it would be difficult to know where the bullet came from."

"That's what your client's pappy was hoping for."

"Move to strike," Maria said, before Dan had a chance. "I will ask the witness to restrict his testimony to what he saw and heard, without speculating on the motives of deceased persons which cannot possibly be known."

"I saw the whole thing," Ellison said.

"Please describe what you saw. Only what you saw."

"Ethan and Jack were behind me and several feet to the right, but I could see Ethan in my driver's side mirror. I could see Jack if I stretched a bit, but as you can probably imagine, I didn't do much of that. I saw Ethan raise his weapon. And he wasn't pointing toward the gangs. He was pointing toward the neighboring cop car."

"Who was there?"

"Only one person. Jack Fisher."

"Did you see Ethan Pike fire his weapon?"

"I did. And I saw Jack fall, right then and there."

"Do you believe Ethan Pike killed Jack Fisher?"

"I know he did."

"You believe that, in the midst of a deadly confrontation with rival gangs, one police officer killed a fellow officer."

"A fellow officer who used to be married to Ethan's wife."

Maria's lips parted.

"Didn't know that, huh? Yeah, Jack and Alice were married, and he didn't treat her too good, either. But some women like the bad boys. Locker room gossip said she'd been seen with Jack again recently, despite being remarried and having this boy who's sitting at the table with us now."

Maria looked at Dan, asking the obvious question.

He answered, nonverbally, but with crystal clarity. He did not know this.

"Ethan wanted Jack dead, and all in all, I can't say that I blame him. Jack was a hothead with a foul tongue. Nasty piece of work. Ethan saw a chance to take Jack out, a time when everyone would assume Jack was an unfortunate victim of this hellacious crossfire. Probably would've gotten away with it, too, if I hadn't been looking in just the right place at just the right time."

"So you testified against a fellow officer. The one you'd been through hell and back with."

"What choice did I have? Can't say that I enjoyed it. But Jack was my colleague too, even if he was a complete bastard."

"I still—"

"Ma'am, I mean no disrespect, but you just don't get it. I'm a police officer. That's who I am. Retired now, but still at heart one of the boys in uniform. I have a duty. Serve and protect. I witnessed a murder. I had to speak up. There was no choice about it."

Dan leaned forward. "You had a choice. You made the wrong one."

"I don't fault you for sticking up for your pa, son. But I saw what I saw."

"Would you be willing to take a polygraph?"

Caldwell jumped in. "Polygraphs are unreliable and we would not advise—"

Ellison cut her off. "Been there, done that. Years ago. I took a polygraph a few days after it all went down. I'm sure you can find the report somewhere. I took the test and I passed. I'm sorry to be the one who tells you, son. I know this has stuck in your craw for a long time. But the facts are the facts. Your father killed Jack Fisher. In cold blood."

CHAPTER ELEVEN

CONRAD SWEENEY DRUMMED A THEME FROM RIMSKY-KORSAKOV'S *Scheherazade* on his desktop. He was anxious and he knew it. This increasing discontent was new to him and he was not entirely sure how to deal with it. He didn't recall ever feeling like this before. Even when he had been poor—and that was a long time ago—he did not recall feeling the same unease. Something was eating away at him. And he needed to get it under control. He had too much at risk to suffer any distractions.

Normally being in his office, this expansive penthouse suite, filled him with an inner calm, a sense of his accomplishment. But not anymore. Now he had this stupid trial to deal with. He was being played by Pike and that cut him like a sharp knife with a serrated blade. He *refused* to be anyone's pawn—

Did he actually almost slam his fist down on the desk?

He needed to do something. Some kind of distraction.

He picked up his smartphone and texted Prudence. STATUS

The reply was immediate. DEPO DONE

AND THE WOMAN?

SHE'S PARKING

BRING HER UP ASAP

UNDERSTOOD

While he waited, he dialed his lawyers. Drake answered. "How was the deposition?"

"Nothing to worry about. And no reason for you to be there."

Not that there was a chance he would give Pike that pleasure. "Did Ellison toe the line?"

"Said what we expected. Held up his end."

"Told Pike he watched his father execute another officer?"

"Precisely."

"Any discussion of cartels or smuggling?"

"None at all."

"Good. Let's keep it that way. Anything I need to know about?"

"I'm telling you, it went without a hitch, sir. No problems. Perfect."

This man might be an ace in the courtroom, but he was a moron in life. He had no sense of what was really going on here. Sweeney wanted the best firm in the city backing him, but he was beginning to wonder if Drake's cluelessness made him an asset or a liability. "There is no such thing."

"Excuse me?"

"No such thing as perfect. Or a perfect deposition, for that matter."

"Well...Ellison did mention that he saw Officer Pike pull the trigger—in his outside car mirror. I thought he'd seen it directly, with his own eyes. But it doesn't matter."

"Don't be an idiot. Of course it matters."

"What matters is that he saw Pike pull the trigger. And an instant later, Fisher went down."

Hmm. That could be improved. "What do you think they'll do next?"

"Take more pointless depositions. Run up the tab."

"There is no tab to run up, you imbecile. Do you think the

firm is going to send one of their partners a bill? These people don't even bill their usual clients."

Drake's voice wavered. "I know they want a lot of depos. And documents."

"But they also want to be in court as soon as possible."

"True."

"Drag your heels. Any way possible. Buy me time."

"I hear what you're saying, Dr. Sweeney, but you know, there are ethical—"

"Don't give me that crap. I know what you are. Delay. Working at a snail's pace should come naturally to you."

"Well, I'll see—"

Sweeney disconnected the line. That call was a mistake. Now he was more agitated than before.

He heard the private elevator arrive. Heard some murmuring. Probably his guest rubbernecking the paintings. Prudence wouldn't allow much of that. She knew he was anxious.

A few moments later Prudence led in their guest, who gawked and gazed as if she were on a tour of the Sistine Chapel. Actually, he much preferred his office to the Chapel. No crowds, and let's be honest, Michelangelo was a better sculptor than painter.

He did not rise. "Please take a seat."

Marjorie McKnight lowered herself into the indicated chair.

"I understand the first deposition is complete."

McKnight nodded. She seemed nervous—a bit hyper. "Yes. What a creepshow that was. I never heard so much arguing at a deposition."

"Did the witness hold up?"

"Absolutely. Stood his ground. He saw that guy's dad fire the gun."

"How did Mr. Pike react to the news?"

"Pretty cool, on the whole. He made a little noise, but not

that much. If I'd heard someone accuse my daddy of murder, I'd have been a lot louder."

"He's heard it before. Many times before. Grew up with it. Made him the fighter he is today." Sweeney paused, staring at his hands on the desktop. "And the lady lawyer?"

"Maria? Supercool. I like her."

His chin lowered. "And when you say you like her...?"

"I'm just saying she's a pro. Even though I know she didn't like what she heard, she didn't let it faze her. Kept her client in check too, which took some doing."

"And they bought your cover story?"

"Oh yeah. No problems there."

Prudence cut in. "No one asked how you financed the journey? No one asked how a newbie court reporter happened to be working for Friedman & Collins?"

"Nope. No suspicions."

"The fact that no one asked does not mean there were no suspicions," Sweeney said. "You're not wearing a ring."

"True."

"You claimed to be married. But you're not wearing a ring."

"I don't think anyone noticed."

"Pike noticed."

"How can you—"

"I know." He and Prudence exchanged a frown.

"Some women are resisting the ring these days," Prudence suggested. "They say it's like wearing a dog collar. A badge of ownership."

"Fine. That's your story," Sweeney said. "If someone asks, you resisted the ring because—" He chuckled out loud. "Because you're a fiercely independent feminist."

"I can do that." Marjorie paused. "If I may ask, do you remember what you promised?"

"About the rest of your family? Your sister? Your parents?"

"I really want them off Staten Island. I don't think they're safe. And I miss them."

"When our business is completed—to my satisfaction—I'll make the arrangements."

"Thank you, sir. I appreciate it."

"But I will expect much more from you in return."

She appeared confused. "I—I thought I was already reporting and—"

"Apparently Mr. Ellison made some foolhardy comments about witnessing the murder through a car mirror, rather than seeing it directly."

"True. But he still—"

"I would like those remarks to disappear."

A sudden silence descended. "Sir, I can't—"

"Of course you can. Are you saying you won't?"

"I—I—the lawyers. They'll remember."

"But they won't be able to prove anything."

"Ellison will remember."

"He'll only remember what I want him to remember."

"They'll know it was me."

"Maybe. But they won't be able to do anything about it. And your family will be safe. Isn't that what matters?"

"If word got out, no one would hire me to—"

"Friedman & Collins will offer you a ten-year employment contract. Payment guaranteed. After a sabbatical starting whenever the depositions are completed and ending after the trial is over. Any other objections?"

She swallowed hard. "I guess not."

"Good." He steepled his fingers before his face. He was feeling better already.

"Dr. Sweeney," Prudence said, "I think it might be good if I sat in on the remaining depositions. As your personal representative."

"Thank you for volunteering. That's an excellent idea. As always, I am indebted to you for your service."

"Always, sir. Is there anything else I could do for you?"

"Yes. I think we should initiate some investigations of our own. Maybe use Ellison. Maybe not, if you think he's too involved to be objective."

"What do you want to know?"

"More about this pack of losers who call themselves the Last Chance Lawyers. We've investigated Pike, but what about this Maria our friend here is so fond of? What about the researcher? The brief writer? I'm willing to bet they all have secrets."

"Everyone does. If you dig deep enough."

"And what about the mysterious Mr. K, the deep pocket who finances this operation?"

"I thought you already knew—"

"I want to know everything."

Prudence nodded. "Specifically?"

"I want to know how to shut down the money pipeline. If we could persuade Mr. K to stop bankrolling this insane excuse for a law firm, all our other problems might evaporate like raindrops on a sunny day."

"I will get right on it, sir."

"Spare no expense. And spare no feelings. We're playing for keeps." His eyes narrowed. "We've toyed and parried with Daniel Pike long enough. We have the means to finish him. Let's drive a stake into his heart and twist it hard. And this time, he will not rise from the grave."

CHAPTER TWELVE

Finding a place to park on 4th Street in downtown St. Petersburg during business hours was always challenging, and to be fair, Dan was more than a little particular about where he parked his Bentley. Not that the crime rate was that bad in this neighborhood but, come on—it's a Bentley.

He'd never been to Great Expectations before. He'd never had any reason to visit. He had no children. Most of his friends didn't have children. He was an only child—or so he believed—so he had no nieces or nephews demanding outings. Why would he visit a children's museum? The Dali Museum, sure, he loved that place. Especially the 3D headsets that made you feel as if you'd walked into a world of paintings. But climbing around in plastic tubes and using ping-pong balls to demonstrate centrifugal force—nah.

He strolled through the museum, dodging children and trying not to touch anything. He passed the Critter Cave, skittered around Build It, then spotted the woman he sought in what looked like a kitchen.

If he'd known there was a kitchen, he might've come sooner.

He took a closer look. No actual food here. In the BellaBrava

Pizza kitchen, children explored how to make a pizza...out of Play-Doh, or something like it. Clay sculptures. Some of them lovely. But probably not tasty.

An older woman explained how the kitchen worked to three children, providing a scientific explanation of why yeast made the crust rise. He preferred flatbread when he made pizza—or rather, Not-Pizza—but still, he found this interesting. He'd used yeast a thousand times but never once contemplated exactly how it worked.

"Yeast is a simple, single-celled fungus," she explained. "And yet it's the secret behind the bread you eat every day."

One of the kids scrunched her nose. "We eat fungus? Eww."

"Not exactly. The yeast consumes sugar and excretes carbon dioxide and alcohol. We call that fermentation."

"She said 'excretes.' Double eww!"

The woman smiled. "Maybe I should just let you make your pizza." She looked up at him. "Dan Pike, right?"

"I am. Beth Kramer?"

"That's me." Red hair, streaks of gray. Peasant shirt. Petite. Tiny mole above her lip. Green smudge on her blouse.

"Former Lieutenant Kramer of the SPPD?"

"Yeah. I worked with your dad. He was my partner." She glanced at her watch. "You're right on time. Just like your daddy. You could set your watch by that man." She gestured toward a corner. "Why don't we go someplace slightly quieter and have a good chinwag?"

"Suits me." They found a spot next to the wall behind a Segway track. He supposed it probably taught some lesson about energy, but the long line of kids suggested they wanted to take it for a ride, not hear a lecture about thermodynamics.

"You favor him, you know."

"You mean—my father?"

"No. Joe Pesci. Yes, of course I mean your father. I can see a little of your mother in there too, but mostly your father. You have his mouth."

He thought about it for a moment. He supposed she was right, but it had been so long since he'd actually seen his father in person, he wasn't sure. "You knew him well?"

"I was his partner for four years. And that's no small thing."

"You spent a lot of time with him."

"And trusted him with my life. Having a partner is like having a brother, except actually, tighter. I got a brother I can't stand to be in the same room with. But your daddy always had my back. And I had his. I never forgot what he did for me. Never will."

That piqued his interest. "What he did for you?"

"Yeah." She fidgeted with her hands. "Remember, this was more than twenty years ago. Women on the force were few and far between. There were more Hispanic men than white women. We had to fight for every crumb we got."

"I can imagine."

"You probably can't. You were a kid back then. And you're a white male now. The world was made for you. Not for women who...wanted something different. Most of the guys on the force wouldn't have me for a partner."

"Did they have a say in it? I thought the Chief made those decisions."

"On cop shows maybe. In reality, pairing someone with a partner they don't like, or can't work with, is like signing their death warrant. The Chief wouldn't force me on anyone. And you wouldn't believe some of the BS excuses I heard. 'What if she starts crying during a fight?' 'What if she trips during a chase?' 'What if I need backup and she has PMS?' You couldn't get away with that blatant sexism today, but back then it happened all the time. Every damn day."

"But my father didn't object to you?"

"He requested the assignment. He knew if I didn't get a

partner I would end up being transferred or turned into the telephone operator or something. He kept me on active duty."

"And it worked out?"

"Fantastically. He was such a good man. So fair. Such a strong sense of justice. Could be a little self-righteous at times, but I didn't care. Best partner I ever had. Not to diss the ones who came after. But he was the best." She paused. "Which is why I'm saddened to see all the troubles you've been having."

"Oh...I do okay..."

"I live in this city, son. You've been all over the news, again and again." She smiled. "Glad you beat that murder rap. Looked like trumped-up baloney from the get-go. I could smell the stink through the TV set."

"Thank you for that."

"Not surprised the bad guys came gunning for you. You're just like your daddy in that respect."

He tilted his head. "Can you explain...?"

"Looks to me like you've been doing the exact same thing he used to do. 'Cept he did it on the streets and you do it in the courtroom."

He hadn't thought about it like that.

"But you both do the same thing. Justice. No one gets rail-roaded. Look out for the little guy." She placed a hand on his shoulder. "The apple did not fall far from the tree. It's good to know there are still some people like you Pikes around."

"Well, thanks..."

"Why didn't you bring your kids with you?"

"I...don't actually have kids."

"A boy your age?" She pulled a face. "Are you—"

"No, I'm not gay. Just...busy."

She rolled her eyes. "Don't be a fool, Dan. Kids are the hardest challenge in the world, but when you get older, they're the only thing you'll care about. And this world needs more people like you and your daddy. Get with it already. Start cranking out those kids."

"I'll...see what I can do."

She shifted her weight from one foot to the other. "I suspect this is not what you came to talk about. Why did you seek me out after all these years?"

"A friend of mine suggested my dad's partner would be a good source of information. She helped me score the police files on his case."

"Find much there?"

"No."

"Didn't think you would. Think they gave you everything?"

He shrugged. "I doubt it. I think the files were expurgated. Probably years ago. Were you there? The night Jack Fisher got shot?"

"Of course. Your dad drove. I was in the passenger seat."

"Did you see it happen?"

"No. Oddly enough, I was looking at the fourteen gangsters shooting at me, not the two cops guarding our rear flank. But I heard the shot. And I saw Jack fall."

"But you don't know who shot him."

She craned her neck. "I know what it looked like."

He thought as much. That's why he didn't notice her for a deposition. He didn't want to record any unhelpful testimony that might not otherwise surface. "Tell me what you saw. Or heard. Or experienced."

"I'm not going to be much help to you. I was otherwise engaged, trying to avoid dying in a rapid-fire hail of bullets. I heard a gunshot. Sounded like it came from where your father was. I'm pretty sure ballistics later traced the bullet to his gun, but you might check that."

"I will."

"I heard Jack shout. Heard him fall. Assumed one and one made two, if you know what I mean."

"Sure." But in his experience, the mathematics of crime could be deceptive. "Anything else you can contribute?"

"That helps you?"

"Either way. Better to hear it now than be surprised at trial."

"I'm sure you've heard this before, but there was some serious bad blood between your papa and Jack Fisher."

"I've been told that my mother…was previously married to Fisher."

"Right. And both husbands were working together on the same police force. Talk about oil and water. Your daddy was a crusader. Jack, I'm sorry to say, was a bigot. He didn't like anyone who didn't look like him. He didn't like women, except maybe in bed. He was brutal, cruel, and tended to draw his weapon first and ask questions later."

"I'm amazed my mother never mentioned her previous marriage."

"I'm not. It was a bad mistake and she probably preferred to sweep it under the rug. Word was…"

"He hit her?"

"Yeah. Pretty bad, from what I hear. Slammed her head into the wall. Made her mouth bleed. Sent her to the emergency room twice. We didn't have Sweeney shelters back then, and sometimes women with no income of their own didn't know what to do. But she eventually got away."

"And divorced him."

"And in time married your dad. And was much happier… till…you know."

"Yeah."

"But your dad and Jack were constantly at loggerheads. Jack was the type who couldn't let anything alone. Shoving Ethan around or bumping into him on purpose. Making innuendoes about how he knew what his wife was like in bed, or that she liked him better because he…you get the idea. I always thought they were headed for a showdown." Her eyes fell. "But I never suspected it would happen like it did."

"Do you know..." Dan wasn't even sure how to phrase it. It seemed impossible. "Did my mother have any children? I mean, when she was married to Jack?"

Beth thought for a moment. "I'm not sure. It's been too long. Why?"

"I just wondered. Did my parents have any children other than me? Maybe someone who didn't survive?"

"Never heard that either. But wouldn't that be an easy thing to check? Public records and all?"

"I have someone working on that. Were you involved in the...aftermath of the shooting?"

"Not much. Your father was suspended. I was reassigned. I was not asked to testify at the trial. They used that turncoat Ellison and kept everyone else on the sidelines."

"You didn't believe Ellison?"

"I didn't know what to believe. But I didn't think much of one officer testifying against another. We just don't do that. There's an unspoken code, you know? And why would he? Hell, even if it was true—if anyone ever asked for it, it was Jack. I think someone got to Ellison. Made him an offer he couldn't refuse, if you know what I mean."

He did. And he knew who the most likely suspect was, too.

"I wanted to reach out to you, Dan, especially after I heard about your mom, but I didn't want to overstep myself. It's not like I was a family friend or anything."

"I understand. You shouldn't feel guilty. I can tell you were a good friend to my dad."

"You should come around more often. You know, we could use some volunteers out here on the weekends. Can't afford more staff, but we get overrun with kids sometimes."

He blinked. "And you think I'd be a good candidate?"

"Why not? I read that you were some kind of gourmet chef. You could help out in the BellaBlaze kitchen."

"Sorry, I've never worked with clay."

"All the better. You can tell them about real cooking. Nutrition. Balanced diets. Forming good eating habits."

"I'm more of an outdoors person."

"Give it a try. You might find you like it. Kids can be amazing."

"I'll keep it in mind."

"You know, Dan, if you learn anything from this whole sorry business, it should be about how precious life really is. And how fleeting. That's why I started working here. My kids grew up and moved away. I missed having young people around. You got to slow down every now and again and sprinkle a little joy into your life."

"I'm sure that's true. But—"

He stopped short. He was gazing toward the front doors...

And saw someone suddenly duck out of sight.

Whoever had been there before was gone.

Was he being watched? *Followed?*

He handed Beth his card. "If you think of anything else that might help, please let me know."

"I will. Good to finally meet you. Keep up the good work."

He made his way out of the museum and back to his car, looking every which way at once.

Had Sweeney decided to engage in some unauthorized discovery by having him followed? Or had the cartel decided they needed to take out the attorney who kept interfering with their operations?

He started his car and blazed down the road as fast as he could manage. Drove all the way home with the top up. He tried to tell himself it was the rumble of the engine making his arms vibrate, but deep down, he knew that wasn't it at all.

CHAPTER THIRTEEN

GARRETT SOMETIMES FELT LIKE THE LEAST APPRECIATED MEMBER of this team. Sure, he was low profile. That was deliberate. One of the aspects of being a prosecutor he had liked least was that he was always on the front lines, getting attention he didn't want that invariably made his job harder to do.

He was better at the computer terminal than he had ever been in the courtroom, where theatrics and strategy seemed to trump research and evidence too much of the time. He preferred his current role as chief research hound—and acerbic commentator on whatever Dan was doing at the moment. He never asked for that role, but the world worked best when there was a system of checks and balances in place. Someone had to play devil's advocate. Or to put it in the common parlance, someone had to call Dan on his BS. He liked Dan, but the man had blind spots.

Sadly, their current case was all about Dan's blind spots, which was why Garrett was currently in his upstairs office laying new skid marks on the information highway. The idea of baiting Sweeney, then suing him for slander, was clever— ingenious even—but fraught with danger and unlikely to produce any result that completely satisfied anyone. It put a target on their backs. And he was convinced Dan's focus was all wrong.

The most important clue The Captain dropped was the reference to Dan's sister.

Why would the man say such a thing? Just to taunt Dan? Like a kid on the playground—*I know something you don't know.* No, there had to be more. Why would this smuggler know anything about Dan's family history? Why spill the beans as he was being taken into custody?

Dan thought the man slipped, that in his anger, The Captain had revealed something he shouldn't. But Garrett had another theory. Was it possible that this dangling reference to an unknown sister was more than a taunt?

Maybe it was a piece of cheese placed on the tripwire of a mousetrap.

At any rate, he was going to look into it while Dan was busy trying to win his case and exonerate his father. Once he knew the truth, he would decide what to do with it, which might or might not involve telling Dan. Garrett was in a much better position to have perspective on this. And if he discovered this was dangerous knowledge, he could bury it before it lured anyone to their doom.

In Florida, most courthouse records were online, which made research almost too easy to be considered a skill. Public records confirmed much of what they already knew. Dan's father, Ethan Pike, married a woman named Alice who had been married previously to Jack Fisher—the man Ethan would later be accused of murdering. Judging from some of the allegations in the Petition for Divorce and how long the action dragged along, it had been an acrimonious split—but then, weren't they all? The Petition alluded to domestic violence without giving much in the way of details.

All divorce petitions required a precise identification of the parties involved, as well as an identification of any children of the marriage. No children were mentioned.

Garrett heard someone sashay by in the corridor outside his office.

"Jimmy!"

His partner stopped and poked his head inside. He held half a sandwich. "You bellowed?"

"Busy?"

"Working on the brief for a Motion to Exclude. Needed to stretch my legs. Get some blood flowing."

"And heighten your blood sugar levels?"

Jimmy shrugged. "A mid-afternoon PB&J is good for you. It's brain food."

He doubted Jimmy's physician would agree.

"You must be on the trail of something important," Jimmy said. "Something about Dan's dad?"

How did he know that? "Are you mirroring my computer?"

Jimmy laughed and took another bite. "Maybe I'm just a mind reader. Maybe that phlegmatic façade of yours is more transparent than you realize."

"Or maybe you heard the voice of God in a burning bush, but I doubt it. How'd you know?"

"There's a Rays game on today. Which"—Jimmy glanced at his phone—"started fourteen minutes ago."

Garrett slapped his desk. "Damn. I was planning to—" He stopped short. "Oh. That's how you knew."

Jimmy tapped the side of his head. "Dan isn't the only one with keen powers of observation."

Apparently not. "You still have a friend in the records department at DHS?"

"I have friends everywhere."

"Yes, but answer the question."

"I do have a contact there."

"Works from home or office?"

"She works from home."

"Can you send her an email? Ask for a favor?"

"Which would be?"

"I don't care. Anything that makes her enter the archived records database. Ten years or older. After you've forwarded her email address to me."

"This sounds a little skeezy. Are you contemplating something inappropriate?"

"It's my opinion that all the records should be public. That's why they're called public records. As citizens, we have a constitutional right—"

"Yadda yadda yadda. What are you planning?"

"You don't want to know."

"Right." He snarfed down the last bite of his sandwich. "I'll forward the email address."

Garrett didn't have to wait long. Once he received the email, he could ID Jimmy's friend's IP address. Once he had that, all he needed to do was get into the DHS database, wait for that IP address to make its appearance, and follow it, mirroring the keystrokes to get past the security challenges.

Hacking public records was astonishingly easy. Granted, he had major computer skills, but he wasn't the only one who did. Given the importance of online data in modern society, you'd think there would be more protection. The government couldn't keep pace with the ongoing exponential increase in hacker skills.

At first, he was disappointed. Just as the petition had suggested, there was no child of the marriage of Alice and Jack. But he kept digging, following links, hopscotching around, searching for connections.

Until he found something. The first problem was that the child was not "of the marriage." The child was born before the marriage and didn't seem to still be living with them when they split.

The second problem was that the records had been erased.

A lesser hacker might've missed this, but someone had entered this database and deliberately expunged everything relating to the child's birth.

A girl. So far as he could discern, never even given a name. The certificate read: BABY GIRL

The trouble with putting data on a cloud storage system, of course, was that nothing ever completely disappeared. Despite someone's best efforts to bury the birth certificate, he found it.

Dan did have a sister. A half-sister, or so it appeared. The certificate listed Dan's mother as the baby's mother, though this was before she married, divorced, remarried, and gave birth to Dan.

And Dan knew nothing about it. Which meant that despite everything that family had been through, no one had ever mentioned the girl to him.

How was that possible? Even if his parents kept quiet, wouldn't someone else know? A sibling, a grandparent, a best friend—someone?

And why would anyone want to cover up the existence of a little girl?

He found no reference to this child anywhere else, though to be sure, his search was severely constrained by the fact that he didn't have a name. The most logical conclusion would be that the baby did not survive. He found no corresponding death certificate, but it was possible it had gone the same way as the birth certificate, except more effectively.

What was the big secret?

He didn't know the answers and he had few clues to move forward, except maybe one. The birth certificate did have the names of the delivering doctor and the attending nurse. A quick search revealed that the nurse had died three years ago, but the doctor was still alive. Retired and in his early eighties, but alive.

Was it possible he remembered something about this? A major long shot—but when all you had were long shots, you played them.

Someone was doing their best to wipe this child out of existence. He needed to find out why—before it was too late.

CHAPTER FOURTEEN

DAN BARELY SLEPT. THE WIND WAS HIGH AND THE WAVES ROCKED his boat all night long. On most occasions, a little weather helped him sleep.

Not this time.

Instead of blaming the weather, perhaps he needed to admit the truth. Conrad Sweeney scared the hell out of him. And he was about to confront the man, face to face.

They had met once before. Sweeney had arranged the meeting in an extremely foggy sauna, and Dan was convinced he did that to undermine Dan's powers of observation, his ability to read faces and absorb minute details. They had never once been seated in a normal room together.

But today that was about to change. Maria was taking Sweeney's deposition.

Sweeney had made excuses and delayed as long as possible. They had taken all the other depos first. But it was finally going to happen.

. . .

As before, the Friedman & Collins receptionist escorted him and Maria to the conference room.

The door opened.

Sweeney wasn't there.

The court reporter, Marjorie, sat before her stenotype, fingers ready. The two opposing attorneys, Caldwell and Drake, weren't there yet.

Dan pulled a legal pad out of his backpack. He was making the all-important decision about which pen to use when he felt a nudge from Maria.

He looked up. She silently tilted her head toward the court reporter.

He widened his eyes. Yes?

She tilted her head again, even more forcefully.

The message was clear. *Observe already.*

He shifted his position casually and gave the court reporter the once-over. Everything seemed much as before...

Wait. She had a new purse. Blue. Compact. Like a combo between a clutch and a regular purse.

He leaned toward Maria. "So?" he whispered.

"Kelly."

He shrugged. "It's a tote bag."

"It's a multi-thousand-dollar accessory."

He scrunched up his face. "For a purse?"

"For a Kelly bag. Named for Grace Kelly. Like the Birkin bag, named for the singer Jane Birkin, who favored them. They're made exclusively by Hermès. You can't get one for less than 7K. And yet they are so in demand there's a long waitlist and a secondary collectors' market. Unlike almost everything else in the fashion world, they increase in value."

"I assume you have several."

"Are you joking? Kellys are not in my budget. And I have a pretty generous clothes budget."

The light began to dawn. "But our court reporter has one?"

Maria nodded her head slowly.

"Maybe she…inherited it from a rich aunt?"

"She'd sell it."

"Maybe it's a knockoff."

Maria shook her head. "Look at it. Saddle-stitched. Swivel latch. Trust my eye, Dan. It's the real deal."

He didn't want to get all class-elitist, but you didn't expect a court reporter to be sporting designer goods. If she was so well-accessorized that Maria was drooling…something strange was going on. And when he combined this bit of informaiton with the fact that she still wasn't wearing a ring…

The door to the conference room opened. Caldwell and Drake entered and took their seats.

Still no deponent.

"Where is he?" Dan said, trying not to growl.

"No cause for concern," Caldwell said, in her usual matter-of-fact manner. "Dr. Sweeney will appear. By videoconference." She pointed at the small video screen mounted on the wall.

"Why isn't—"

Maria laid a hand on his shoulder. A gentle reminder. I'm the lawyer here, not you. "We thought the witness would appear in person."

"Read the local rules. A deponent may appear by videoconference."

"If approved by both sides," Maria added.

"Do you object? I don't know why you would. You'll be able to ask him any question you want."

"But you neglected to obtain my consent."

"You've been pushing for this deposition since you filed the case. I thought you were ready to do it."

"I am, but—"

"Dr. Sweeney is a busy man. He has three major deals pending plus a new Sweeney shelter in the planning stages. It's a miracle he could carve away enough time to do this by teleconference. If you want an in-person appearance..." She shook her head. "I don't know. It might be months."

"We'll get a subpoena."

"Suit yourself. It won't free up Dr. Sweeney's schedule, and I don't see Judge Fernandez asking him to put aside his business for your convenience. Especially after the judge hears that you had a chance to take the depo by videoconference and turned it down."

Dan pursed his lips. The opposition lawyers were violating one of the fundamental principles of professional collegiality—and didn't care. But if they didn't take this opportunity to depose Sweeney, they might not get another one for months.

"Give me a minute." Maria leaned toward Dan and whispered. "Why is he doing this?"

"Same reason our last meeting was in a steam bath. He heard that I can read people. He doesn't want to give me the chance."

"You'll still be able to see him."

"It's not the same."

"Do you want me to object?"

"No. I'm ready to get this done."

She nodded, then turned back to face the lawyers on the other side of the immense conference table. "Very well. Let's proceed."

Caldwell nodded. "The usual stipulations?"

"We will show you precisely the same professional courtesy you have shown us," Maria replied.

"Meaning?"

"No stipulations."

"As you wish."

Caldwell flipped a switch, and a picture appeared on the video monitor.

Conrad Sweeney was seated in a dark room. It might be his office. It was impossible to tell. He was in front of the camera but not all that close to it. They could see him—but just barely.

"I'm not going to get a damn thing," Dan muttered.

"You never know," Maria whispered. "You're amazing some-times. You might get a clue without even realizing it."

Dan shook his head. "Not unless he holds up a Kelly bag."

Maria spent the first ten minutes asking preliminary questions, establishing the witness's identity, address, occupation, and educational history. Some attorneys spent more than an hour on this kind of material, but he personally thought that was more to run the clock than because it produced useful information. Maria kept it to a minimum. Sweeney remained responsive and polite. He wasn't friendly, and he didn't elaborate. He was in complete control of the situation.

"Mr. Sweeney, I'd like—"

"Excuse me," Drake said, leaning in. "But it's Dr. Sweeney."

She knew that, of course. "I'm sorry. Is he a medical doctor? Does he have a Ph.D.?"

Sweeney chuckled. "It's an honorary degree. They made such a big deal out of it. Named a student center after me too."

In gratitude for a sizeable donation, no doubt.

Sweeney continued. "You may call me whatever you like, young lady. Call me Connie, if you prefer."

"Connie?"

"That's what my friends call me."

He has friends? "Thanks, but we should probably keep it professional. You made a public statement that my client's father, Ethan Pike, was a murderer."

"Matter of public record. Man was convicted for first-degree murder. Died in prison, as I understand it."

"Are you aware of any other criminal activities by Ethan Pike?"

"I haven't looked into it."

"Do you have any personal knowledge pertaining to the murder?"

"Depends on what you call personal knowledge."

"Were you there?"

He hesitated. Only an instant. "No."

"Have you talked to anyone who was?"

"As I think you're aware, I know Bradley Ellison."

"How do you know him?"

"He's one of my oldest acquaintances. I knew him when he was a young rookie officer and I was just starting in tech. Back when wireless meant 300-baud dial-up modems and computer screens only came in green. We worked on some charitable projects. A policeman's retirement fundraiser, I believe."

"You've employed him, haven't you?"

"Yes. Bradley has worked for me in the past."

"On what?"

"To which I will object," Caldwell said. "Relevance."

Maria nodded. "You may answer the question, Dr. Sweeney."

"But she objected."

"Objections are reserved until the time of trial."

"Are they?" Drake said, eyebrows arched. "I never heard you agree to that stipulation."

Maria's face made it clear she was tired of dicking around with Sweeney *and* his lawyers. "You decide how you want to play it, Nick. But your decision sticks for the rest of the case."

He waved his hand in the air. "Fine. You can answer the question, Dr. Sweeney. If the deposition is used at trial, we'll renew our objection."

Sweeney nodded. "I had some concerns about our city government. As you'll recall, our mayor, Camila Pérez, was accused of criminal activity. More than once. I asked him to look into it."

"You were spying on the mayor."

Sweeney was nonplussed. "If you choose to put it that way."

"And you thought that was appropriate?"

"I thought it was necessary. And given what we now know— I was right. I was awake while others were sleeping. In fact," he said, letting his eyes wander, "some people were sleeping with the enemy."

Dan bit down on his lip. "Smart ass," he muttered.

"Emphasis on the 'smart,'" Maria muttered back. She addressed the television screen. "Do you have any more information about the murder?"

"No. Just what Ellison told me."

"Has Ellison ever spoken poorly about Ethan Pike?"

Another meaningful pause. "That's a complex question. I've heard Bradley say he liked Ethan Pike and considered him an excellent officer. But he also thought Pike was ...unnecessarily violent. Which proved to be true in the worst possible way."

Maria tapped her pen on her legal pad. "In the public statements that form the basis of this suit, you mentioned organized crime. Do you have reason to believe my client's father was involved in organized crime?"

"Again, it would be best if you deposed Bradley."

"I already did. He didn't mention this."

"I guess you didn't ask the right questions."

Maria tucked in her chin. "You've known Ellison a long time. What about Dan's father? Did you know him?"

"I...knew of him."

Something about the way he said it triggered something in Dan's head.

"Did you know Jack Fisher?"

"I...did, yes."

"How did you know him?"

"Bradley introduced us. I believe Jack was having some financial problems, but so many years have passed, it's hard to recall all the details."

"Do you have any additional information to support your claim that my client's father was a criminal?"

"Nothing comes to mind."

"What about my client himself? You also claimed he was a criminal."

Sweeney glanced down. Did he have notes on his desk? Talking points? "Your client has a reputation for being... dishonest and disreputable. He has spent his adult lifetime consorting with criminals."

"And when you say consorting, you mean, *representing?*"

"Among other things. He dated a criminal. He defended a woman who was in clear violation of immigration law. And of course, he himself has been accused of murder."

"And exonerated."

"But the situation would never have occurred if your client didn't spend so much time with the criminal element, the kind of people who hire hitmen on the internet or pay money to be excited by leather-clad dominatrices. As my father used to say, 'When you hang with sleaze, you become sleaze.'"

Dan could feel Maria's frustration. Sweeney was choosing his words carefully, defending himself without saying anything that could lead to additional claims. The man had been baited once. He would not be baited again.

"Do you have any evidence suggesting that my client aided a South American cartel? Or any other criminal organization?"

"Not at this time."

"Does that mean you're looking for some? That you might get some later?"

Sweeney shrugged. "You're conducting discovery. So am I."

"I'm not aware of any outstanding discovery requests."

"Court-sanctioned discovery rarely leads to much, in my experience."

Maria's back stiffened. "Are you talking about private investigators? Are you having my client investigated? Or followed?"

Sweeney appeared completely unruffled. "He initiated this attack on my character."

"Don't you mean, this defense of his character?"

"He came after me. Quite deliberately. Threatened my business. My livelihood. Did he think I would take that quietly? My business empire was not built by taking things quietly."

Maria turned to the opposing lawyers. "I'm formally requesting the production of any and all reports, documents, photos, or anything else in the possession of or obtained by Dr. Sweeney that relates to my client."

Sweeney answered for them. "I regret that I will not be able to comply."

"Why not?" she snapped.

"Because I don't want to."

Drake jumped in. "Anything obtained through a private investigator in preparation for trial would be privileged work product and thus not subject to discovery."

"That's crap and you know it."

"I don't know that at all."

"I'll file a motion to produce."

"Feel free. You'll lose. You want to see what we've got? Come to trial and find out." Drake's eyes wandered to Dan. "You're going to be sorry you started this mess."

Dan knew he should keep his mouth shut, but as usual, didn't. "Is that some kind of threat?"

"I don't make threats. I win cases. The smartest thing you could do is drop this suit. Right now. Before it goes one minute longer. But if you choose to proceed…" Drake shook his head, and for a moment, almost looked genuinely distressed. "I won't be responsible for the consequences. To you. And everyone you know."

On the video screen, Sweeney simply smiled.

CHAPTER FIFTEEN

FABIAN FUENTES TRIED TO HIDE HIS DISGUST. HE WAS NOT successful.

They had waited until well past midnight to make sure the port authorities would not be watching when the secret compartment in his ship was opened. No one would notice who went in or out of the dock. No one would ask them to complete tax forms as huge sums of cash exchanged hands.

His purchaser was nervous. He had been told the man had done this before with other suppliers, but he saw no evidence of that. He had Jose and Roberto close but out of sight. He did not anticipate trouble, but there was always the possibility of a double-cross, someone getting too greedy for their own good. The jittery nature of this buyer did not suggest deception, but it was always best to be cautious. His instincts were the reason he had survived this pirate life for so long. Cartels rose and fell. El Chapo was caught and arrested. Even the great and mighty Captain ended up a blood splatter on a courtroom wall.

But Fuentes still stood tall. Part of that was his innate intelligence. Part was caution. And part was that he understood why he was doing this. He did not seek fame. He did not want to be perceived as a big man. He did not want a huge show house. He thought of himself as an artist. He wanted to create something that would last. Security for his children, yes, but more importantly, security for his people. He did not care about American morality or their arrogant attempts to serve as policemen for the entire world. What Americans considered crimes were commonplace occurrences elsewhere in the world. Prostitution has been with us since the dawn of time. No amount of morality would change that. For that matter, if people could afford to purchase organs, why shouldn't they be allowed to do so? As in all things, the strong survive and the weak perish. No amount of piety would change that.

His purchaser, Albert Gomez, was ready to complete the transaction. "You have it?"

"Indeed. And you have the money?"

Gomez passed him the gym bags. It appeared to all be there. It would be gauche to count. And needless. He knew where Gomez lived.

"It's all there," Gomez said. "Where's the product?"

Fuentes led him to the other side of the boat. Placed a key in an unobtrusive cargo hold and opened the door.

Sixteen plastic bags rested in dry ice.

It did not look like much. But it was worth almost half a million dollars.

Gomez peered inside one of the bags. Fuentes waited anxiously. He had no reason to believe the federal authorities knew anything about this—but of course, The Captain thought the same thing. And he was now buried in an American grave.

Gomez chuckled. "They don't look like delicacies, do they?"

Fuentes shrugged. "I prefer tomato soup myself."

"Bisque?"

"Campbell's."

Gomez grabbed one of the bags and loaded it onto his dolly. "Fortunately, Florida's significant Asian population feels differently. The ultra-elite cannot get enough shark fin. They will pay almost anything for it."

This seemed to be true, which was why, in the wake of the disruption of first, the sex-trafficking network, and now, the organ-smuggling network, they had become shark hunters.

Unwillingly.

Shark fin soup was considered a rare delicacy, particularly in wealthy Asian communities. Chinese emperors supposedly ate shark fin soup and served it to guests, in part to impress upon others that the emperor was so strong he could even conquer sharks. Shark meat was in demand as well, but transporting and selling shark meat, in and of itself, was not illegal. Selling shark fins were, especially when they were unaccompanied by the rest of the shark. After a wave of hunters took the fins and left the carcasses behind, the ever-present American overlords passed a conservation law forbidding the finning of sharks. You could be arrested for having shark fins aboard a fishing vessel without the corresponding carcass.

The safest approach would be to simply take the entire shark and sell the meat, but those carcasses consumed valuable and limited space in the cargo hold. Though shark meat could be sold, it fetched nothing near the same price. Some believed it had medicinal qualities, but Fuentes' people said it was completely without nutritional value and, due to mercury poisoning, could be dangerous. The big money was in the fins. So that was what they smuggled.

Gomez finished loading his dolly. "When will you return?"

"Give us three weeks."

"The usual arrangements?"

"I will contact you when we are ready."

Gomez gave him a small salute. "Been a pleasure."

Fuentes watched as Gomez hauled his pathetic loot away, teeth clenched.

It had not been a pleasure. Nothing about this had been a pleasure. He was a pirate.

And now he had been reduced to a fisherman. Just as his own father had been a fisherman.

A different type of fisherman. Considerably less prosperous. But a fisherman, just the same.

After Gomez left the site and the area appeared secure, Roberto and Jose joined him on the boat.

"Any signs of trouble?" he asked his associates.

"None," Roberto said. "I believe we are completely under the cop radar."

Fuentes pursed his lips. "I recall once hearing The Captain say almost the exact same thing."

"Maybe this shark-fin business is beneath their notice."

"It is beneath my notice." Fuentes said, voice rising. He recovered himself immediately. He was usually in better control of his emotions.

"I just meant that, for Americans, kidnapped girls and kids needing transplants raise emotional issues. Few people are emotionally attached to sharks."

"And yet Clinton passed the shark-fin law."

Jose smiled. "Creating a new crime that did not exist before. Another stream of income for us."

That part was true. "Did you make your appointment this afternoon?"

Jose puffed out his chest. He obviously liked being given assignments he thought important. He was too young and too stupid to realize that he was given the riskiest jobs most likely to attract law-enforcement attention. "I did."

"Was the report informative?"

"I learned everything that happened in that deposition. And I have been promised a recording."

Always useful to have an ear on the inside. Another consistent trait of Americans—having been raised in a culture that worshipped only wealth, they were all too easy to buy. "Did Sweeney behave himself?"

"He barely even mentioned the cartel. Said he had nothing to do with it."

"Erasing more than twenty years of history. Amazing bravado."

"He's a hard man to ruffle."

"What about the lawyer? The one they all think is so smart, so dangerous. The one who helped bring down The Captain."

"He barely spoke. Let his woman do all the talking."

"Is he a man or a mouse?"

Jose shrugged. "He is a lawyer. It is much the same."

"Does he understand that Sweeney is involved in this matter he is investigating?"

"He suspects. He cannot prove anything."

"He is still being followed? Watched?"

"Of course."

"Any concerns?"

"I have noticed a...discrepancy."

"Which is? Don't speak to me in riddles."

"There are some witnesses Pike quizzes in an official way. With a reporter taking down each word. But there are others he speaks to in private."

"And what is the difference between them?"

Jose appeared embarrassed. "I do not know. I cannot even speculate."

He could speculate, especially given the sensitive matters being discussed. Pike's father was a convicted murderer. He might prefer to hold some conversations in private, without a reporter taking down each word.

"Will they take a deposition of Jaquith?"

"He is not on the list."

Did Pike not know about him? Or did Pike know more than they realized? "Watch them both carefully. If those two meet—"

"I do not believe Pike has learned anything of value. This lawsuit is an enormous fishing expedition that has produced no fish."

"We cannot assume that will last forever. We cannot become complacent. That is what happened to The Captain. And you see where that led."

"I have worked for both of you," Roberto said. "You are much smarter than The Captain."

"Smart is not always enough."

"If you want this man silenced, you need only give the word."

"The lawyer? Or Sweeney?"

"I thought you meant the lawyer." Roberto's eyes narrowed. "But I would do anything you asked."

Fuentes almost smiled. "Your loyalty is appreciated. But I think there is a better way."

"The dark web?"

"What am I, a child? You cannot solve all your problems by staring at a screen." He paused, laying a hand on his associate's shoulder. "Americans love to talk. They talk and talk and talk. But I am much better at silence."

CHAPTER SIXTEEN

DAN PASSED THROUGH THE GLASS DOORS OF REVEL 18, ONE OF the city's swankiest salons, not far from Coffee Pot Bayou. He hadn't been in this area for a long time, not since a case brought him to a then-closed bakery—and most of that experience he preferred to forget.

The perky woman behind the front desk beamed at him. Orchid neck tat. Six piercings in her left ear. Spot of something white on her blouse. Powdered sugar? Cocaine? She appeared to be around twenty and to have perfect teeth. Was that a service they provided at the salon?

"Do you have an appointment?"

"Sort of. I'm not here for a makeover." Although maybe he should. He was looking ragged. Stress, he supposed. Stress, plus the fact that Maria, who normally chided him for sartorial and grooming errors, was keeping quiet. Because she thought he had enough problems? Because she didn't want to upset him during this tricky time in their relationship? Because she thought he was hopeless? "I'm here to see Erica."

"She told me someone was coming. She's on break. You can go on back if you want."

He nodded. She led the way.

The salon was an impressive large-scale operation. He'd had a pedicure not long ago—only way to meet a witness, long story —but that place looked like a dive compared to this one. On the left were the expected berths where people got their hair cut and styled and colored, but on the right were an equal number of nooks with chairs and foot boxes, so mani-pedis could be delivered simultaneously. He also spotted some rooms with curtains where he assumed facials and massages and such took place.

Peeking between the curtains as he passed, he spotted something he couldn't identify. "Is she putting...wax in that guy's nose?"

"On a cotton swab." The receptionist smiled. "Ear and nose waxes. The latest rage."

"But...why?"

"Why does anyone get waxed? To remove hair."

"It will grow back."

"Then it's time for another wax. Come on—no one wants to look at your nose hair. It's super-gross."

"That's why God invented tweezers. How do people breathe during this procedure?"

"They only do one nostril at a time."

"And did you say ears? Ear wax? Why would anyone do that?"

"Ask me again in twenty years."

She opened the door to the break room. Predictably small and lined with vending machines, though the options were healthier than what he usually saw in break room vending machines.

A woman in her late fifties rose when he entered. She was generous in figure and comfortably dressed. Big strand of fake pearls. Flip-flops. Dangling earrings.

"Danny!" She rushed toward him with arms spread wide and

wrapped them around him, squeezing tightly.

He stood there wordlessly, not sure how to respond. *Danny?*

"I have heard so much about you," she explained, hugging all the tighter. "And I wanted to reach out. But it didn't feel right, you know? Not fair to your mom."

He took a step back and gave her a closer inspection. She looked good, not only for her age but for any age. "You knew my mother?"

"How could I not? We were all thick as thieves back then. Even lived together for a while. One big weird wife-swapping household."

"Um, excuse me?"

"Aw hell, kid. It was a long time ago. Why keep secrets? Turned out poorly, sure, but we had some great times while it lasted. Your dad and Jack were both major up-and-comers in the police force. Your mom taught kindergarten. I was fresh out of cosmetology school and had my first gig as a hairdresser."

"I'm a little confused. My dad's former partner described you as Dad's ex-girlfriend."

"That's one way of putting it. We lived together."

"But my mother lived in the same house?"

"Yeah. Your mom was with Jack."

"She was married to Jack before she married my father."

"Correct."

"But she later divorced Jack and married my father."

"Also correct."

"And you all lived together?"

She waved her hand in the air. "It was another time. Have a seat."

He took a chair at the card table. Between the vending machines he noticed a brown door, closed and locked. Dust on the doorknob.

She followed his gaze. "Hungry?"

"No. Just curious. Nice that you offer your employees healthy options."

"It's important for people working in the beauty industry to appear, if not necessarily beautiful, at least not haggard and unhealthy. I encourage my staff to eat well—to the extent that anything that comes out of a vending machine can be called eating well."

"My friend Garrett tells me you own this place."

"True. Started as one of many hairdressers, and now, all these years later, it's mine. I turned it into an enhanced, much cooler, full-service salon."

"I got the quick tour. It does look like you offer everything there is to make a person look better."

"We don't have plastic surgeons on the premises yet, but we're working on it." She winked. "Believe me, this didn't happen overnight. I had to scrape together a lot of pennies. Make some smart investments. Had to find people willing to take a chance on me, including a few I didn't particularly like. But money is money. Your father taught me a lot about business, you know. If not for him, I'd probably still be cutting hair."

That was surprising. So far as he knew, his father had no actual business experience. "What did he teach you?"

"Little stuff. Mind you, when we were together, I knew nothing. He told me to start an IRA. I did. He told me to pay myself first, to save and invest the first ten percent right off the top. Basic stuff, but I didn't know any of it. Till Ethan taught me."

"Did he live the same way? Far as I know, he never amassed much cash."

"Because he was generous. Always giving it away. And because he chose to be a police officer, not a—"

Dan arched an eyebrow. "A lawyer?"

"Or anything likely to bring in big bucks. Now Jack was a different story."

"Jack had money?"

"Every now and again. Not every day. Not regularly. But occasionally he would pop up with big wads of cash and no one had the slightest idea where it all came from."

"Did you ask?"

"He always blew the question off with some silly answer. Won the lottery. Inheritance from a rich uncle. Yeah, sure. He didn't want to talk about it. And he never saved any of it, so what did it matter? He spent some on your mother, but mostly he just frittered it away."

"Ever heard anyone mention it since?"

"No. Didn't matter to me what the roomies did. Your daddy took care of me. I preferred a strong man with a steady income to a flashy guy with unexplained spikes of wealth. After your dad left me and took up with your mother, Jack made some moves toward me. Like we should all just change lobsters and dance, you know? But I wasn't having any of it. Your dad was the man for me. If I couldn't have him, I certainly wasn't going to settle for the inferior clone."

"Sounds like you really liked my father."

"I adored your daddy." Her eyes lit. "Did I say that strongly enough? I *adored* him. I got goosepimply when he walked into the room. I still think of our two years together as the happiest time of my life. I've had other relationships since, and I've had some business success. But no one ever made me feel the way he did. He was a good man, your daddy. Through and through. They don't make many like that."

Dan didn't know what to say. It was great to hear such positive comments about his father. But it also made him feel as if there were gigantic holes in his family knowledge. More he didn't know than he did. "I...don't recall my father ever mentioning you."

"Why would he? He married your mother, and I suspect she didn't want to hear about his old girlfriend. You were just a kid back then. I can't imagine any reason he would start talking to his little boy about ex-girlfriends."

Valid point. "Where was this house you all lived in?"

"Not far from the beach. Your daddy loved the water."

Just like he did.

"Old Victorian-style thing," Erica continued. "It needed lots of work, but it was the best we could afford. The boys did a lot of much-needed repairs. We had our own lives, but we all ate dinner together almost every night."

But not forever, apparently. "When did things start to change?"

"You mean, when did your dad drift from me to her?" Her smile faded. "Too soon. I saw it coming. But there was nothing I could do to stop it."

"Was he unhappy?"

"Not that I was aware. But in many ways...we were an odd couple. Truth is, I was the odd person out in the whole house. I was the only one of the bunch who hadn't been to a real college. They were professionals. I was a hairdresser. They talked about books I'd never read. They used words I didn't know. Don't get me wrong—your daddy was not a snob. He was completely down-to-earth. He was a cop, after all, not a physics professor. But still. There was a...divide."

"And eventually he drifted to my mother?"

"Yeah. And I kept telling myself not to let it get to me. She was a better match for him. I wanted him to be happy, I told myself." Her eyes lowered a bit. "But I'm not quite that selfless. I wanted to be happy too."

"Nothing wrong with that."

"It just wasn't meant to be. I was lucky to get the time with Ethan that I did."

"Do you know what happened...that night? When Jack was killed?"

"Sorry. I don't. That was long after your dad and I stopped

seeing each other. I read about it, but I don't know anything about it personally."

"Do you think my dad did it?"

"Like I said, I wasn't there."

"But you knew him. And Jack. What do you think went down?"

"I don't know." Her voice became more forceful. She looked away, blinking rapidly. After a few moments, he realized she was blinking away tears. "When I read about the shooting in the papers, I was horrified. I knew how hard this was going to be on everyone involved."

"Was there bad blood between my dad and Jack?"

"What do you think? Your father took his wife and married her. Left Jack in the cold. But the two men still had to see each other almost every day at work. No way that was going to be a happy experience. I know Jack thought about getting a transfer but...for whatever reason, it never happened."

"Do you think—" Dan swallowed. "Do you think my father was capable of killing Jack?"

She fidgeted. "Your father was a strong man. Very strong."

"What does that mean?"

"It means he was capable of doing anything, if he had to."

"But was he a murderer?"

"For the right reason?" She wiped her eyes. "I know this isn't what you want to hear. Ethan wasn't a bad person. But he could do anything if he felt it needed to be done."

"Even murder."

She didn't reply.

Dan waited a few moments before he pressed ahead. "Do you know anything about me maybe...having a sister?"

She hesitated a moment, then looked at him levelly. "Dan... are you sure you want to get into this? 'Cause let me tell you— it's nasty. You're not going to like what you hear."

"I want to know the truth."

She nodded. "There was...a daughter. Your mom's daughter. But not with your dad. With Jack."

"So...my half-sister?"

"Yeah. I guess that's right."

"What happened to her?"

"I don't know the details. They never wanted to talk about it. I think they considered abortion—your mom and Jack weren't married yet—but she decided to have the baby. They kept her a while, then gave her up for adoption."

"Why?"

"I don't know all the ins and outs. But she resurfaced again, several years later...and there was some trouble. I don't know much about it, but she came back into their lives in the worst possible way."

"Which is?"

She bit down on her lower lip. Her eyes went into deep focus.

"Please. I need to know what happened."

She hesitated for a long moment before answering. "You know who you should talk to? Gerald Jaquith. Jack's old partner. Back in the day."

"Would he have been at the shootout? When Jack was killed?"

"I assume so."

"He must be retired now. Do you know where he is?"

"I don't." She flashed a smile. "But you found me. I bet you can track him down too."

"I have a friend who is an excellent researcher."

"From what I read, you do pretty darn well yourself. You got dealt some tough cards. But you played them right and turned yourself into a superstar. Who helps people. Just like your dad did."

He did not reply. He couldn't. He decided to change the subject. "What's behind the door?"

"Huh?"

"The brown door. Between the vending machines."

"It's just...storage...and..."

He gave her a long look. "I've learned to watch people. Carefully. I saw the expression on your face when we came in, as if you were expecting someone else, even though I arrived at the arranged time. I see how you've positioned yourself. No one can get in or out of that door without going through you. And I can tell from the building layout that there's more back there than a mere storage closet. It's at least the size of a massage room. Maybe bigger."

She looked worried at first, then all at once, burst out with a huge grin. "Damnation. You *are* your father's boy."

"Well..."

"If I were thirty years younger, I'd throw myself at you right here and now."

He tugged at his collar. "I'm...seeing someone..."

"Just an expression, kid."

"What's the hustle? Smuggling?"

"Nothing quite that nefarious."

"Then what?"

"Off the record?"

"Does it relate to what happened to my dad?"

"Not in the slightest."

"Then off the record."

She took another deep breath. "You know anything about stem cells?"

"I know President Bush discontinued medical research using them."

"Embryonic stem cells, yes. But others quietly restarted the inquiry. The FDA has approved stem-cell procedures for treating cancer. But there are other uses."

His forehead creased. "Is this some kind of...secret beauty treatment?"

She touched her finger to her nose. "Ding ding ding. Medical researchers think stem cells could be used to treat heart disease or diabetes. But others believe it could have cosmetic benefits. Kinda like the crowd that started taking human-growth hormone. People will shoot themselves up with anything if they think it will keep them young."

"I see."

"We're not the only ones providing this service, though I think we're the only ones in St. Petersburg. Hard to know for sure, since no one's exactly advertising it. Supposed to take years off you. Erase wrinkles."

"I did notice you don't have much wrinkling."

"Because I eat right and take care of myself. I'm not injecting myself with anything risky. One lady in California got a $20,000 facelift that put her own stem cells into her face, especially around her eyes. But the stem cells turned to bone in her eyelid and suddenly she couldn't see any more. Paid a fortune to undo what she first paid to have done."

"Ouch."

"Yeah. We don't do that. But we will inject people with stem cells in low threshold doses."

"Do you think it helps?"

"I personally think it's mostly perception. People want to think they look better so they do."

"Like an expensive placebo?"

"More or less."

"Is this illegal?"

"Not to my knowledge. But nothing to brag about. The Association of Plastic Surgeons has warned against unsubstantiated claims and procedures that might put people at risk. But no laws have been passed. Want to give it a try?"

"No thanks. I like my face just fine the way it is."

"You might feel differently one day."

"Nah. I like my wrinkles. I earned these wrinkles. I don't

think they're anything to be embarrassed about." He rose. "But I do thank you for talking to me."

"The pleasure was mine. Seeing you takes me back to another time. A happy time. Before the shooting. Before the breakup. Life seemed simpler then. A place to live, food to eat, a man you loved. I thought I had it all."

He turned toward the door. "Maybe you did."

"Not surprised you would say that. You know what? You're just like him. You probably don't see it, but I can."

"Well...maybe."

"And you know what else?" She smiled, as broadly as it was possible to smile. "You've got your mother's eyes."

CHAPTER SEVENTEEN

DAN ENTERED THE COURTROOM WONDERING WHY HE FELT SUCH acute anxiety. Today should be a snap. He wasn't the attorney of record, so technically he didn't have to do anything except sit in a chair. He didn't have to make a brilliant argument. Jimmy wrote a fabulous brief and he knew Maria would argue it well.

But there were stakes. Enormous ones, even if they weren't the usual stakes. He was fighting not only for his name, but his family's name. His father's name. And he knew Sweeney was gunning for him. And his friends. And his law firm. Sweeney was determined to wipe him off the face of the map. And even that might not be enough to satisfy the man.

Jimmy barreled through the courtroom doors, swinging his satchel like a deadly weapon.

"Whoa, slow down, pardner," Dan said, raising his hands. "The courthouse deputies are already on edge. Keep moving like that and they're gonna draw on you."

"Sorry," Jimmy said, gulping air. "Important."

"You can't help us if you stroke out."

"I'm...not...gonna..."

"Of course, getting some exercise is probably good for you,"

Maria said. "Those desserts do tend to add up. But next time you decide to work up a sweat, you might take off the cardigan."

"Would you two clowns listen to me?" Jimmy asked. "I found two invoices."

Maria twirled a finger in the air. "Hurray. More bills to pay."

"You're not getting it." Jimmy reached into his satchel and withdrew a file folder. "Two invoices from investigators."

Maria opened the file. "Where did you find this?"

"In the documents our worthy opponents produced."

"Why didn't we see this sooner?"

"Because it was buried in a morass of more than twenty-thousand pages of garbage. This was in a box that looked completely irrelevant. And most of it was. But not this."

Maria nodded. "It would be contempt of court not to produce requested documents. But there are no rules against producing so much the other side can't possibly wade through it all." She scanned the first invoice. "This does confirm what Sweeney alluded to in his deposition. Private investigators."

"If they're claiming this is privileged work product, why produce invoices?" Jimmy asked.

"The results of the investigation may be privileged, but the existence of the investigation is not," Dan explained.

"Won't they have to tell all if they want to use the info at trial?"

"Sadly, no," Dan replied. "They'll tell as much or as little as they like."

"But we can cross-examine their witnesses," Jimmy said, "if they put them on the stand."

"I can try," Maria replied. "But paid witnesses tend to be loyal to the person who's paying them. Of course, the fact that they hired people doesn't mean they found anything. This could be a giant charade designed to distract us from more important matters." She tucked the invoices into her notebook. "But this is good work, Jimmy. Thanks for bringing this to my attention. Now sit down and rest. We need you healthy."

They all took a seat at their table. Dan waved at Drake and Caldwell as they entered. Still no client. He was beginning to wonder if Sweeney would show up for the trial.

A few minutes later, Judge Fernandez entered the courtroom. After addressing a few preliminary matters, he drew his attention to the motion. "If I understand this, Ms. Morales, you want to compel production of documents and witnesses pertaining to private investigations?"

She rose. "Yes, your honor. During the deposition, the defendant, Mr. Sweeney—"

"Dr. Sweeney," Caldwell corrected.

Maria rolled her eyes. "Whatever. He admitted that he has hired people to investigate matters pertaining to this suit. We immediately requested the production of all documents relevant to these investigations, but they stonewalled us."

Caldwell stood. "Not entirely—"

"Yes, we know you produced the invoices, buried in a box of documents pertaining to something else entirely, but that only tells us, once again, that the investigations exist. Our motion to compel relates to all documents pertaining to these investigations. We assume that will give us the names of the investigators, and then we'll likely take depositions."

Judge Fernandez adjusted his gaze. "And I suppose you object to this, Ms. Caldwell?"

"Indeed, your honor. Those investigative reports are privileged work product."

"That's not what Sweeney said," Maria cut in. "He said *he* hired people."

"He was speaking figuratively. That was actually a reference to the work of his legal team. I know, these abstract concepts may be difficult for you to—"

"I still want the documents."

"As those invoices make clear, the investigators were hired by my law firm. They were paid by my law firm. Any work generated by them is by definition work product and thus protected from oppositional discovery."

"Unless it isn't," Maria said. "Those invoices could be a smokescreen, which would explain why they were produced. Sweeney hired the investigators, the lawyers realized it was a mistake, so they're trying to avoid discovery by claiming they did the hiring. We really have no way of knowing. Unless we depose the investigators."

Judge Fernandez lowered his head and rubbed his temples. "Have any of you read the decisions of Judge Wayne Alley?"

Caldwell hesitated. "I...don't think so."

"He was handling a case like this. For some reason, his words come back to me today. He wrote in his opinion, 'If there is a hell to which disputatious, uncivil, vituperative lawyers go, let it be one in which the damned are eternally locked in discovery disputes with other lawyers of equally repugnant attributes.'"

Maria didn't take the hint. "We all hate discovery disputes, your honor. The easiest way to resolve them is to adopt a liberal approach. Make them produce the documents. There is little to no harm in producing them, but a great deal of harm if important information is kept secret."

"As a general rule," Fernandez said, "I do adopt a liberal approach. But when client confidences are involved, or attorney work product, I have to be stricter. Clients must be able to tell their lawyers matters in confidence, and lawyers must be able to prepare a case without worrying that the opposing side will seize everything they scribble on a piece of paper. Or quiz everyone they hire."

"This is entirely different," Maria said. "Here we're talking about the results of an investigation. We're talking about evidence. Not trial strategy. Not confidential discussions. Evidence."

"If I may," Caldwell interrupted, "it's only evidence if we decide to present it as evidence at trial. And if we do, they will receive notice and copies of relevant materials in advance. If we use any witnesses obtained as a result of an investigation, they will see the name on our witness list and they can depose before trial and cross-examine at trial. But the idea that we have to share everything we learn as we investigate a case is absurd."

"If the court takes that position," Maria insisted, "then basically, you're saying the defendants can decide for themselves what's important and what isn't. Which basically means they can bury anything that helps us or hurts them."

"Do you have evidence of any relevant documents being buried?" Judge Fernandez asked.

"Well...no."

"Have they done anything to prevent you from conducting investigations of your own?"

"Not to my knowledge."

"In fact, you have conducted your own independent investigations, haven't you?"

"Of course."

"Have you shared those reports with your opponents?"

"Well...no. But that really *is* attorney work product."

The judge gave her an arched eyebrow.

"Because the work was conducted by an actual attorney," she continued. "Garrett Armstrong, a member of my firm."

"I'm not seeing a distinction."

"At his deposition, Sweeney made veiled references to his discoveries, suggesting they are relevant and threatening us with them. Saying they were going to make us look like fools at trial."

"I can see where you would want the reports, given those facts," the judge said. "But I don't see that you have a right to obtain them."

"Your honor," Caldwell said, "I can assure you that this is

legitimate work product. I personally hired the investigators and I personally communicated with them. And to the extent that we found anything threatening, the plaintiff will know about it as soon as we exchange witness and exhibit lists."

Judge Fernandez tilted his head. "That is the way it usually goes."

Maria did not relent. "Your honor, that's not satisfactory in this case. When we exchange lists, it will be a few days before trial. We need to know everything these people have up their sleeves now."

"Ms. Morales," the judge said, "let me remind you again that you are not in a criminal court. The civil courts are a completely different kettle of fish."

"I am aware that—"

"Seriously. Completely different. A defense attorney can demand that the prosecution turn over all exculpatory evidence. But a plaintiff does not have the same rights. In civil cases, where no one's liberty is at stake, we have a much leveler playing field. A plaintiff is expected to prove his own case. In fact, a plaintiff is expected to already have that proof before filing. Otherwise, the lawsuit is brought in bad faith and could be seen as a tool for harassment rather than genuinely seeking reparation for damages suffered."

Dan didn't like the sound of that at all. Was the judge trying to send them a message?

"You have the burden of proof. A considerably less stringent burden than the one you're accustomed to, but still a burden. Which you must meet. Without a lot of whining."

Maria did not respond.

"Your motion is denied."

"But your honor—"

"Yes, Ms. Morales, I know you disagree, but I'm the one wearing the black nightgown, so I'm the one who makes the rulings. I'm not ordering any additional discovery, but I'm not having a trial by ambush, either. When can the parties be ready to exchange witness lists and exhibits?"

Caldwell spoke loud and clear. "We're ready now, your honor."

He nodded. "Ms. Morales?"

"We can be ready...very soon."

"Good. And I don't want endless laundry lists of every document in your possession. Do your work in advance of trial and produce a list of the items you think might actually be introduced. After you've exchanged those lists, look them over carefully. If you see any names you don't know or exhibits you didn't expect, notice some depositions. But stop with the discovery disputes. They are irritating, unproductive, and frankly, make you look rather desperate."

Maria looked like an ice sculpture.

The judge scooted back in his chair. "Is there anything else? Good. I don't expect to see any of you before the pretrial. Submit your trial briefs, which by the way are limited to twenty pages. I do not want any Homeric epics. Just tell me what the case is about and the issues to be addressed. I expect everyone to be ready to go to trial on time." He paused. "Without a lot of whining."

The judge left the courtroom.

Maria fell into her chair in a heap.

Jimmy leaned closer to both of his partners. "What...just happened?"

"I'm not sure," Dan said.

"Was the judge being sexist? The stuff about whining?"

"I think he just doesn't like discovery disputes."

"Or me," Maria added.

"I didn't perceive any animus toward you," Dan said, hoping it was true. "But he is a Bush appointee. Probably leans toward the conservative. And let's face it—Sweeney is a prominent citizen with a lot of connections. No one wants to be on his bad side. I know Sweeney thinks he controls judicial appointments around here. Maybe Fernandez would like to be on the Fifth Circuit one day."

"You think Sweeney got to the judge?"

"I don't think Sweeney has to say a word. Everyone knows the kind of power he wields. No one with ambition wants to be on the wrong side of that."

"Bottom line this for me, Dan."

"You won't win over the judge with the bleeding-heart stuff."

"Then what?"

"Prove Sweeney is a liar. And a criminal. If you do that, then sucking up to him becomes a liability, not a career move."

Her head dropped. "I don't have that kind of proof."

Dan pushed himself out of his chair. "Then I guess we know what we need to do. And the sooner the better. I feel relatively certain Judge Fernandez is not going to be amenable to a motion for a continuance." He paused. "Or anything else."

CHAPTER EIGHTEEN

DAN STROLLED DOWN THE BOARDWALK THAT SERVED AS THE MAIN drag at St. Pete Pier. He was embarrassed to admit that this was his first time out here, though to be fair, he had been busy of late. The Pier was the grandest step yet in St. Pete's ongoing effort to attract more tourism and to create recreational opportunities for residents. Its planned grand premiere had been delayed by the coronavirus lockdown. St. Pete was disproportionately impacted by the disease, so they had to take all possible precautions.

Fortunately, that national nightmare passed, a vaccine circulated, and once again people could remind themselves what it meant to have fun. He had read that the Pier comprised more than twenty-six acres. There were many places for children to play, plus a discovery center and what they called a "wet classroom" for learning about marine life. Local artist Janet Echelman created a spectacular billowing net sculpture, and there were areas to bike, swim, eat, drink, or shop. All kinds of ways to have a fantastic day with family and friends. In many ways, it reminded him of the famous Santa Monica Pier, except without the cheesy carnival rides. Or Chicago's Navy Pier, without the wind.

St. Pete Pier was packed this Saturday morning. He was pleased to see so many people, tourists and locals alike, enjoying the sunshine and the sea. It was almost too crowded to have anything resembling a serious meeting—but perhaps that was what the man had in mind. Little chance of attracting much notice, given the hustle and bustle.

"Pike?"

He heard the voice and swiveled around. He thought the call came from someone standing outside a gelato store.

The beard altered the man's appearance, but Dan was almost certain it was Gerald Jaquith. Torn, loose-fitting jeans. Small scar beneath his left eye. Gnarled fingers. Looked like the intervening years had not been all that kind to him. Dark circles around both eyes. Blue windbreaker he did not need.

He approached. "I'm Dan Pike. Gerald Jaquith?"

A small smile played on the grizzled man's lips. "You're Ethan's boy?"

"I am."

"Wow." The man shook his head slowly. "You look just like him. I guess people tell you that all the time."

"Not really."

"You've got the same fire. Ethan was one of those guys who didn't just drift through life, you know what I mean? He was always in active mode. Never let anything slip by."

"Thank you for speaking with me. You didn't have to."

"And I didn't want to. I've spent the last few decades trying to forget all about that mess. And wishing everyone else would."

"What changed your mind?"

"About talking to you? You're Ethan's boy. I respect that. I have a son too but...that didn't turn out too well. I read about your lawsuit against Sweeney."

"And you wanted to help?"

"I understood what it was really about. You don't care about money. You're trying to learn the truth about what your dad did."

"True enough. You were Jack Fisher's partner."

"I was. Just got the assignment a few days before...well, you know. The day everything changed."

"The day my father was wrongfully accused of murder."

"The day my partner died. The worst thing that can possibly happen to a cop. Worse than if I'd died myself. Much worse, in fact."

Dan drew in his breath. Note: stop being so self-centered. You're not the only person in the world with feelings. "I'm sure that was horrible."

"I doubt it was a picnic for you, either. Wanna walk? I prefer to keep moving."

Because he was paranoid about eavesdropping? Afraid someone was watching? Dan was happy to oblige. Since he was almost certain someone had been watching him, too.

They walked side-by-side down the long boardwalk. Most of the traffic was headed the other direction, but passersby tended to curve around them.

"How well did you know my father?"

"Well enough to really like him. As cops went, your dad was the best. The crème de la crème. Which is what made what happened later...hard to believe."

Dan decided to postpone asking the ultimate question. "How did he get along with your partner?"

Jaquith let out something between a laugh and a choke. "Now that's a whole different thing. Complex. Multifaceted. Even a great cop has weak spots."

"Like...?"

"Ethan and Jack hated each other."

Not what he wanted to hear. "I know my dad married Jack's ex-wife."

"And the rumor around the station was that their relationship started...before her first marriage ended. If you know what I mean."

That corresponded with what he'd heard from Erica. "They were all living in the same house."

"Right. Weird from the start. The only thing that could possibly make it weirder would be if they started swapping partners."

"They didn't exactly swap..."

"True. Your dad got Jack's wife. Jack got nothing."

"Was there more to it than just the divorce and remarriage?"

"Oh, much more. So much more."

"Did you ever hear about...Jack having a daughter? I mean, with my mom?"

"You don't know whether you have a sister?" Jaquith snapped his fingers. "You know, I do kinda remember hearing something." His eyes went up and to the left, and if he were trying to pull a memory out of deep storage. "Like some gossip, maybe when I was out drinking with the other officers. It's like...there was something bad about it."

"What? Birth defects? Some kind of disease?"

"I don't know. I can't pull it up. I may not have ever known the details. But there was something people were whispering about. Something Jack wouldn't talk about. Like...maybe he was doing something he shouldn't." Jaquith took a breath. "I'm sorry. I just don't remember. But if you had a sister, wouldn't your father have told you? Or your mother?"

"You'd think. If they didn't—there must've been a reason."

"Agreed. Of course, sometimes the new husband prefers not to be reminded about kids by another spouse—but your dad wasn't like that. He'd be more likely to adopt the kid. But I guess that didn't happen?"

"Definitely not. I grew up an only child. Any idea where that daughter is today?"

"Sorry. No clue."

It seemed no one did. Every time he tried to learn more, he hit a dead end. "Any other grudges Jack might've had against my dad?"

Jaquith exhaled slowly. "Jack...was not the world's greatest cop. Your dad was. Your dad became a cop by choice. He had a passion for justice."

Somehow, that sounded familiar...

"Jack was just imitating others and trying to survive. He'd gotten through college—barely. Didn't exactly set the curve. Lucky to get on with the SPPD. If he failed as a cop, he'd be driving a truck or working fast food."

"He felt...insecure? Inferior?"

"And rightly so. About a month before the shooting, your father started having some problems at work. Reports went missing. Evidence didn't stay in the locker. Made no sense. Your father was not the type to make careless mistakes."

"You think Jack was sabotaging him?"

"I wasn't the only one who suspected that. These mistakes seemed completely out of character for your dad—but exactly like the kind of petty weaselly stunts Jack would pull. Your dad thought so too. He finally confronted Jack about it. In public."

"That can't have been pleasant."

"It wasn't. They had a huge knockdown drag-out. Right in the middle of the station. Probably twenty witnesses. Nasty. Name-calling. Accusations. Jack used the f-word more than once and called his ex—your dad's wife—a slut. Your dad threw the first punch. Landed a good one on Jack's solar plexus. Jack made a half-hearted effort to reply in kind, but others broke it up."

"Sounds intense."

"And remember, this was me, punk rookie, with my new partner, watching him mix it up with another officer. I just stood and stared. Couldn't believe it. And then, a few days later, Jack's dead."

"And my father is the lead suspect."

"After the big fight, that conclusion was inevitable." They reached the end of the boardwalk, gazed out at the sea, then turned and headed back the way they came. "With an eyewitness confirming what everyone already suspected, there was no way your father could escape. The police never even considered another suspect."

"When you mention an eyewitness, you're referring to Bradley Ellison, right?"

"Yeah. Mister Clean, that's what they called him."

"But you didn't think so?"

"I'm suspicious of anyone who's that perfect. I'm suspicious of anyone who rats out a fellow officer, even one he thinks committed murder. Cops usually protect one another. He didn't."

"Did you have reason to doubt his testimony?"

Jaquith slowed. He looked at Dan out the side of his eyes, brows knitted together. "Have you talked to Ellison?"

"I have."

"Did his testimony seem...right?"

He tried to peer into Jaquith's eyes, to read his mind. What was he saying? "Ellison testified that he was crouched outside his patrol car. He saw my dad fire in his driver's side car mirror."

"Let's think about that for just a moment. They're caught in a horrendous crossfire. A hail of bullets. Gang leaders firing at them relentlessly, some with automatic weapons. But is Ellison looking ahead at the people trying to kill him? No, he's looking behind at other police officers." Jaquith tucked in his chin. "Is that what you would be doing?"

"Probably not. But maybe he heard something..."

"Who could hear anything in that chaos?"

"Maybe he had some reason to suspect—"

"That your dad would take this moment to off a fellow officer? Come on. Even given the fact that they hated each other,
that's a stretch. A secret assassination in the midst of a
shootout? How could Ellison anticipate that?" He paused and let
his voice go quiet. "There was no reason for Ellison to be
looking backward. Unless, of course, he knew something was
about to happen. Or he made the whole story up afterwards to
disguise what truly occurred."

Dan let the words sink in. Jaquith illuminated a lot of what
had been nagging at him, even if he hadn't yet been able to put it
into words. "What about you? Did you see anything?"

"No."

"You were Jack's partner, weren't you?"

"So?"

"Weren't you there?"

"No. Why would you think that?"

"I assumed—you said you were his partner—"

"But I wasn't with him that night, thank God."

"But—someone must've been with him. Someone must've
been riding shotgun."

Jaquith took a tiny step closer. "Oh my God."

"What? What is it?"

"You don't know."

"Stop talking in riddles."

"You don't know who was—did Ellison cover that up, too?"

Dan grabbed him by the shoulders. "What are you talking
about?"

"The other person in Jack's car—"

Dan heard the shot the same instant he felt Jaquith stiffen in
his hands. Jaquith's eyes rolled back into his head.

"Talk to me. Finish your sentence!"

He heard another crack and this time he realized it was
gunfire. Someone was shooting at them.

Blood spilled out from a wound in the back of Jaquith's head. His body went completely limp. He started to fall. Dan tightened his grip and lowered him slowly to the boardwalk.

Another shot rang out. This time Dan heard the shrill wasp-buzz of a bullet whizzing past him so close it stung.

Wait—there was more to it than that.

He clasped his hand against the side of his face.

Blood.

The bullet had creased his head. Another inch or two to the side and he'd be dead.

"Talk to me!" he screamed, but he knew he was only making a bad situation worse. Jaquith was in no condition to be interrogated, and every second he remained out in the middle of the boardwalk his life was in danger.

Who was the target? Jaquith? Him? Both? Someone else?

It was impossible to know and he didn't have time to ponder mysteries. Another crackle of gunfire boomed, even louder than before.

The crowd panicked. Everyone looked around and tried to understand what had happened, but after that explosive burst, no one had any doubts.

There was a sniper. They were under fire. It was Las Vegas and the Beltway all over again.

"Run!" someone shrieked, and everyone did. The boardwalk descended into chaos. Parents scooped up their children and darted out of the stampede. People raced into stores and restaurants, trying to find cover.

Another shot rang out, and this time the crowd became dangerous. People pushed and shoved, desperate to get out of the line of fire. Dan saw a man near him topple and fall. People shouted, adding to the pandemonium.

Dan dragged Jaquith to the side while scanning the skyline, trying to determine where the shots originated. There were too many possibilities. The Learning Center. The restaurants. The gift shops. Any of those could give a sniper the needed height and a nest to hide in.

Jaquith looked bad. His eyes were open, but barely.

"Jaquith. Who was in the car with Jack?"

Jaquith grabbed his shirt. His voice was barely a whisper. "She...needs you...."

He looked as if he were trying to purse his lips, trying to form more words. But he didn't have the strength left. A few moments later, the light went out of his eyes.

"Don't leave me!" Dan screamed, but he knew it was too late. Once again, he'd come close to learning something useful, and once again, the knowledge had been snatched from him at the last possible moment. The trial would start Monday morning and he had no idea how he could win it. And an innocent was paying the price for his curiosity.

It was becoming increasingly clear that someone wanted the secrets of the past to remain secret. And was willing to kill to keep them that way.

NOT EVEN PAST

CHAPTER NINETEEN

DAN STARED INTO THE BATHROOM MIRROR. THE WIND ROCKED HIS boat like a strand of straw in a hurricane. What brought this turbulent weather? St. Pete got high winds from time to time, but this was like something in a Gothic novel—where the turmoil in the environment reflected the turmoil within.

He took a deep breath and tried to steady himself. He could not appear in court for the first day of trial without shaving. But he could not shave with a shaky hand, at least not unless he wanted to appear with bandages across his face. He was already bruised and battered from the shooting at the Pier. He couldn't afford to go in looking like a rough character.

But he also couldn't get his hand to stop shaking.

He liked to feel he was in control of his environment, that he knew what he was doing and was prepared for what would happen next. Because you're a control freak, Maria would say, but he felt that was somewhat overstating the case. He was cautious, and he had learned the value of being prepared. Of leaving no stone unturned. Of belt-and-suspendering every possible contingency.

This case had started as his masterplan to uncover the truth, but it had soon descended into near chaos. He did not control any aspect. He didn't have all the answers and he was putting his friends in danger. He was putting everyone in danger. Three innocents were shot at the Pier. Not fatally, but still. He had no idea who did that, or why. He kept waking in the middle of the night, sweating, imagining himself back in the tourist attraction that in a split second had turned into a war zone.

Jaquith was in a coma, barely alive. Doctors said it was a coin toss whether he would survive. The man hadn't said a word since he left the Pier.

Maria had suggested asking for a continuance. Given the publicity the shooting had received, they might be able to convince Judge Fernandez the plaintiff was suffering from some version of PTSD. It was tempting.

But he couldn't do it. He'd started this mess, and he was going to end it, on schedule, one way or the other.

He steadied himself with both hands on the sink and peered into the mirror. People kept remarking on his eyes.

Whose eyes were they? And how far did they see?

All he wanted was the truth. Was that too much to ask?

He pressed a hand against his forehead. Maybe it was. Maybe he was being selfish. Maybe he should let the past be the past. Move forward. Focus on the future.

But even as he thought it, he knew he wouldn't let it be. He couldn't let it be.

Maybe he would never know the truth. Maybe he would never learn everything there was to learn about his past, his sister, his family, his father.

But it wouldn't be because he didn't try. And it sure as hell wouldn't be because he quit.

DAN STOPPED BY THE HOSPITAL ON HIS WAY TO THE COURTHOUSE. No change, and he didn't detect much optimism about Jaquith's future. He tried to keep a poker face while the doctors spoke, but it wasn't easy.

By the time he arrived at the courthouse, he was barely able to think about the trial. And he knew where that led. An attorney who didn't have his head in the game was destined to go down in flames.

"Dan!" Near the courtroom doors he spotted Jake Kakazu, and with him, Jazlyn. "I was hoping to bump into you," Jake said. "I want you to know we're doing everything possible to find out who the shooter was. Following all the leads. The Chief has every available man on this."

Dan nodded. "You won't find him."

"What makes you so sure?"

"This didn't start yesterday. This is part of something larger that has been going on for a long time. And no one has stopped it yet."

"We can try."

"Sure. You can try. Give me a heads up if you find something."

"Of course. How are you?"

"Fine."

Jazlyn gave him a stern look. "Yeah, yeah, but seriously. We have counselors working with others who were at the Pier during the shooting. But someone actually took a shot at you. How are you holding up?"

"I'm fine. Back on the job."

"You don't look fine."

"You don't like my suit?"

"The suit is fabulous. But you look like you didn't sleep a wink and are having flashbacks after being caught in a vicious sniper attack."

"I've seen worse."

"*When?* You've seen bad, sure. But worse? What could be worse?"

"Jazlyn, I appreciate your concern. Truly. But I think it's best if I plow ahead with the case. Keep my mind occupied."

"What I hear you saying is, you think the best way to get over trauma is to ignore it."

"No..."

"Pretend it didn't happen."

"I'm not—"

Jazlyn laid a hand on his arm. "Dan, that is not the best way to get over anything. That's how it gets worse. That's how it festers until it creates permanent scars."

His voice soared. "Do you people understand—"

He closed his eyes, took a deep breath, then slowly released it. "Whether I like it or not, I have a trial starting today. I need to focus."

Jazlyn did not release his arm. "When you're ready to talk, I'm here."

"I appreciate that."

"These aren't just words. You've done so much for so many. You've made my life immeasurably better. Let me help you."

He gently shook off her hand. "I'll keep that in mind. Thank you for the update, Jake."

He turned abruptly—and had barely taken a step before he bumped into someone else. Someone impossible to miss.

Conrad Sweeney. Live and in person. No steam, no video monitor.

The huge man stood before him. Glowering.

Sweeney's attorneys hovered in the background. They looked enormously displeased, as if they had advised against this encounter but he insisted on it. And not far behind them, Dan spotted Prudence Hancock. Also glowering.

"Mr. Pike, I'm so sorry about what happened," Sweeney said. His arms were outstretched, his eyes wide and earnest.

Seeing the man clearly and up close for the first time sent Dan's brain into overdrive. He tried to observe what he could but his head felt fuzzy. Sweeney missed a button on his shirt. Missed a spot that proved he shaved his head. Armani suit. Gucci shoes. Red socks. "That shooting sounds nightmarish."

Dan tried to respond but found his tongue frozen in place, as if he were in the presence of his favorite celebrity, or the middle-school vice-principal, or God.

"I want to assure you I had nothing to do with this. Nothing whatsoever, and I don't know who did."

Dan gazed at him. If he couldn't speak, he could at least use his eyes to express how little he believed this.

"I've known Officer Jaquith for decades. Horrible to hear what happened to him. If we're not here all day, I plan to visit him at the hospital."

Concentrate, Dan told himself. Don't stammer like a schoolboy. "I...was there this morning."

"Of course you were." Sweeney's eyes knitted together. "I also want you to know that we will not object if you'd like a continuance. We can put this trial off till a later date." He smiled, then glanced at his legal team. "Viewed in perspective, it all seems rather trivial now, doesn't it?"

"Not...to me."

"Maybe we could come to some kind of settlement. We could issue mutual retractions. Let bygones be bygones. Work together on some kind of community charitable endeavor."

He wasn't sure if his head was disagreeing or trembling. "I can't do that."

Sweeney sighed heavily. "Then the show must go on? A pity." He glanced at his lawyers. "I see very little benefit in perpetuating the hostility."

Maria appeared beside them. "Does that mean you'll release those investigator reports?"

Sweeney's eyebrows knitted. "I fear that would...aggravate the hostility rather than abating it."

"All we want is the truth. Tell us everything you know. Then we might be in a position to consider settling. And not until."

Sweeney looked at her wearily. "I'm sorry to hear that. If you have a change of heart...as this case unfolds...please let me know. We're always willing to talk. No matter how nasty it gets."

Sweeney turned and took his seat at the defendant's table.

As soon as the man was out of his immediate vicinity, Dan found it much easier to speak. And think. Why did Sweeney have such a powerful effect on him? He felt embarrassed about how easily he'd been intimidated.

He turned to Maria. "Where did you come from?"

"You didn't think I was going to let you talk to that monster alone, did you? I noticed he had his lawyers close at hand."

"I could've handled it."

"Yeah, I noticed you were winning the debate. Or would've, as soon as you said something."

"You learn more by listening."

"Is that what was going on?"

"Did you notice what Sweeney said? Or didn't say?"

"I'm not sure what you mean."

"He told me he'd known Jaquith for decades. I told him I'd just been to the hospital."

"Yes. And?"

"Wouldn't most people ask how Jaquith was doing?" He paused. "But Sweeney didn't."

Maria pondered a moment. "Meaning he didn't care? Or he already knew?"

"For that matter, he didn't appear surprised when I said I'd already been to the hospital this morning, early though it is."

"Meaning he already knew?"

Dan cast a steady gaze toward the other table. "Meaning we need to be careful. And not buy into his show of concern. This man is playing hardball. An oily, behind-the-scenes hardball, but no less hard for it. We need to bring our A-Game. Or he will bury us alive."

CHAPTER TWENTY

JUDGE FERNANDEZ ENTERED THE COURTROOM AND BRISKLY plowed through the preliminary matters, making sure the parties were ready to proceed and eliminating anything that might slow the trial once it started. He clearly knew about the shooting at the Pier but made no direct reference to it, simply asking if the parties wanted to proceed at this time.

They did.

Dan was amazed at how briskly jury selection went in this civil suit. Compared to criminal cases, there were fewer peremptory challenges, less leeway in the questioning, and more judicial intrusion. He was astonished to find they had selected a jury in about an hour and a half. The judge gave the panel some preliminary instructions, then called for opening statements.

Another first—since he was the plaintiff in this action, they got to speak before the opposition. Dan was glad Maria was doing it. He was accustomed to absorbing what the opponent said and basically offering an extemporaneous rebuttal.

"First of all," Maria began, "I want to thank you all for your service." She proceeded with a few more platitudes and niceties.

They all seemed like time-waste to him, but he knew studies showed jurors liked a little warmup. It helped give them a feeling that the lawyers understood they were real people surrendering precious time to hear this case.

It didn't take Maria long to get to the heart of the matter. "This case is all about words, the power of words, the enormous potential words have to do damage to others. In America, of course, we have the First Amendment. Everyone has the freedom to speak their mind—but that doesn't mean you can't be held accountable for what you said after you say it. That's what this case is all about. The defendant, Conrad Sweeney, made statements before a group of more than a hundred people, statements later broadcast to a larger audience on television and on the internet, that damaged my client, Daniel Pike, both emotionally and economically. As a lawyer, Mr. Pike's career and livelihood are dependent upon his reputation. The defendant did his best to destroy that reputation. Let me play you a recording of precisely what was said."

At the pretrial, both parties and the judge had agreed that a video recording could be used in openings. It would later be formally introduced as evidence by a sponsoring witness.

The jurors stared at a monitor placed behind the witness stand and watched an edited video of the relevant parts of the conversation at the press conference.

"Just for the record, the arrogant young man speaking is Daniel Pike, a criminal lawyer who has put dozens of drug dealers and murderers back on the street, including the man responsible for the horrendous Trademark Massacre."

"That's not even—"

"The Pike family has been a blight on this city for generations. His father was a dirty cop and a convicted murderer. And what a coincidence—the son has been accused of murder as well. I guess what they say about the murder gene is true. The apple doesn't fall far from the tree."

"My father was a hero."

"Only to the underworld. He was a crook who, like you, had signif-icant ties to organized crime. What a coincidence—whenever a new story breaks involving this smuggling cartel, you're always involved."

Maria shut off the recording. "We will play the entire conversation during the trial, but I hope you've already heard enough to be shocked. Just to be clear, the defendant accused my client of being a criminal because he represents accused criminals. In other words, every defense lawyer in the country is a criminal because he does his job. Worse, the defendant suggested that my client and his family are connected to orga-nized crime. The mob. South American cartels. Because he helped the police *stop* the cartel. That is simply vile."

She pivoted slowly and scanned the jury box. "To be sure, my client's father was convicted of murder—though that sadly does not prove he was guilty. The other accusations, however, are completely baseless. They are lies. They are unsubstantiated lies, and they were lies told in public for the specific purpose of hurting my client. Ask yourself—would you hire a lawyer who was suspected of being connected to the mob? Of course not. You can readily see how serious and potentially damaging these claims are.

"We will submit evidence at trial to help you assess the damage. We have been hampered by the fact that the defendant refused to produce certain reports in his possession relating to the case. You will hear more about that later, but ask yourself, why would someone withhold information? There's only one possible answer, and it isn't because the reports support your slanderous lies. That would make them eager to produce the reports."

Maria continued. "Is there any doubt that damage to my client's reputation occurred? The evidence will make it clear, if this recording hasn't already, that unlawful slander was perpe-trated by the defendant. The defendant believes that his wealth, his connections, and his influence will immunize him, that they put him above the reach of the law. I hope you will take this opportunity to send a strong message to the contrary. No one is above the law. Not even the rich and powerful. No one."

She stepped back to give the jury a clear view of Sweeney, who sat impassively at his table. Not quite grinning. But almost.

"This man believes he can get away with anything." She turned back to the jury, giving heavy emphasis to each word. "Prove—him—wrong."

DAN WAS NOT ENORMOUSLY SURPRISED THAT DRAKE DELIVERED the opening. Caldwell might be the better attorney, but her robotic demeanor wouldn't resonate with jurors or incur much empathy. She would have trouble driving home the drama. As it happened, Drake was all about the drama.

"Just to be clear, I agree with exactly one thing my worthy opponent said, and one thing only. We do have the First Amendment in this country. We have freedom of speech. Supposedly. But what does that freedom mean if people can haul you into court for stating facts that are well known and mostly a matter of public record? We live in a time of vile words. They're everywhere. People tweet lies every day, but Congress says they're immune from liability. Troll farms pump out fake news and they aren't stopped. But one man, perhaps the most prominent citizen of this city, tries to alert people to a possible danger, a family that has repeatedly aligned itself with crime and criminals, and what does he get for his service? A lawsuit, of course. No matter how frivolous your claim, there's some lawyer somewhere willing to bring it to court."

"Objection," Maria said. As Dan well knew, objections during openings were rare, but this crossed the line. "Among other problems, this is argumentative."

"I have to agree," Judge Fernandez said. "Please stick to previewing your evidence and witnesses for the jury. The court does not appreciate attacks on the justice system. Remember that you are an officer of the court."

"Understood," Drake said, then turned back to the jury as if he hadn't heard a word. "Here are the facts. The evidence will show that the plaintiff's father, Ethan Pike, was a police officer convicted of murdering a fellow police officer, a man named Jack Fisher. Pike was given a life sentence and died in prison. Fact. The evidence will show that his son, the plaintiff, Daniel Pike, is a criminal lawyer who has represented many drug dealers and other felons. Fact. He also represented the man who, after Pike got him released, started the Trademark massacre. Fact. Pike has represented gang members on many occasions, and even more recently has handled two cases that involved organized crime, specifically, South American cartels. Fact. And that's important. Because, thank God, in America, we still have the right to speak facts, even if someone else finds those truths unpleasant or some liberal conspiracy wants to make it illegal to say what's so. You see, statements can only be slanderous if they're false. Truth is a defense."

Drake leaned against the rail separating him from the jury. "That's the key here. We will show that every statement made by our client, Dr. Conrad Sweeney, is true and has strong support in documented fact. We will also show that the plaintiff made statements that have no basis whatsoever in fact. That's why we asserted a counterclaim. In this case, it's not just the plaintiff asking for damages. The defendant is also seeking damages, and believe me, Dr. Sweeney's reputation is worth a great deal more than this criminal lawyer's. If anyone has suffered damage, it's Dr. Sweeney, the man who has done more for this city than any other living person."

Drake hesitated, as if ready to conclude, then spoke again. "Let me say a word about those reports the opposing lawyer mentioned. Those reports were generated by us, Dr. Sweeney's lawyers, not Dr. Sweeney. As the judge will explain in his final instructions, they are privileged work product. The court has ruled that they do not have to be produced to the other side in advance of trial. But to the degree that they're relevant they will be produced during this trial. These suggestions that we're hiding something are nonsense. As with most investigations, the lion's share of what we learned is not that interesting. But we did dig up a few nuggets that shine a whole new light on Mr. Pike and his...associations. And prove once and for all that Dr. Sweeney has not committed slander. He has merely shined a light on reality. He should be praised and thanked. And the plaintiff—"

In an almost direct mimicry of Maria's final move, Drake took a step back, inviting the jury to look at Dan. "This man, this son of a convicted murderer, this defender of murderers, this man who always seems to be in the middle of whatever crime gang, crime lord, cartel or"—he paused—"crossfire is taking place, has very little reputation to worry about. Even if his claims were true, he couldn't suffer damages, because his reputation has no value. But I will ask you to hold him accountable for his actions, something that has been far too long in coming."

CHAPTER TWENTY-ONE

GARRETT LIKED TO THINK OF HIMSELF AS A WELL-ROUNDED ADULT male, open to new ideas, flexible and fun-loving, if not frivolous. But he was on the conservative side, and there were some aspects of modern society he took exception to. He refused to become his father—or worse, his grandfather. But come on—that alleged music they play on FM radio stations is corporate claptrap. He didn't mind same-sex couples, but he was tired of seeing them gratuitously forced into television dramas in percentages that far exceeded reality. He was a healthy male who enjoyed heterosexual sex in monogamous relationships. And he felt certain that if he ever had any problems in that department—not that he ever had—he would seek the appropriate help.

But visiting a professional sex researcher? That was not on his bucket list. That was modern society and its obsessive focus on pleasure reeling out of control.

He had tried to make an appointment with Dr. Elliot Harrison at a neutral location, like a diner or a donut shop. But Harrison said he was busy and didn't have time for this, so the meeting was either at work or it wasn't happening.

A sex researcher. He should get hazard pay for this one.

After a few minutes, an elderly man wearing the traditional white coat and a bow tie emerged from a doorway. As if the cliché weren't quite fulfilled, he was actually holding a clipboard.

"Dr. Harrison?"

The man smiled. He was short, a little stocky, balding at the top, and wore thick plastic glasses. "Last time I checked."

Ha ha. "I'm Garrett Wainwright. Thank you for meeting with me. I'm sure you're very busy."

"Depends on your measuring stick. Nothing like when I was an OB-GYN. Much calmer lifestyle. Care to step inside?" He led the way and Garrett followed.

Although the exterior of the building was modest—plain square stucco, boring—the interior was more modern and high-tech. As they walked down the corridor, Garrett spotted a number of small lab units. He had no idea what the researchers inside were doing, but they looked smart and appeared to have the equipment they needed to complete their tasks.

"We do all kinds of work here," Harrison explained. "But my lab is in the rear. Some of my volunteers prefer privacy. I'm sure you understand."

Privacy for sex research? He definitely understood. Harrison escorted him into what appeared to be his office. Small but adequate. A desk piled high with file folders took up most of the space, but the far window permitted a view of another room beyond. One equipped with a small bed. He couldn't be certain from this perspective, but he thought the window was a one-way mirror.

"I called you because I believe you used to deliver babies at St. Petersburg General," Garrett explained.

"True enough. I didn't have or want my own practice. I took what came. ER work, too. You'd be amazed how many pregnant women don't have a regular doctor and haven't made any advance plans. Hell, I've had women who didn't even know they were pregnant till the baby started making its way into the world. And somehow I'm supposed to take these random elements and turn them into a successful childbirth. Too stressful for me."

"So you switched to...sex."

Harrison chuckled. "I guess that's one way of putting it. I got into pure research. What happens before the baby is born. It's what always interested me most. As you get older, you have to accept some things about yourself. I'm not a people person. I don't need patients. I do like helping others...but perhaps in a less immediate way. I didn't start with the sex stuff, but strangely enough, that seems to be what I'm best at."

Given his "class nerd" appearance, Harrison might not appear threatening or intimidating. People might be able to discuss their intimate issues more readily with him.

"I rose in this field far faster than I ever did at the hospital," Harrison explained. "Everything changed after I attended my first orgy."

Garrett blinked. "Your *first* orgy?"

"Yeah," Harrison said matter-of-factly. "The amazing thing is, you think it's going to be all sexy and exciting, lots of screaming and wailing and orgasmic ecstasy."

"But it isn't?"

"Nah. Mostly silence. Little conversation. The occasional sound of a belt buckle hitting the floor."

"You actually...attended? Observed? Participated?"

"Observed. I had this idea it would be a crazy free-for-all, but no, there's a bouncer with an iPad keeping everyone in line. This was a formal affair sponsored by a private club. You had to be approved in advance and you had to pay an admission fee. A hundred bucks for a single guy, fifty for a married guy bringing a spouse, and ten bucks for a woman."

"Seems rather sexist."

"Sexist but necessary. That fee doesn't guarantee you're going to have sex with anyone. You still have to find someone who wants to. It's a lot like a singles bar, except you don't need clever banter and you don't have to go anywhere once you're ready to hook up."

Garrett felt a chill. "I don't think I'd enjoy it."

"Imagine how I felt. Not only there but administering the penile gauge."

"The...uh..."

"You heard me right. To measure arousal. I was working on an ongoing study, and the fact that I didn't mind doing what others found embarrassing made me indispensable. I don't know why I didn't mind. I think it's because those people didn't mind me. Maybe they were just preoccupied, but I think there's something that makes me sort of...invisible. Someone people overlook."

Garrett could almost see that, actually. "What were you researching?"

"There's a psychological theory—a whole branch of research actually—called 'cads vs. dads.' Which is related to the 'sexy sons hypothesis.' Have you read about it?"

"I'm afraid I have not."

"But I bet you've wondered, do women always go for the bad boy? Or do they want a stable partner, a good husband and father?"

"And?"

"The answer depends upon the age of the woman, her background, and her personality, but as a general rule, once women reach a certain age and maturity, they look for a stable partner, someone who will be a good provider or parent. But after a while, it's possible they might stray–even if only for a night— with a hunkier guy with ripped abs. She keeps the reliable guy but gets to have sex with the hunkier cad. You know, the Fifty Shades of Grey fantasy."

"I really don't—"

"And then the kids from this union with hunky Daddy become ripe candidates for the exact same thing, since they inherited the hunky genes, thus perpetuating the cycle."

"And this is a real scientific study? How would women find these beefcake one-night stands?"

"That's part of what I was researching. Years ago, at Florida State, someone ran a study where someone walks up to a person of the opposite sex and says, basically, 'I've noticed you around. I think you're attractive. Would you sleep with me tonight?'"

Is this a study, or a frat house prank?

"Most men were ok with it," Harrison continued. "Even the ones who said no apologized and made an excuse. But all the women said no. 'You must be joking.' Or 'Leave me alone.' The study has been repeated elsewhere with almost identical results. Initially people said this proves men are sexual hunters, they're ok with casual sex, they always want more, and so forth. Women, supposedly having less interest in sex, especially casual sex, and more concerns about becoming pregnant, say no. But my partners and I think the people conducting this study got it wrong. We think women would say yes to exactly the same degree as men—if they could eliminate the fear factor."

"Which is?"

"When we conduct this experiment, the women get to choose a potential partner from an array of photos. Polaroid Grindr, if you will. Then they get to chat with their selection for half an hour to break the ice, watch for red flags. Eliminate the fear of the unknown."

"Did it change the results?"

"Completely. Eliminate the fear factor, and women opt for casual sex only slightly less frequently than men. The numbers are almost statistically identical. We still need to do more research but, when I publish, I think this is going to change everything we thought we knew about sex."

"Could we talk about Alice Pike? I mean—Alice Fisher. When you knew her. You do remember the case?"

"How could I forget?" Much of the light that shone in his eyes when he talked about sex faded. "That was a tough one. The lady initially said she wanted to put the baby up for adoption. But she'd made no plans."

Dan did have a sister. Confirmed. "I'm sure you knew how to contact the proper authorities."

"I didn't have a clue. But I educated myself fast. Got the social workers and adoption agency people on the scene pronto."

"Was her daughter born...ok?"

"Rough delivery. Roughest I've seen that didn't lead to either mother or child perishing. We got through it...barely. I thought the worst was over. Wrong."

"What happened next?"

"Dad showed up. Jack."

Who might not have been the dad, given that the child was conceived before Alice and Jack married. "What did he do?"

"Acted like a complete douche. Ranting and raving. He didn't want to give the baby up."

"What name did they give the baby?"

"I never heard. They ended up taking the child home, but then, several years later, Alice came back to me and wanted to put the child up for adoption again. She said their home wasn't a safe place for a child. She didn't give any specifics—but it wasn't hard to guess. That's when the adoption actually happened."

"Did you ever see the parents again?"

"Oh yeah. Why do you think I remember the case so well?" Something happened to Harrison's face as he told this part of the story. Like a shadow descended over his entire countenance. "Years after the adoption, the dick returned."

"What did he want?"

"The baby. He thought I could tell him who the adoptive parents were so he could get his little girl back. And he couldn't give me a rational reason, nothing that made any sense. It was more like someone stole his toy and he wanted it back."

"I assume you didn't help him."

"I didn't want to, but remember, he was legally the father. He claimed the adoption took place without his consent, in secret. And he threw his weight around because he was a cop. Threatened to have me arrested."

"Did you believe him?"

"I doubted the adoption was a complete secret. But it might have been without his consent."

"Why come after you? Just because you delivered the baby? You wouldn't know anything about who adopted the child."

Harrison's eyes drifted downward. "Except actually...I did." He cleared his throat. "Once again, I let my heart work harder than my head. This thing was such a mess." He blew air through his lips. "I didn't think the adoption was going through. Not without the father's active participation. But I knew a wonderful couple who lived a few doors down from me. Nice people, good jobs, smart. Childless. Weren't having any luck adopting because he had a criminal record. Trivial stuff. Marijuana, like anyone cares these days. I sort of..."

"You arranged for them to adopt Alice's baby."

"In an unofficial, Ma and Pa Kent sort of way. Private adoptions are not illegal in Florida. And no money changed hands. Well, okay, not much."

"Tell me you didn't take money for arranging this."

"Me? No. I was just trying to help. But I thought Alice could use a little something. Frankly, I was hoping she'd use it to go to a women's shelter or blow town, but I don't think she did. Too bad. That guy was an abuser if I ever saw one."

Garrett took a step closer. "Did you tell that man where his daughter was?"

"He held a gun on me, for God's sake! And as if that wasn't enough, he pulled out a knife, a big one, and pressed it against my throat. Told me he was a cop so he could get away with murder, no questions asked. What could I do? I didn't want him to get the kid. But I didn't want to die for it, either."

Garrett remained silent, his jaw clenched. What he was thinking was unspeakable.

"Apparently Fisher filed some kind of lawsuit to regain custody of the child he claimed he had never agreed to give up. Claimed she forged his signature."

Because fraud would allow his lawyers to reopen the case or set aside the adoption. "Did he succeed? What happened to her after Jack was killed?"

"I never heard anything about it again. That man scared me. I didn't want anything to do with him. That was when I decided to get out of the ER. Too dangerous. I much prefer the academic world."

"Thank you for your time. I'm sure you had no great desire to talk about this incident. But it's important to my friend. And to me."

"No problem. Hey, you got a girlfriend?"

"Not at the moment."

"If you'd like, I could sign you up as a volunteer. There might be some...advantages."

"Absolutely not interested." He tried not to slam the door on his way out.

CHAPTER TWENTY-TWO

DAN SAT AT THE DEFENSE TABLE, HANDS FLAT, TRYING TO STAY calm. He knew what was coming next. He and Maria discussed it, debated it, play-tested it, and analyzed it. He was convinced this was the right way to go. But that didn't stop his stomach from churning.

Was he doing the right thing? Was he being selfish? Who was so desperate to keep him from the truth that they would resort to murder?

"Showtime," Maria whispered. "Put on your game face."

"Understood." In the courtroom, game face was no face. Attentive but unresponsive.

Judge Fernandez leaned back in his chair. "Ms. Morales, you may call your first witness."

"Thank you, your honor. The plaintiff calls Conrad Sweeney."

The surprise at the other table was evident. Good. That was what they wanted.

Caldwell slowly rose. "Your honor...this is highly improper."

Fernandez looked back at her. "How so?"

"We had no notice that they would be calling the defendant. Much less calling him first."

Fernandez glanced down at his bench. "He's on their witness list. For that matter, he's on your witness list, too."

"Yes, but..." She struggled for words. "He's not *their* witness."

Maria jumped in. "We'll be asking the court to let us treat him as a hostile witness."

"I figured you would. Ms. Caldwell, you still haven't stated a basis for an objection."

Sweeney leaned forward and spoke to Caldwell, but did it loudly enough that everyone could hear. Including every member of the jury. "It's not a problem. I'll be happy to tell them whatever they want to know."

Nice. Sweeney knew he couldn't prevent himself from taking the stage. Instead he played it like he hadn't a care in the world, nothing to hide.

Sweeney strode to the witness stand. For a man of such immense size—Dan guessed he was at least a hundred pounds overweight—he did not look fat. Part of it was the immaculately tailored double-breasted white suit. But part of it was his bearing—strong, upright posture, shoulders pulled back, confident. He did not waddle or jiggle. He seemed powerful, not blubbery. Strong. Like someone who knew what was up. Someone you didn't mess around with.

Maria asked him to identify himself and provide a little background. Given how well-known Sweeney was locally, it was probably unnecessary, but she had to establish a foundation for his testimony. She tried to keep the questions pointed, but inevitably, this gave Sweeney an opportunity to brag about his business accomplishments as well as his ongoing civic activism. Dan suspected Sweeney's financial picture was not as rosy as he portrayed it.

"Were you engaged in one of those civic activities last April at the new women's shelter?" Since the court allowed him to be treated as a hostile witness, she could ask leading questions, as if this were cross-examination rather than direct.

"Yes. That is the seventh shelter I've had the pleasure of opening since the program began. I either contributed or fundraised all the money—"

"Thank you. You've answered the question." She had every right to cut him off when he started rambling, but of course, anytime you did, you risked irritating jurors who wanted to know what he had to say. "Did you hold a press conference after the ribbon cutting?"

"That is traditional. The reporters like to have some quotes to put in the articles or television spots."

"And during that press conference, did you engage in an exchange with my client, Daniel Pike?"

He gave her a sturdy look. "You know that I did."

"But it isn't in evidence. Yet. Was that a yes?"

"Yes. Even though he wasn't a member of the press, he interrupted the proper business and started slinging—"

"Thank you. You've answered the question, Mr. Sweeney."

Caldwell rose. "Actually, your honor, my client has a doctorate degree, so he should be addressed as Dr. Sweeney."

"Honorary degree," Maria grumbled. "From a college he gave a lot of money."

Fernandez raised his hand. He appeared to be hiding a small grin. "I'm not the language police. I will let counsel decide which honorific they choose to employ."

Good thing, Dan thought. Maria would fall on her sword before she would address that man "Dr. Sweeney."

Maria continued. "Did you hear the recording I played during my opening statement?"

"I did."

"That was taken from a Channel 8 News recording. They had a minicam crew at the event." Of course, Jimmy recorded it too, on his phone, but it sounded less staged if the footage came from somewhere else. "Did that appear to be an accurate record of the exchange between you and my client?"

"I can't tell that the recording has been doctored, if that's what you mean."

"Then as far as you're aware, what the jury heard is what happened. The words they heard were the words that were spoken."

"Yes."

"You did in fact call my client a criminal."

"That was a statement of opinion, not fact." Sweeney had no doubt been coached by his lawyer. The First Amendment granted every American the right to express an opinion, with relatively few exceptions. It was only when you claimed something was true that was factually untrue that you could be liable for slander. "In my opinion, an attorney who systematically puts dangerous people back on the street is performing a criminal act. It may not be the kind of crime that prosecutors go after, but it is an enormous disservice to the community I have worked hard to make better and safer. I have a constitutional right to speak out on issues I feel strongly about."

The whole speech sounded as if it had been scripted by counsel and memorized by Sweeney. "But when you call someone a criminal, don't you imagine most people take that to mean that he has committed a crime?"

"Pike was charged with murder only a—"

"And completely exonerated, as you well know. After the true criminal was identified."

"He has consorted with criminals. Dated a woman who—"

"But your comment was not about women he dated. It was about him."

"He put Emilio López back on the street, which led to an incident that killed six St. Pete citizens."

There was much more to that affair than Sweeney was

explaining, but the fact was, Dan had done a stupid, reckless thing and he still felt enormous guilt about it. Last thing he needed was this bloodsucker ramming it down his throat.

"Is it a crime for a criminal defense attorney to win an acquittal for his client?" Maria asked. "Or is that simply doing his job?"

"He's in a position to choose his clients. I believe it was an immoral act."

"But that's not the same as a criminal act, is it?"

"In my opinion, it is."

Maria might as well move on, Dan thought. Sweeney was never going to budge. She'd made her point, and he was not likely to agree with her.

"On the recording," Maria continued, "the jury also heard you allege that my client was involved with organized crime. True?"

"We all heard it."

"Now you're saying the plaintiff is not only a criminal, but a mobster. A gangster."

"I didn't use those words."

"Those are the words that describe someone who participates in organized crime."

Sweeney raised a finger. "Ah, now you're changing what I said. I didn't say that he participates in organized crime. I said he was involved with it. Which is completely different and unassailably true."

"I'm not seeing the distinction."

"How many times has your client been involved with some cartel or organized crime scheme? He cleared the murder charges against him by producing witnesses from a human-trafficking cartel. He's been all over the news for his activities involving an organ-smuggling gang."

"You're referring to his efforts to *stop* the gang. At the risk of his own life."

"Objection." Caldwell rose, obviously pleased to have an excuse to interrupt the flow. "Counsel is testifying."

The judge granted her point. "Sustained."

Maria continued. "You have not identified a single instance when my client worked *with* a criminal organization."

"And I never claimed that I could."

"You deliberately suggested to your audience that Daniel Pike was a participant in organized criminal activities."

Sweeney shrugged. "I can't be held accountable for what other people think. I'm not a mind reader. The legal question is whether I slandered your client. And I did not."

"Are you familiar with the legal concept of holding someone to a false light?"

"Again I object," Caldwell said. "Dr. Sweeney is not a lawyer, nor is he an expert witness."

"He just offered his legal opinion on slander," Maria said. "I think I should be entitled to follow up."

"I'll have to grant her that point," Fernandez said. "I'm sure the witness can handle himself. Objection overruled."

Maria took a step forward. "Please answer the question."

Sweeney sighed. "I am familiar with the concept, sure."

"If you've suggested to a great number of people that my client is a participant in organized crime, even if you did not use those exact words, that would be holding him up to a false light, right?"

"I do not agree."

"Did you think your comments would cause people to see him in a positive light?"

"I didn't think about it one way or another."

Maria pounced. "Now that part I believe. You spoke in anger and said things you shouldn't."

"Not true."

"Are you willing to apologize to the plaintiff for the damage you've caused?"

"Absolutely not."

"But you acknowledge that you've caused damage."

Sweeney leaned forward. "I don't—acknowledge—" He drew in his breath. He was becoming visibly heated. "How could you damage a reputation like that? An accused murderer. The son of a convicted murderer."

"But Dan's father was never accused of being involved with organized crime, was he?"

"The man was sent to prison for first-degree murder. That is an unassailable fact."

"And if you had stuck to the facts, we wouldn't be here today. But you didn't. As you've admitted, you spoke in anger and made accusations that far exceed the facts."

"I only said what everyone—" He stopped short.

Dan watched Sweeney, wondering what was going on. Why did he stop? Did he realize he was blowing it? Did he get a hand signal from his lawyers?

Sweeney took a deep breath and dialed it down. "Look, Daniel Pike is a dishonorable man. Time and again he has engaged in activities I consider harmful to the community, while I have been doing everything within my power to improve it. It would be safer in this modern-day litigious, Twitterstorm world to simply keep my mouth shut. But as an American, I had the right to speak my mind, and you can surely see why I would not appreciate someone else putting criminals back on the street and leading this town in the worst possible direction." He raised his hand and pointed. "Daniel Pike is a menace. That is my opinion and I stick by it."

Maria simply smiled. "If you consider my client such a menace, why did you offer him a job?"

"Uh…excuse me?"

"You've met my client prior to this trial, haven't you? Prior to the encounter at the women's shelter?"

Sweeney frowned. "On one occasion. At his request."

"And during that encounter, you offered my client a job working for you as in-house legal counsel. Do you deny it?"

"I'm a problem solver, not a complainer. Pike is obviously smart, talented. He just lacks direction. A moral compass, if you will. I thought that if I gave him an opportunity to work at my direction, I might steer his talents in a more positive direction."

Maria looked as if she were about to barf. "Give me a break. You were trying to buy him off."

"Not true."

"He's been a constant problem and you were trying to seduce him to the dark side."

"I was trying to turn a dishonest man into an honest one."

"You believe the plaintiff is dishonest?"

"No doubt in my mind."

"Then why did you offer him a judicial appointment?"

That slowed Sweeney down a beat. Dan could almost see the wheels turning in his brain. Sweeney could deny it. But he might've mentioned it to third parties, and Dan mentioned it to several people. "I don't have the ability to dish out judgeships."

"Don't you, though?"

Judge Fernandez' eyebrows rose an inch.

Maria continued. "You sit on an advisory panel that makes recommendations to the state Bar Association, don't you?"

"As I have said, I like to give back to the community."

"And you are known to have backed judicial candidates in the past."

"That is my right, if not duty, as a citizen."

"And you would never recommend that anyone dishonest be given a judgeship, would you?"

"Of course not."

The pieces were falling into place like a well-crafted syllogism. "Did you offer my client a judgeship?"

Sweeney squirmed a bit. "I may have...mentioned the possibility. I certainly didn't offer any guarantees."

"Fine. Now please turn to the jury and explain to them why you would offer the possibility of a judgeship to someone you consider dishonest."

A moment of silence.

Maria eventually filled the gap. "And don't bother to tell them you were trying to improve his morals. Because that doesn't even make sense. Judgeships aren't on-the-job ethics training. You were offering a bribe to a perpetual thorn in your side to get him out of your way."

"That isn't true."

"And since it didn't work, because my client wouldn't be bribed, you framed him for murder. And when that didn't work, you slandered him in public."

Sweeney started to speak, but Caldwell cut him off. "Objection, your honor. That wasn't even a question. More like closing argument."

"I'll sustain that objection. Anything more, counsel?"

"No," Maria said, turning away. "I'm done with this man."

"Looks like it's your turn, Ms. Caldwell. Would you like to inquire?"

"Only briefly." She walked around the table and stood between Sweeney and the jury. "Dr. Sweeney, did you intend to bribe the plaintiff?"

"No. I was trying to help him turn his life around. Put it to better purpose." He smiled a little. "But you know Kepler's fourth law of thermodynamics."

"Which is?"

"No good deed goes unpunished."

"Did you intend to slander the plaintiff?"

"I did not. But I am entitled to express my opinion. And I made no statements of fact that were inaccurate. Daniel Pike has spent most of his adult life associating with criminals. He has freed dangerous people. And his late father was a convicted murderer who died behind bars."

Sweeney turned and peered directly into Dan's eyes. "No one has ever proved anything different. And no one ever will."

CHAPTER TWENTY-THREE

JIMMY HAD BEEN TRYING TO TIE SHAWNA DOWN FOR A MEETING for weeks without success, so he was surprised when he got a text saying she had a few minutes. She probably knew he would be in the courthouse, since Dan's trial was in progress. But still —why now?

That was the insidious thing about suspicion, or as his husband Hank called it, paranoia. Once you start suspecting people, you're tumbling down a slippery slope. You reinterpret everything. Like Lex Luthor. First Lex suspected Superboy intentionally used super-breath to make his hair fall out, then he suspected the Kryptonian must be pretending to be good so he could take over—and then he was an insane super-villain.

Jimmy did not want to become an insane super-villain.

Regardless of the doubts flooding his brain, he couldn't pass on this chance to chat up the Pinellas County Court Clerk, a woman whom others might perceive as a glorified file clerk but who actually wielded a great deal of power. If anyone could give him insight into the strange administrative occurrences that seemed to plague them every time they had a major case, Shawna would be the one.

To his surprise, she asked him to meet not in her office but outside the day-care facility provided for parents who worked at the courthouse. He found her peering through the window in the door. He tried to read her facial expression, but he lacked Dan's gift. He'd have better luck reading her thoughts if she'd been drawn into a comic book.

He stood beside her. "Do you have someone in there?"

Shawna seemed startled. She turned awkwardly. "Oh no. No kids. Never married. I just like to...watch. I don't see children much these days. I used to play with my sister's kids, but they're mostly grown now."

"Regrets?"

"Not really. I've had a good life. Better than most."

"And you have a nephew, right? The one you're putting through college."

"Oh yes. Morgan. Good boy. Wants to be a doctor. I try to help when I can."

"I'd say you help a lot. College tuition these days? I don't know how you afford it. He must be a major expense for you."

Her eyes turned downward. "You have no idea. Wanna go for a walk?"

"Sure." They passed the metal detectors and exited through the back double-doors. A few moments later they were on the street. He turned left on the sidewalk. If they needed a table, he knew a great coffeeshop that way.

"All right," Shawna asked, "what did you want to talk about?"

"Do you know the court reporter who took the depositions in Dan's case? Marjorie?"

"I've met her."

"Know anything about her?"

"Not much. Why?"

"I don't know. I get a bad vibe."

"Seriously? A vibe? What are you, a surfer dude?"

"Maria says her purse is too expensive."

"Oh, well then. Lock her up."

"Come on, Shawna. Give me something."

Shawna drew in her breath, then slowly released it. "Your instincts are good. Keep a careful eye on her. Get a different court reporter if possible."

"Too late. What did she do? Or what is she planning to do?"

"I don't know. Just keep a close eye on her. That's all I can tell you. And I'm only telling you that because you're a friend. And because you make fabulous brownies."

He acknowledged the compliment—even though Dan made the brownies.

Shawna continued. "And because...unlike most people, I think you actually care."

"Surely you can give me more. There's been some weird stuff going on in this case. All our cases, really. Everything major since Dan joined the team."

"Maybe you should be talking to Dan."

"I do, constantly. But I think the problem is that ever since Dan joined us, he's been on Conrad Sweeney's radar."

Shawna definitely reacted to the mention of the name, but he wasn't sure how to read it. "Dan's got Sweeney in the court-room. Isn't that enough?"

"Depends. Dan is convinced the courtroom consultation rooms—basically the only place in the courthouse lawyers can go for a private conversation—have been bugged."

"We did an electronic sweep. We found nothing."

"So you reported. When Dan defended Camila, he became convinced that even conversations held in chambers were being overheard."

"That's ridiculous."

"Did your electronic sweep include the judges' chambers?"

"Of course not. They would be offended by the suggestion."

"Did you ask them?"

She turned her head. "Are you accusing me of criminal activity?"

"I'm...giving you an opportunity to talk to a friendly audience. If you have something you'd like to say. And I think you do."

She looked edgy, but she wasn't running away. There was something she wanted.

"We still don't know who stole that silver flask from the evidence locker," he added. "During Camila's case."

"You think I did that?"

"I do not. You wouldn't have access to the police station, much less the evidence locker. But I thought it was just possible you might know...who did."

She stopped in the middle of the sidewalk. "I'm getting seriously offended. You're accusing me of being a criminal."

Jimmy licked his lips. "I don't think you're a bad person, Shawna. In fact, I know you aren't. But I think it's possible...you got in over your head. And now you can't get out."

All at once, her eyes appeared wide and moist. "Stop. Please. Just stop." She turned away.

He took a deep breath, thinking hard. "You know what Superman says? In the first Christopher Reeve movie?"

"I'm sure I do not."

"Confession is good for the soul."

"Confession is what gets you put away for life."

Now he understood her concern. It probably started small, nothing of great consequence, but once Sweeney had her under his thumb, he pushed for more and more and she couldn't risk saying no. He'd expose her without incriminating himself, and there would be nothing she could do to stay out of prison. It all made a gruesome sort of sense—and was exactly how Sweeney liked to do business. Making offers people couldn't possibly refuse.

"Did you read about the big bust? Dan helped the cops nail some organ smugglers."

She didn't say anything.

"Can you imagine? Live cargo. Kidnapping young women to be sliced up for their organs."

He could still see the tears trying to break out. "I believe it. I can definitely believe it."

"Do you know...something about that?"

"No. But the black market for organs? Unfortunately, I do know about that. Lots."

"How?"

"You remember that nephew of mine?" The first tear slipped through the sluice. "There's more to it than tuition. Much more. He has a serious genetic condition. A kidney ailment. By the time he was fifteen, he needed a transplant. The hospital put him on a list, and he was on dialysis for months. In bad shape. We were worried that he would die before a kidney became available."

He stopped and peered at her. He liked to believe he had his ear to the pavement, that he knew what was going on in the community. But he'd never heard a word about this.

"My sister is a wonderful caring mother...but not a strong person, if you know what I mean. I had to take the reins. I had to make decisions and seize opportunities that I would later regret." She wiped away some tears. "I learned everything there was to know about the black market for human organs."

"Shawna...I had no idea."

"Organ traffic is strictly regulated in the US. But that didn't prevent a black market from forming. In a way, that created it. Last time I looked at the statistics, there were over 120,000 people waiting for organs in this country—and eighteen of them die every day because they can't get an organ in time. One organ donor could potentially save eight lives. You see why donors are so valuable—especially live donors. That's why that cartel was smuggling people. Organ harvesting is only viable if the organ still has blood and oxygen flowing through it when harvested. A dead donor can't donate. But a living donor can give a kidney, intestine, pancreas, corneas, and a part of their liver."

"I wondered about that. Transporting live bodies seems so much more complicated."

"Also far more profitable." She started walking again, eyes straight forward. "These cartels are new to the game. Most black-market organ donors have arrangements with funeral-home directors. The rich can buy organs. But not everyone is rich. People have been killed for their organs. A Georgia teenager was found dead a few years back. Looked like a freak accident, like he got trapped under a gym mat and suffocated. But when the pathologist did an autopsy, he found the corpse stuffed with newspaper."

Jimmy winced. "You're joking."

"I'm not. The boy was missing his liver, heart, lungs, and brain."

"That's...hideous."

"It's not an isolated event. Every year there are suspicious deaths involving victims who turn out to be missing vital organs."

He took a moment to collect himself. "Are kidneys hard to find?"

"The most in-demand body part. It's reached epidemic level. In the US, almost 100,000 people are waiting for a kidney. Half will die before they get one. Rich buyers pay around $150,000, though some have paid more, especially when time is of the essence. Of that, about $5000 typically goes to the donor. The rest goes to the broker. In countries like China, brokers openly advertise. 'Donate a kidney, get a new iPad!' People sometimes advertise their kidneys for sale on Craigslist. On the dark web, you can buy organ packages from overseas sellers costing thousands of dollars. With that kind of profit margin, it was inevitable that organized crime would get involved."

"Like the cartel."

"Exactly. There have been cases of US doctors treating patients for non-existent ailments as a means to remove organs without their knowledge or consent. A few years back, I talked to an agent from the World Health Organization. He told me that about 11,000 organs are obtained on the black market every year. That an illegal organ is sold every hour of every day."

"Why would he tell you that?"

She looked straight into his eyes. "Isn't it obvious?"

"He was telling you to make a black-market deal."

"He was telling me that if I didn't, Morgan was going to die."

Now it made sense. "And to make that happen, you needed money. A lot of money."

"And unfortunately, charitable organizations won't give you money for an illegal transaction. Make-a-Wish could send Morgan to Disney World—but it couldn't get him a kidney in time."

"So...you did."

"With help. Financial and otherwise."

He took the giant leap. "Because Sweeney has been involved with this cartel for decades. He would know exactly where to go. And could afford to go there."

She looked at Jimmy with sorrowful eyes, but said nothing.

"Once you were in deep with Sweeney, you couldn't get out. He had you where he wanted you. He threatened to expose you if you didn't give him everything he wanted. And no matter what you did, he always wanted more."

"But Morgan is alive. And healthy. On track for medical school."

Jummy laid his hand on her shoulder. "Shawna...I don't

think there's anyone on earth who would blame you for doing what you did."

"I'm pretty sure the FBI would."

He knew what she meant. They might be sympathetic. But she'd still committed a crime. And the FBI couldn't overlook that. Especially not if a cartel was involved. "Come clean. We'll protect you. We'll represent you if charges are filed."

"You can't win if your client is guilty. And confesses."

"You'll never be happy—or safe—until you come clean."

"You just want me to help Dan's lawsuit. To get even with Sweeney."

"It's not about vengeance. It's about learning the truth."

"Sometimes the truth is best left buried." She checked her phone. "Look, my break ended ten minutes ago. I need to get back to the office."

He held tight to her wrist. "You don't have to live like this."

"I'm fine."

"Get this noose off your neck. We need a level playing field in the courtroom. We're not going to win this suit if Sweeney knows every move we make."

She shook her head. "There is much more at stake than your little lawsuit."

"What do you mean?"

"You think you've seen or detected all of Sweeney's skull-duggery—but you haven't even come close."

"What? What does he have planned?"

"You can't even imagine. He wouldn't be in that courtroom if he didn't see an advantage. He would've paid you a little money and made it go away. But he doesn't want that. He wants to destroy Daniel Pike. And every member of the firm. Including you."

"What is Sweeney planning?"

She twisted away. "I have to go."

"Tell me what you meant."

She glared at him. "Have you not been paying attention? People have been shot. And not just your buddy and his informant. Random people whose only crime was being near Daniel Pike. Like you are every day. Like Maria. And Garrett. You cross Sweeney and you're dead."

"That's not—"

"I don't want to end up dead. I don't want Morgan dead. Or my sister. Or anyone else." She pulled away. "Just leave me alone!"

"Shawna, stop."

"If you have any sense," she said, backing away from him, "you'll let this lawsuit go. Because you will get nothing good from digging around in the past. The truth will not make anyone happy. Especially not if they're dead."

CHAPTER TWENTY-FOUR

WHETHER DAN LIKED IT OR NOT, HE KNEW THE JURY WOULD SEE this case as a grudge match between two men who despised one another. Maria did her best to call other witnesses and to suggest other ideas, but that wasn't fooling anyone. This was Pike vs. Sweeney, strong men who had crossed each other's paths and interfered with each other's plans too many times. One of them was telling the truth and one of them was lying. Possibly both were lying. But the jury would be forced to choose sides. Did they believe the wildly successful tech magnate and philanthropist, or the lawyer who'd made a career out of protecting the accused?

Maria called a law professor, Philip Morrison, who had reviewed Dan's father's case and the courthouse files. He testified that although Dan's father was convicted of murder, there was never any suggestion of a connection to organized crime, nor was there any reason to suspect that he had any such connection.

Despite the fact that they normally sat on opposite sides of the courtroom, Jake Kakazu agreed to testify for Dan. He talked about several of the cases he and Dan had worked on and noted that Dan had always cooperated with the police. He primarily talked about the organ-smuggling raid. He said Dan was the one who brought the lead to law enforcement. According to Jake, he asked Dan to act as their front man. Past events had made Jake concerned that the department had a mole, so any of their officers might be made. Jake asked Dan to pretend to be the buyer and he agreed, despite the obvious danger. Jake also noted that when the shooting started, Dan did not run. He stood his ground, which was more than he might expect from some trained police officers.

That had to improve the jury's opinion of him at least a little, didn't it?

Despite her best efforts, Maria was only delaying the inevitable. Dan had to take the stand. Sweeney had already said his piece. He needed to do the same.

Maria announced that their final witness would be the plaintiff himself. Dan took his place in the hot seat, marveling at how nervous he was. He was in the awkward position of trying to convince people to believe *him*—and he didn't like it.

Maria wasted little time unveiling his background. He was a criminal defense attorney, he had worked on several controversial cases, and he had helped the police on more than one occasion.

"Mr. Pike." Maria was doing a good job keeping a straight face. It was probably a challenge to call someone "Mr. Pike" when not long before you'd planted a big hot wet one on his lips. "Why did you go to the shelter on the day in question?"

"I wanted to speak to the defendant. Mr. Sweeney."

"Why?"

"I'd been investigating what happened to my father and became convinced there was much more to that story than came out at trial. I also found indications that Sweeney was involved. He knew Ellison and most of the other officers involved. He may have even known my father. I wanted to ask him about it."

"Was that all?"

"No. As I mentioned, I've worked with the police to derail a South American cartel involved in sex trafficking and organ smuggling. I'll be the first to admit I don't know everything there is to know about these crooks, but time and again, when investigating the cartel, I've seen Sweeney's fingerprints. I don't know the full extent of his involvement. Some members of the police believe he—"

"Objection," Caldwell said. "Hearsay."

The judge nodded. "Sustained."

Maria continued. "What happened when you arrived at the shelter?"

"I asked a question. The defendant spotted me in the crowd. He started making statements I thought were defamatory. I replied."

"You interrupted the press conference?"

"He asked for questions. I gave him one."

"Are you a member of the press?" Maria was asking the questions she knew Caldwell would ask on cross. Better to get it out of the way up front.

"No. But nothing Sweeney said restricted questions to members of the press. He said, 'Are there any questions?' So I asked him a question."

"What did you ask?"

Dan watched the jury with a little side-eye. They did appear interested. He couldn't be sure how much they believed, but at least they weren't dozing off. "I asked about his connection to the cartel."

"Did he deny it?"

"You heard the recording. I don't think he ever actually denied it. Instead, he launched into a completely unrelated attack, first on my father, then on me."

Maria took a few steps toward the jury box. "Mr. Pike, I'm sure you know what some people may be thinking. What you call attacks, the defendant calls facts. Or his constitutionally protected opinion."

"If he had stopped at saying my father was convicted of murder, I might agree with that. There is much we don't know about that case, much I believe was covered up, but he was convicted. Sweeney didn't stop there. He said my father was a dirty cop. That's just a flat-out lie. He was never even accused of misconduct the entire time he served the public as a police officer. In fact, his record was exemplary and he was up for promotion."

"I'm sure they will say the murder conviction makes him dirty."

"No. The term 'dirty' suggests he did something dishonest as a police officer. That he was on the take. That's a lie."

Maria nodded. "Was there anything else in the defendant's statement you found slanderous?"

Dan leaned forward a bit. "Much. He talked some nonsense about a murder gene."

"And what is that?"

"That's a reference to a pop psychology idea currently in vogue in some circles. I might add that there is no scientific basis for this and it has never been asserted by any reputable scientist or scientific agency. But the theory has been used in television programs and shows up on the internet in tweets and such. The idea is that an inclination toward violent crime is hereditary. He was basically saying my father was a murderer and therefore so was I. Which is a complete lie on all counts."

"Just to be clear, Mr. Pike, have you ever committed a murder?"

"Never."

"Do you have violent or murderous tendencies?"

"Just the opposite. I have a reputation for keeping a level head when others might lose theirs."

"Was there anything else Mr. Sweeney said that you found offensive?"

"Yes. He suggested that both my father and I have ties to organized crime. We don't. We never have. No one, other than the defendant, has ever suggested that we do. It's a complete falsehood. And an ironic one since, as I said, there are many indications that Sweeney has ties to a South American cartel and has for decades. This could be the true explanation for his enormous wealth and—"

"Objection," Caldwell said. "The witness has answered the question."

"Sustained." Judge Fernandez looked at María directly. "Anything else, counsel?" Clearly, he thought her job was done.

"Just one more question, your honor. Mr. Pike, do you believe these statements by the defendant have injured you?"

He didn't miss a beat. "I know they have. I've had no new potential clients contact me since the incident. I normally get several a week. Part of it, I think, is the defendant's suggestions that I'm dishonest or associated with crime lords. But part of it is simply that the defendant is a rich and highly prominent member of our city—with a reputation for taking strong action against his enemies. No one wants to get on Sweeney's bad side. Similarly, no one wants to be associated with the lawyer he has declared to be public enemy number one."

"Any other damage you've suffered?"

"Yes. I...personally have experienced a great deal of mental anguish. As you can imagine, this is a painful memory the defendant gratuitously trotted out in public. I know my father was wrongfully convicted. That's why I've devoted so much time to investigating it. Sweeney did this for a specific purpose. To hurt me. Which it did."

"Thank you. Pass the witness."

He took a deep breath. He'd survived the direct examination, which was the softball part of the game, but he was breathing deeply and his heart was racing. He feared sweat was trickling down the side of his face. He'd practically melted, and that was with a friendly face asking the questions.

The worst was yet to come.

CHAPTER TWENTY-FIVE

FABIAN FUENTES WAS PERHAPS THE ONLY MEMBER OF THE CARTEL who appreciated Zoom conferencing. Perhaps that was because he was younger than most of the Old Guard smugglers he assisted. They still favored meeting in bars and restaurants and smoke-filled hideaways—which were increasingly difficult to find these days. But Zoom conferences were possible anytime you had an internet connection, and as far as he knew, the FBI had not yet discovered a way to hack into them. As long as he remembered to cancel the automatic recording, this was the safest way to do business with people from a distance.

Roberto watched the door outside his hotel room. A cheap joint like this was more likely to attract attention from panhandlers and the homeless than law enforcement, but he wanted no interruptions of any kind. Jose set up the conference, and once he was done, Fuentes sent him on a pointless errand. Little pitchers have big ears, as his father always said.

The image that appeared on Fuentes' laptop was grainy, but he supposed he shouldn't complain given that it originated on a different continent.

His leader was not one to mince words. "Report."

"We completed the first round of deliveries. All went as planned. We will send the take by the usual means."

"Will I be pleased?"

Fuentes chose his words carefully. "It cannot compare to our previous operations. But something is better than nothing."

"That is not sufficient."

"Agreed." Fuentes stared at the man, almost eighty, yet just as sharp as he had been twenty years before. Grayer, more wrinkles around the eyes, thinner lips. But if anything, these changes made him appear more foreboding. "When you are ready to resume our previous enterprises, I will be prepared to assist."

"It's too soon. Tell me about the Great White Whale."

That could be a reference to only one person. "He has been weakened. He attracts too much attention."

"You will have to deal with him."

"He has served us for more than two decades. And until recently—"

"You will have to deal with him."

Fuentes drew in his breath. "Understood."

"His new enterprise threatens us. Just as the lawyer does."

"That man survived the assassination attempt, though his witness did not."

"Who was behind it?"

"There is only one possibility."

"Another reason to deal with him. He is not stupid. He must realize we have lost faith in him."

"I will meet him as soon as the lawsuit is complete. When he is no longer in the limelight and being followed by reporters. If he does not—"

Fuentes stopped mid-sentence. He heard something outside the motel room door.

He drew a finger to his lips, silencing his leader.

Was it his imagination?

No. Someone was out there. What happened to Roberto?

He slowly pivoted toward the door...

A sudden burst of gunfire slammed into the thin wooden door like pistons shredding Swiss cheese. Fuentes flung himself behind the bed, barely dodging the bullets. They pummeled the walls and dresser and bed for half a minute.

Then it stopped.

Was the shooter still there? After making so much noise, he could not remain exposed for long.

All at once Fuentes heard a thunderous thudding sound, followed by the door slamming open.

The assassin's foot was still raised. He strode forward, automatic weapon in hand, scanning for his target.

Fuentes did not give him time to find it. He withdrew his knife from a holster inside his right pant leg and flung it with expert speed and accuracy. It hit the assassin's carotid artery. He made a gurgling sound. His eyes rolled up into his head. Then he collapsed, staining the crappy carpet.

Fuentes slowly rose. The bullets had destroyed his laptop. He would have to complete—to update—his report later. He needed to flee before the authorities arrived. After so much noise, police were an inevitability.

He paused briefly, staring at the dead man on the carpet. This was the assassin, the one who had killed Jaquith and almost killed the lawyer. He was certain of it.

And now the assassin had been dispatched to kill him.

This could only mean one thing.

To his sorrow, he found Roberto's body outside. Of course, the bastard had taken him out quietly. Probably snuck up and stabbed him in the back. His most loyal lieutenant. Dead.

He rose, his lips thin, his jaw set.

The game had changed. The players on the chessboard were forming new alliances.

And no one would be safe until the game was over. No one.

CHAPTER TWENTY-SIX

CALDWELL ROSE BUT REMAINED BEHIND HER TABLE. WAS SHE afraid of getting too close? Dan wondered. She seemed as robotic as ever, but then again…on closer inspection, did her lip curl just the tiniest bit when she spoke his name? Was there just the slightest hint of a sneer on those lips?

"Mr. Pike, let's start with your sad story about all the anguish you've suffered since this incident that you instigated. How many calls from new clients do you normally get per week?"

"I've never counted. Several."

"What's several?

"As I said, I've never—"

"Two?"

"More than two."

"Four?"

"I've never counted."

"And how many of those new clients do you normally accept?"

"As many as I choose. And time permits."

"Mr. Pike, isn't it true that you receive a regular salary from the managing partner of your firm?"

"Yes."

"Are you still receiving it?"

"Yes."

"And isn't it true that he assigns your cases?"

"Yes. But we're free to take additional cases as time permits."

"Don't you normally take those on a pro bono basis?"

"If I want to."

"Then how can you claim that you've lost money? At best you might have lost clients that you weren't going to charge anyway."

He tried to keep his cool. "I might have taken a case for a fee if the right case came along."

"But you can't say with any certainty that this would have happened?"

"I can't predict the events of an alternate universe in which your client didn't slander me, no."

"You can't calculate the amount of your alleged loss."

"Not with that degree of precision. But damage to my reputation is an impairment to my work. An attorney lives and dies by his reputation."

He regretted saying it as soon as he did, but the words were already out of his mouth.

"Ah," Caldwell said. "If that's true, then your reputation probably died the day you got Emilio Lòpez off the hook—and he started a gang war that killed six people."

Dan licked his lips, trying to recover. "I obtained an acquittal for Emilio because he wasn't guilty of the charges. The so-called eyewitness couldn't see clearly and was being misled by the police. I'm not responsible for everything the man does for the rest of his life. My job was to make sure he wasn't railroaded for a crime he didn't commit. Which I did."

"How do you know he didn't commit the crime? The charges were dropped, weren't they? After you pulled some courtroom stunt?"

He knew what she was doing. Playing on ignorant stereo-types about criminal lawyers. "After I impeached a witness whose eyesight made it impossible for him to positively identify my client, there was no credible evidence against Emilio. Because he didn't do it."

"So you say. But there's no question about the fact that he participated in the later shooting that killed all those people, is there?"

"No."

"Could your association with that mass murderer perhaps be what damaged your reputation?"

Maria rose. "Objection. Argumentative."

"I'll withdraw the question." Because the jury had already heard it and knew exactly what she was implying. "You've been accused and tried for murder yourself, haven't you? Just like your father?"

He could see concerned expressions on the jurors' faces. "Accused and, as we've already mentioned, exonerated. Throwing that at me shows how completely disingenuous—"

"My point is that a highly public trial on a murder charge might do some damage to your reputation, don't you think? Might be a reason clients stop calling."

Or they might think, if he can get himself off the hook, he can get me off, too. But Dan wasn't going to say that. "I suppose it's possible."

"More than possible. Probable."

"I don't know that."

"And as my colleague mentioned in his opening, for a long time you were romantically involved with the mayor of this city. And what a surprise—she was accused of murder too. Twice."

"That was a complete frame. My case may have been an honest mistake. The case against Camila was a calculated conspiracy."

"Except as it turned out, she wasn't exactly pure as the driven snow, was she?"

"Now you're referring to an entirely different—"

"Answer the question. Was your girlfriend Camila completely law-abiding?"

His lips tightened. "No."

"Do you suppose that relationship might've done some damage to your reputation?"

"Not for anyone who bothered to get the facts."

Caldwell raised a finger. "We don't live in a world where all people take the time and trouble to get the facts, do we? We live in a world where people make ill-informed judgments based upon snippets and factoids they find posted to online bulletin boards or tweets. So let me ask you again. Is it possible your relationship with the mayor could've prevented clients from calling you?"

His jaw clenched. "I suppose it is possible."

"During that murder investigation against you, it emerged that some evidence stolen from a police-evidence locker was found in your office."

"I had nothing to do with that. It was planted."

"Mr. Pike—how many fairy tales do you expect this jury to swallow?"

"I didn't steal the flask. I would never do that. And quite frankly, even if I did, I wouldn't leave it in my own office. That's just stupid."

"Was dating a criminal smart? You have a long history of doing things that most people wouldn't consider smart. And yet, you still do them."

"Objection," Maria said.

"I will sustain that one," Judge Fernandez said. "It wasn't really a question."

"And then there was the remark about organized crime. Dr.

Sweeney didn't actually say you were a participant in organized crime, did he?"

"He strongly implied it."

"You mean, that's what you heard. But your paranoia is rather clear at this point. Have you heard anyone else say they took this remark to mean that you're some kind of gangster?"

"My colleagues all thought—"

"Other than your close personal friends. I don't think they were likely to toss you much business."

Dan drew in his breath. This was not going well and he knew it. She was scoring point after point, very effectively. How could someone who was so good at conducting cross-examinations be so poor at being cross-examined? "I haven't discussed it with other people."

"Then you don't know whether these comments have caused you any damage?"

"Common sense tells me they have. People don't hire lawyers associated with organized crime."

"Someone in organized crime might. They need lawyers too. More than most people."

"That's not the kind of client I want."

She leapt onto that. "Now you're saying it's not that you can't get work. It's that you're turning down work because you're choosy about your clientele."

"That's not—"

"In fact, there are many factors that could have damaged your professional reputation that have absolutely nothing to do with my client."

"Your client has been at the heart of every—"

"Let me rephrase. There are many factors that could have damaged your reputation before my client made the statements that are the basis of this lawsuit, right? Is that at least theoretically possible?"

He shrugged. "Anything is possible. That doesn't—"

"Mr. Pike, can you identify a single client who would have hired you but didn't because of Dr. Sweeney's comments?"

"I have no way of—"

"So your answer is no. You can't identify any specific damages you've suffered." She turned a page in her notebook. "You also objected to my client's comment about a 'murder gene.' But your father was convicted of murder, and you have been accused of the same crime. Correct?"

"The murder gene idea is pseudo-scientific balderdash. There's no evidence to suggest such a thing exists."

"Let's not be too hasty, Mr. Pike. There is in fact a great deal of evidence to suggest that genetic destiny can override free will."

"There's a difference between genetics and 'genetic destiny,' which suggests some biological hand of fate that we're powerless to fight. This isn't Huntington's Disease, or some other biological aliment that can be traced to a single gene. Doctors can perform a test to see if someone has the specific mutation that increases the likelihood they will develop Huntington's. There is no isolated, deterministic gene that makes someone more likely to become a murderer."

"I believe the theory is that the murder gene makes someone more likely to commit a violent crime. A combination of anger, rage, lack of impulse control—"

"That's a lot of baloney. Almost anyone could be capable of murder, given the right circumstances. It has nothing—"

"Remind me, are you a licensed psychologist?"

He exhaled heavily. "You know I'm not."

"A medical doctor?"

"No."

"These opinions you're spouting are just your...pseudo-scientific baloney?"

"No, it's me trying to prevent you from misleading the jury.

Just as your client was trying to mislead people at the press conference."

"You've acknowledged that various factors can make someone more likely to commit murder. Like perhaps a lack of empathy. Neuroticism. Do you think those factors could be inherited?"

"I don't know. Perhaps."

"And some genetically inheritable genes"—She glanced at her notes—"such as monoamine oxidase A, sometimes called MAO-A, can mutate and cause Brunner syndrome, which has been linked to a wide variety of psychiatric disorders, including extreme antisocial behavior, correct?"

"I've read about that."

"Could those be called murder genes?"

"Your client implied that I've inherited something from my father—who was completely innocent."

"According to you. The jury in your father's case felt differently." She flipped another page in her notebook. "You have made statements suggesting that Dr. Sweeney is involved with a South American cartel."

"I've seen his fingerprints all over the sex-trafficking ring I helped bust. I believe there are ties between Sweeney and the organ-smuggling ring I also helped bust."

Caldwell gave him a patronizing look. "Then why haven't the police pressed charges against Dr. Sweeney?"

"I'm still gathering evidence."

"Which is a lawyerly way of saying you can't prove it, right?"

"Not at this time." He turned his head toward Sweeney. "But the time will come. Just wait and see."

"Is that some kind of threat?"

"More like a guarantee." He could see Maria signaling him to be quiet, but he couldn't stop himself. "Justice will prevail. I will make sure of it."

"You have a personal vendetta against my client, don't you?"

"I wouldn't put it that way."

"In your own juvenile way, you blame him for your father's arrest."

"I know he was involved. He put Ellison up to his false testimony."

"But you can't prove it."

He bit down on his lower lip. "Not yet. But soon."

"More threats. I know you see yourself as a crusader for justice, but you know what I see? A little boy who was torn apart when he lost his daddy. As a coping mechanism, he created a scapegoat. My client. To assuage your pain, you created an arch-villain, a Professor Moriarty. You set up this confrontation at the shelter to instigate a vengeance lawsuit. But you know what, Mr. Pike? Your father is dead. I'm sorry to be blunt, but he's dead and there's nothing you can do to help him now. When you attack my client, one of the leading citizens of this city, you not only do not help your father, you dishonor his memory."

"Objection," Maria said, but Caldwell kept on rolling.

"Here are the sad blunt facts. Your father was a murderer. He passed some of his violent, law-flouting tendencies to you. And no matter how many problems you cause for Dr. Sweeney, your father will remain dead. Another jury just like this one found him guilty by unanimous verdict and quite properly convicted him. Nothing can change that."

Maria raised her voice. "Objection. This is an—"

Caldwell pivoted toward the judge. "Your honor, I have no more questions. At this time, I would like to formally make a motion to dismiss the plaintiff's claims. He has not proved his case. Not even close."

CHAPTER TWENTY-SEVEN

DAN TRIED TO SIT STILL ON THE SOFA BUT FOUND IT IMPOSSIBLE. He paced, not that pacing made anything better. Normally he enjoyed team meetings, but he didn't like this one. For one thing, he should be leading the meeting, but he wasn't.

For another thing, they had finished putting on their case and it sucked. It wasn't Maria's fault. He filed this suit to get people talking, to gather evidence, but it wasn't working. They had barely survived the motion to dismiss, probably only because Fernandez was a cautious judge and wanted to hear all the evidence before he reached any suit-ending rulings.

He'd put his friends in danger. Someone shot at him and for all he knew they might be next. He was certain Sweeney had targeted everyone he knew.

Garrett confirmed what Jaquith told him. He might have a sister, or half-sister, he knew nothing about. Who was caring for her? If Fisher got custody long ago, what happened to her after he was shot? And why had no one ever mentioned this to him before? He couldn't stand the thought that she might be in...a bad situation. Something he couldn't even speculate about.

Jake Kakazu came by to give them a status report, an unusual courtesy. More and more he realized he hadn't given that man the credit he deserved. Unfortunately, there wasn't much to say. None of the young women saved from the organ smugglers knew anything useful. And Jaquith had died during the night.

"Any closer to finding out who your mole might be?" Dan asked.

"Unfortunately, no. It's hard to believe someone on my squad might work with these vile people. But I suppose money turns heads."

"This might be completely unrelated, but do you remember the silver flask in Camila's case? The one that disappeared from the evidence locker?"

"That I later found in your office?"

"Yeah. I'm sure you don't believe this, but I didn't put it there."

"Actually, I do believe it. I never thought you were dumb enough to hide it in your own office. But why would you take it at all? You won the case in the courtroom, as you usually do, by paying attention to people and figuring out what truly happened. You don't need to resort to stealing evidence. That wasn't even the most important piece of evidence. It makes no sense."

"I appreciate that, Jake. My point was, if you could figure out who had access to that evidence locker—"

"I might find the mole?"

"Makes sense that Sweeney would have a confederate in the police department. He does everywhere else. And the same man who stole the flask is probably also feeding Sweeney info about your investigation into the cartel."

Jake made a note on his phone. "I'll check into it. We're still moving heaven and earth to figure out who took potshots at you at the Pier. The Chief has made that investigation Priority One."

"And…?"

"So far, nothing. We know where the sniper crouched. There's a gift shop near the entrance where we believe he fired. We found what looks like a rudimentary sniper's nest. It's the perfect location, and it would be easy to get in and out without attracting much notice."

"Spent shells?"

"Don't I wish. This guy wasn't that careless."

Jimmy shook his head. "We'll probably never learn who fired those shots."

"But we already know who hired him," Dan said. "Why was it so important to silence Jaquith?"

"Or you," Jake said quietly.

"If the sniper wanted me dead, I'd be dead. Possibly he wanted us both dead and didn't have time to get to me before I ducked out of sight. But I think Jaquith was the main target."

Jake made his way toward the door. "In any case, I wanted to assure you that we're still working on it. And we'll keep you informed. Are you taking safety precautions?"

"Like you wouldn't believe," Jimmy groused. "We have security everywhere. Someone dogs my steps every time I leave the office."

"Good. Let me know if you see anything suspicious. And…" He hesitated. "Good luck in court."

That surprised Dan. Was it possible Jake cared about the outcome? Was it possible the cops, who normally despised him, were actually rooting for him this time around? That they wanted Sweeney taken down just as much as he did?

Made him feel good to think so, anyway.

After Jake left, they returned to the case. "As I see it," Maria said, "we have to accomplish two things. Obviously, we have to undermine Sweeney's counterclaim. But we also have to take every possible opportunity to bolster our own case. I don't think we've convinced the jury."

"We'll have a chance to call rebuttal witnesses," Dan said, "after Sweeney finishes his case. We should be prepared to make the most of it."

"Anyone in mind?"

"Not yet. I need to see what Sweeney's lawyers have up their sleeves. I've gone over their witness and exhibit lists, but I still only have the vaguest glimmer of an idea what they plan to do."

"Just got an email from Mr. K," Garrett announced. "He can't phone into the meeting, but he wants us to know he's following the case and supports us one hundred percent. He's glad we survived the motion to dismiss. He wants us to treat this as we would any case he assigned. No holds barred."

"Best boss ever," Jimmy commented.

"How does he follow the case?" Maria asked.

"How does he do anything?" Dan replied. "And yet, he always seems to know everything about everything."

"True. And a little scary."

"What do you see as Sweeney's problem proving that he's been slandered?"

"Much the same as yours. Damages."

Proving slander was hard enough. But to be entitled to any monetary award from a jury, you had to show you had been injured financially. That's why Caldwell spent so much time inquiring about whether there was any damage to Dan's professional reputation. The jury could award punitive damages to punish the offending party—but only if there were actual damages.

"Sadly," Garrett said, "I think Sweeney's case is stronger than yours."

Dan's eyebrow rose. "Excuse me?"

"I'm talking about damages. Your income stream is fine. Sweeney, on the other hand, has suffered some serious financial losses. I don't know everything because he keeps a tight lid on his financials. And I don't have access to IRS records."

"What?" Jimmy said. "Our master hacker can't get into the IRS databases?"

Garrett tucked in his chin. "I didn't say I couldn't. I said I don't. It's a federal crime."

Dan smiled. "How much do you know?"

"Sweeney lost a bucketload on that bad deal with the Coleman heir. Like half a billion bucks in bad investment. I think he's lost a lot of illegal income—what he normally launders through his tech companies. I suspect the cartel will be looking for a different place to bring their goods in the future. With a different contact on the mainland."

Maria jumped in. "Is there any evidence that Dan's statement at the press conference impacted Sweeney's income?"

"Not that I'm aware of. But I'm sure Caldwell and Drake have something up their sleeves. They're too smart to let an essential element of his claim drop without trying to prop it up."

"I don't have enough to salvage Sweeney's business," Dan said.

"He would derive a great deal of pleasure from driving you into bankruptcy."

"I'd survive."

"If his sniper reappears, you might not."

That sobering comment put a damper on the meeting. Even persuaded Dan to finally sit down.

"The truth is," Garrett continued, "this is an extremely dangerous case. I know you want the truth. I know you think the truth shall set you free." He paused. "But it isn't worth dying for."

"I think it is."

"Do the rest of us get to vote?"

Dan's jaw tightened. He had about reached his limit with Garrett's constant criticism. But he also knew there was some truth to it. "Ok, change of topic. Garrett, have you learned anything more about my...sister?"

Garrett pushed away from his laptop. "A little. I've verified most of what Dr. Harrison told me. And found copies of some of the records that mysteriously disappeared." He hesitated a moment. "You're not going to like this."

"Skip the trigger warning and spill."

"Since her last foster home, she's lived on the streets. Committed a lot of petty crime. Understandable, really—after Fisher died, she was completely alone. And now I think she's homeless."

Dan felt his stomach drop. "That...can't be right. My mother would've done something. After Fisher died—"

"I think your mother had enough on her hands dealing with a husband in prison and a little boy she had to raise on her own."

"But that's...horrible."

Maria reached out and took his hand. "It's okay, Dan. It's not your fault."

"That she's out there alone? When she has a brother who could give her anything?"

Garrett shook his head. "She probably doesn't even know you exist. She's had a tough life. First taken from her adoptive parents by Fisher. Then abandoned after his death. Then..."

"Spit it out, Garrett."

"You can imagine as well as I can. Drugs. Shoplifting. Juvie court. Maybe even...worse things."

"If she's out there," Maria said, "we'll find her. As soon as we finish this case, we'll make it our top priority."

"I'm making it my top priority now," Dan said. "Garrett, do you have any more leads?"

"I know where the largest concentrations of homeless people are in this city. I can't be sure she hasn't left town. But it's a good place to start. I thought I'd go out tonight—"

"I'll go."

"I'm not sure that's such a good—"

"I'm doing it."

Maria jumped in. "I'm not saying you shouldn't, Dan, but I am saying that right now, you should be focused on the trial."

"The trial will be over by five."

He didn't need special skills to read her face. She wasn't pleased. But she knew the futility of arguing with him.

The room fell silent. They stared at one another wordlessly. After several seconds, Dan spoke.

"About my sister, Garrett. Did she have a name?"

He nodded. "Dinah."

"Of course." His eyes drifted down. "Like the cat in *Alice's Adventures in Wonderland,* my mother's favorite book." A line creased his forehead. "That's the name she would give her daughter. And she would expect me to protect my sister to the best of my ability. She would count on me to look after her." He drew in his breath. "So I will."

CHAPTER TWENTY-EIGHT

DAN ENTERED THE COURTROOM, DISTRACTED AND DISTRAUGHT. Just as well he wasn't lead counsel. He probably wouldn't be in top form. Let Maria deal with motions and objections and cross-examinations. His brain was still obsessing over Sweeney and cartels and snipers.

And Dinah.

As soon as he and Maria passed through the courtroom doors, Drake headed their way. He stopped them before they got to their table.

"Okay," Drake said to Maria, "I've got a deal for you. I assume that since your client is a lawyer, it's okay if I discuss this in his presence."

"Of course."

"And by the way, Maria, I love that outfit. G&B?"

"Versace. I thought the jury might appreciate it if I improved the view a bit. What's the offer?"

Drake wore an aftershave so strong Dan wanted to pinch his nose. "Just to be clear, this is a one-time offer. You take it now or never. Five-minute window. After that, it's gone."

"Offer rejected," Dan said.

Drake blinked. "Wait—don't you want to hear it first?"

"Nah. Anything offered that obnoxiously I'm going to turn down just for the hell of it."

Maria laid her hand on Dan's arm. "I believe we have an ethical obligation to listen to offers and to make a good-faith effort to settle the case if possible. Remember—civil court. Not criminal."

He shrugged. "Whatever. You're the boss."

"Wait," Drake said, "let me get out my phone. I want to record that. Daniel Pike, showboat lawyer and control freak, says his female co-counsel is the boss."

Dan tried not to roll his eyes. "She's lead counsel. I trust her instincts."

"No, no," Drake said, fumbling with his phone, "I'm not letting you walk it back. You said she was the boss."

Maria smiled. "He meant in bed."

That shut Drake up.

Dan covered his smile. "You still haven't made the offer."

Drake stumbled to find words. "It's simple enough. We both walk away. No one takes anything, not on your claims or our counterclaims. No money, no admission of wrongdoing. We just stop the bleeding."

"I'm not bleeding," Dan said. "Are you bleeding, Maria?"

"Nope. I'm enjoying myself."

Drake frowned. "I'm talking about legal fees."

"I'm not paying any."

"You must provide your lawyer with some form of compensation."

Maria smiled again. "In bed."

Drake's eyes widened.

Dan spotted Sweeney sitting at counsel table acting as if he weren't paying attention, but at this point, he turned and addressed his lawyer. "I believe they rejected the offer, Drake. We gave them a chance to salvage themselves and they didn't want it. Everything that happens from here on out is on their heads. Sit down."

"Funny that you should be making this offer now, Sweeney," Dan said.

"A good citizen tries to resolve disputes. Not exacerbate them."

"But why now? And why this nonsense about legal fees? You know this isn't costing me anything. You, on the other hand, are paying the most expensive law firm in town." He paused, the wheels in his head turning. "Are your financial problems even greater than I imagined?"

Drake cut in. "We need to terminate this conversation."

"You initiated it, remember? I'm just finishing it. Why now, Sweeney? Is it the money?" He snapped his fingers. "Or is it something you're afraid we'll learn?" Everything was clicking at once, and when his instincts kicked into high gear, he couldn't think fast enough.

Drake stepped between them. "This conversation is over. Finished. Done. Do I need to call a bailiff? I can guarantee I'll be filing charges with the Disciplinary Committee."

Dan took a step away, though he kept his eyes locked on Sweeney's. "This is all starting to make sense. For the first time in a very long time."

———

Sweeney's defense team first called an expert witness. An unusual move, but Dan was sure they had some reason. For the defense in a civil suit, the whole case was a protracted game of Jenga. Keep pulling out the support blocks, one by one, until eventually the entire tower crashes to the ground.

Dan knew Dr. Folsom because she testified when Dan was accused of murder. She hadn't changed much. Late sixties or early seventies. Mandala pendant. Close-cropped hair. A bit slimmer than the last time he'd seen her.

At the previous trial, Dr. Deanna Folsom had testified that DNA proved Dan committed the murder in question, so he held the woman in contempt before she even spoke. If that case had proven anything, not only to him but he hoped everyone paying attention, it was that DNA was not nearly as conclusive as many people believed it to be.

Folsom was a forensic scientist, a skin-and-scalp expert by training, but she had developed a knowledge of DNA evidence and the use of genealogical data to support it. She appeared regularly in criminal cases, but Dan was willing to bet this was the first time she'd made an appearance in a civil case.

Caldwell took the lead for the direct examination. In a few minutes, she established Dr. Folsom's credentials, including that she had previously worked for an online genealogy site called FamilyTree. Folsom discussed several cases in which she had successfully teamed with forensic genealogists to create DNA profiles—including, she emphasized, some arising from old DNA samples. She then uploaded these profiles into various genealogy databases like CODIS until she found what she wanted. She traced the Y-chromosome DNA of the suspect's sample to link it to relatives who might have voluntarily submitted genetic information while trying to get a more complete family background. Sometimes that produced results, she explained, but not always.

"The huge breakthrough," Folsom explained, "was autosomal DNA testing. I first learned about this about two years ago."

Caldwell nodded as if she understood every word of this, but many of the jurors looked baffled. "Could you please explain what that is?"

"Sure. But I can't take credit. Dr. Colleen Fitzgerald did a lot of the pioneering work in this field. She opened it up for use by law enforcement. Autosomal DNA is inherited from both parents. It's much more useful from a research standpoint than Y-chromosome DNA. We barely even use the latter anymore. Autosomal DNA can find your relatives, cousins, and cousins of cousins, along every branch of your family tree. If anyone related to you has submitted a sample to one of those genealogy services—we're going to find you."

Caldwell nodded. "Using layman's terms, can you please explain how this is done?"

"It's not as complicated as it sounds. In this case, I used a skin flake found on the murder weapon after Officer Fisher died. When Ethan Pike was tried for the crime, DNA evidence was in its infancy. We can do more with it now than they ever dreamed."

"Did you get a match?"

"Almost immediately. I sent it to GEDMatch. The plaintiff, Daniel Pike, has a DNA sample on file—from when he was arrested not long ago on a murder charge. No question about it. The person who pulled the trigger on Fisher was closely related to the plaintiff."

Dan saw the jurors looking at one another, nodding.

"Did you do any other work on autosomal DNA relevant to this case, Dr. Folsom?"

"Yes. I used a new technique called phenotyping."

"What is that exactly?"

"It's a process by which we can determine what a person looks or looked like based upon their DNA."

"That's amazing."

"Agreed. But scientists have created composite images based upon DNA information that are so accurate they have led to the apprehension of many criminals."

"Alleged," Dan muttered under his breath.

Folsom continued. "This process was created by a company called Parabon Nanolabs. I contacted them and asked them to run the sample obtained from the murder weapon. They created some amazing composite images."

"May we see them?"

"Of course." Caldwell activated the television monitor behind the witness's head. "This first image is an actual mug shot taken of Ethan Pike after his arrest on murder charges."

An image appeared on the screen—thick brown hair, square jaw, slight smile. Gazing at the illuminated photo on the big screen, Dan was struck by how much it was like gazing into a mirror.

"And now," Folsom continued, "let me show you the composite image created from the autosomal DNA courtesy of Parabon. They did not know the name of the DNA donor and had no reference photos."

A new image appeared, sharing the screen with the first one.

The similarity was uncanny. These could be photos of brothers. In fact, Dan mused, they could be photos of twins. They were not identical. But close enough to support a familial identification.

"There's no question about this," Folsom said. "Yes, we aged the composite image to be the same age Ethan Pike was when the first photo was taken. But there's no serious doubt here. That DNA sample on the gun came from Ethan Pike. The defendant's father."

Caldwell smiled and sat down.

Dan leaned close to Maria and whispered. "I'm not sure there's any reason to cross."

"There is," she said, pushing herself to her feet. "Though I may live to regret it." She walked toward the witness stand and stood a few feet away, in full view of judge and jury.

"Dr. Folsom, did you obtain the permission of the people whose genetic material you surveyed?"

Folsom tilted her head slightly. "I'm not sure what you mean. I obtained permission from GEDMatch."

"I'm asking about all those people who submitted their genetic material. Kids who gave grandpa a kit for Father's Day so he could read about his German-Russian ancestors. Do you think they ever imagined this information could be used against other people? Other members of their family?"

"If they committed a crime—"

"So in your Big Brother view, someone could be nabbed for trespassing because a remote relative submitted a DNA sample for completely different purposes."

"I don't know that—"

"These companies make it sound like this is all just good fun. A curiosity. Learn where you came from. They don't inform people that your associates are assembling a huge database and releasing their genetic makeup to the entire world. Including law enforcement."

"Objection," Caldwell said. "This is not relevant."

"I think it is," Maria responded. "This evidence raises huge privacy issues. And if it was collected in violation of the privacy protections inherent in the US Constitution, the evidence should be excluded."

"This is a smokescreen," Caldwell said. "It's obvious why the plaintiff wants to exclude this evidence. It proves beyond question that the plaintiff's father was a murderer."

"Not true," Maria shot back. "But I am concerned about the precedent we might set if the court allows this evidence. This is a case of first impression in Pinellas County. The court's ruling could have major ramifications. Imagine a world where anyone can upload your personal DNA profile to this GEDMatch database, and that information can be accessed and used by anyone who wants to do so. For any reason they want to do so."

"I hear what you're saying," Judge Fernandez replied. "But I have to agree with the objection. This is terrifying, but not relevant."

Maria frowned and proceeded. "Dr. Folsom, you seem certain your evidence has proven who killed Jack Fisher."

"There's not the slightest doubt in my mind."

"I heard you testify on a previous occasion. When my client was falsely accused. You recall that?"

"Yes..."

"I believe on that occasion you also testified that the DNA evidence proved with absolute certainty that my client had committed murder. Except, as you surely know by now—he didn't."

"I'm not convinced—"

"The actual murderer admitted his guilt on the witness stand."

"But my DNA analysis was 100% correct," Folsom said. "The problem was that the scalp flakes were planted at the crime scene."

"Indeed. And isn't it just as possible that a skin flake was planted on the murder weapon in the case we're discussing today?"

"Objection," Caldwell said. "This is ridiculous. And desperate. The Fisher murder occurred more than twenty years ago. How could the witness possibly know the answer to this question?"

"I asked her if it was possible," Maria clarified.

"Then I object because it calls for speculation."

"Dr. Folsom is an expert witness, as my esteemed colleague went into great detail to explain. As such, she's entitled to offer an opinion based upon her expertise."

Judge Fernandez nodded. "I have to give this one to the plaintiff. The witness may respond."

Maria repeated the question. "Is it scientifically possible that the DNA evidence could have been planted on the gun?"

"It's...certainly possible. Though—"

"And you would still get the same match and the same

composite image. It just wouldn't be an image of the murderer. It would be the image of an innocent man who was framed. Right?"

"It's...remotely possible."

"Possible and, as the judge says, terrifying. Since this could potentially happen in every case, every time a DNA sample matches someone who foolishly sent their genetic material to a public database, never dreaming it could be used against them or someone they love." She closed her notebook. "No more questions."

CHAPTER TWENTY-NINE

DAN STARED AT THE SOCKLESS MAN IN THE BLACK NIRVANA T-shirt that looked as if it hadn't been washed in weeks. Possibly ever. He wore a tattered bandana across his forehead and both sneakers had holes at the toes. He stood before an eight-foot stretch of concrete tunnel decorated with debris, mostly trash discarded by travelers whizzing by overhead.

It wasn't much, but he called it home.

Dan had deliberately dressed down for the occasion, wearing only an untucked Polo, jeans, and of course, his Air Jordans. He still felt overdressed.

"I'm looking for someone," Dan explained.

"Haven't seen him," the man replied, not looking up. He appeared to be occupied with something, but Dan couldn't tell what. Whittling, perhaps? His movements were so slow and deliberate it was hard to imagine he would ever finish anything. Perhaps that was the point. He had a lot of time on his hands.

"It's a woman, actually. Maybe a few years older than me."

"Haven't seen her."

"Look, I'm not a cop."

"You look like one."

"I'm not. I'm a lawyer."

The man almost smiled. "You gonna sue me for everything I'm worth?"

At least he hadn't lost his sense of humor. "I don't want to cause anyone any harm. In fact, if I can find her, I think I could do her a lot of good."

"You chasin' tail?"

"What? No! Why would you even think that?"

"Lot of guys do. They come down thinking them homeless gals'll be easy. They'll do it for a buck, probably."

"I can assure you that's not why I'm here. I'm looking for my sister."

"Oh." Nirvana Man put down his whittling stick. "One of them deals."

"What's that?"

"Chasing down the prodigal daughter. Gonna stick her in a home or something?"

"Wouldn't that be an improvement?"

"In some cases, family is why people are here. What they're running from. Mix bad family and bad drug habit and..." He glanced over his shoulder. "You get what you're looking at now."

When Garrett first gave Dan this location, he didn't believe it. He'd read about people living in underground tunnels in Las Vegas, or even San Antonio—but here? These weren't really even tunnels. Underpasses. Flood channels, which were increasingly unsafe places as the climate warmed unpredictably. For that matter, a heavy rainstorm could send water rushing through these tunnels at thirty miles an hour.

Flooded or not, these underground tunnels had to be the worst place anyone could live. This man was the fourteenth person he'd spoken to since he arrived, and the backstories he heard, the patterns he detected, were distressing. Veterans. Addicts. Black sheep. He found a chain of dark passages that comprised a huge drainage network that had apparently been adopted by the homeless community. During the day, many of them travelled to the streets to beg for cash or table scraps, but this is where they lived.

There were dozens of them. He hadn't counted, but he thought he'd seen close to a hundred so far tonight. More men than women, but both. What he found particularly distressing was how young many were. In their thirties, even. They couldn't all be drug addicts—they couldn't afford it, at least not anymore. They couldn't all be vets. What caused this hideous phenomenon?

He'd seen two social workers here too, a young husband-and-wife team trying their best to care for people who either couldn't or didn't want to care for themselves. They were distributing socks and sandwiches and wristbands with an emergency contact number. Most took the socks, some took the sandwiches, and almost no one took the wristbands.

He'd seen a police officer too, which probably explained why many of the residents were skittish about talking to him. The cop was trying to get them to move out because a big rain was predicted, but few listened.

"Some of these people don't want to leave," the officer said. Maybe, but Dan suspected there was more to it than that. They didn't know where else to go. They didn't want to be dependent or beholden to others.

He continued walking through the tunnels. A few minutes later, he heard someone trying to get his attention. "Psst. Mister?"

He did an about face. A woman beckoned in the darkness. Dirty hair. Dark circles around her eyes. Paper-thin. "You lookin' for someone?"

"I sure am." He took a cautious step closer. She sported a buzzcut and a military fatigue shirt five sizes too big. She was supermodel-thin but not in a healthy or attractive way. She had a large scab or sore on the left side of her chin. "Can you help me?"

She hunched forward and beckoned, as if she feared she might be observed by the secret police. "Come over to my place. We can talk there."

He followed. She pushed a large piece of plywood to the side —her makeshift door. Beyond it, he saw her eight-foot stretch of paradise. Knickknacks and fake flowers tacked to a board. A Snoopy toy. Several candles, none lit.

"My name's Mandy," she explained.

"Dan." He almost offered her a hand, then stifled the instinct. He had heard the homeless were skittish about being touched, and after the coronavirus scare, they weren't alone.

"Nice place," he said, and all things considered, he meant it. "Been here long?"

"'Bout a year." She sat on a large pillow on the ground and offered him the same. "Used to be on the streets. This is better."

"I can see that. It's more private. But I hear it's going to rain."

"Always survived so far. That's what we Mole People do."

"Mole People?"

"That's what the cops call us. 'Cause we live underground."

"A big rain could wipe out this nice place you've got."

"Wouldn't be the first time." She was somewhat difficult to understand. He wasn't sure if that was because she was unaccustomed to talking out loud, or because drugs and alcohol had addled the language centers of her brain.

"Must be a lot of crime down here."

"Yeah. But not from Mole People. We don't steal from each other. Kids come down and cause trouble. Nothin' better to do. They steal from us, then go back to their Snell Isle mansions. They do most of the graffiti you see on the walls."

"Not the Mole People?"

"Why would we do that to our homes?"

Valid point.

"Worst is, someone reports the crime, the neighbors blame us Mole People, then the cops hassle us, try to make us move out. Just to please those rich SOBs who don't have to worry about what they're gonna eat tomorrow. Or *if* they're gonna eat tomorrow."

"I'm sorry."

Mandy smiled. "Nothing else, least a good rain will get me clean. I haven't had a shower in years."

"Seriously?"

"And that was at some shelter where I could only stay two days. I tell you—the last time I felt an honest-to-God shower pouring down on me—I cried."

Dan closed his eyes. He was afraid he was going to start crying himself. "Where did you live before...the streets?"

"Oh, I had me a little apartment downtown. Tiny. But it had a bed. Then I got in with this guy. He said he'd take care of me, but all he really did was get me hooked on that crystal meth. And that..." She waved her arm around the small area. "...led to this."

He nodded.

Her voice dropped to less than a whisper. "Had me a little dog once, too. But I lost him." She reached up and took down the Snoopy figurine. "Now I got this."

"I'm...sorry."

"He got a hot shot."

"A...what?"

"Poisoned. Bad food." She sniffed. "Don't matter. This is no place for a puppy."

"No."

"Some days I think I'm gonna get heatstroke. Other days I think I'm gonna drown. No good any way you go." She looked up and tried to smile. "Did I hear you were looking for your sister?"

"Yeah."

"Bout your age?"

"A little older."

"She got a name?"

"I don't know what she might be calling herself now, but her birth name was Dinah."

"Dinah? Like, Dinah blow your horn?"

"That's right."

Mandy shook her head. "Curiouser and curiouser."

His eyebrows knitted together. That was one of the most famous lines from his mother's favorite book. "What makes you...use those words?"

"That's what she used to say. All the time."

"Who?"

"Dinah."

"You know my sister?"

"I knew a gal named Dinah. Lived here in this tunnel for a while."

"What did she look like?"

Mandy shrugged. "Big eyes. Brown hair. Thin." She peered at him for a moment. "You know, I think she favors you a bit. You got the same eyes."

He felt his lips tremble. "Those are my mother's eyes."

"What'd you do to her? Why'd she have to run off?"

"I didn't do anything. Truth is, I've never met her. At least not that I recall."

"You never met your own sister?"

"I didn't know I had a sister until recently. Even now I don't know the details. But my friend has been investigating, and he thought she might've...had some bad experiences. And become homeless. Do you know where she is?"

Mandy gave Dan a quick up and down. "You got money, don't you?"

"I...do."

"Lots of it?"

"Enough to take care of my sister."

"And maybe a finder's fee for old Mandy?"

Old Mandy who was probably in her mid-forties. "I would be grateful. Among other things...I could find you a place to live."

"I got a place to live."

"You know what I mean."

She nodded, and all at once her eyes got watery. "You can't go back in time."

"But you can build a future."

"I don't need no fancy home but...I do miss that dog of mine."

"We'll go to the kennel. Get you the best rescue dog that ever was. And a collar and vet and shots and everything else."

"And some food. Safe food?"

His voice choked. "Mandy, if you help me find my sister, I will personally come down here and feed that dog every damn day for the rest of my life."

She nodded slowly. "I believe you. You're one of the good ones."

"I try."

"Where were you when I was just a kid?"

He refrained from mentioning that they were probably more or less the same age. "Too wrapped up in myself to be good for anyone else. You wouldn't've liked me."

"I don't know. You're pretty cute."

He cleared his throat. "Where's Dinah?"

Mandy drew in her breath. "She lived here for a time, but then she got wrong-ways with some cop. He kept coming around, bugging her. I think he wanted what she had, if you know what I mean. Your sister's a cutie. Even in bad shape, she's the type of gal who catches a man's eye."

His face hardened. "What did this cop do?"

"Kept getting fresh. Touching her. Wouldn't let her be. Finally, she said she was leaving."

"She didn't tell anyone?"

"Like who? The cops? The cops were the problem. They usually are, for folks like us. No one was gonna help her against one of their own."

"Where did she go?"

"Well, I didn't follow or anything, but I know what she said."

"And...?"

"She said she was going to Wal-Mart."

He blinked twice. "For...groceries?"

"Nah. To live. They let folks like us spend the night in the parking lot. I prefer to be a Mole Person myself, but a pretty thing like her should be out and about."

"Do you know which Walmart? There are several in town."

"Sorry. I'm not much of a shopper."

"Right." He pushed off the pillow, then checked his watch. He needed to get at least a few hours of sleep before the trial resumed. "I'll get on it tomorrow. Right after sunset."

"You tell her I said hello, ok? I liked that girl."

"If I find her, I'll tell her. And—" He wanted to give Mandy a hug, but he restrained himself. "I can't tell you how much this means to me."

"Old Mandy was able to help a fancy Dan like you. This is a strange world. Hey, did I hear you say you're a lawyer?"

"You did."

"You talk to judges and them folk?"

"Constantly."

"If you get a chance...tell them about us Mole People, would you? I think most folks don't have any idea. They rush past every day on their way to something else. Tell them our story. The world already pushed us into the tunnels and sewers. Don't let them forget about us."

CHAPTER THIRTY

DAN KNEW THE DEFENDANTS WOULD CALL BRADLEY ELLISON. HE was in many respects their star witness, even more important than Sweeney himself, at least on the subject of whether Dan's father was wrongfully convicted.

Ellison seemed cool and collected, but perhaps not in the best shape ever. Maybe Dan was imagining it, but Ellison seemed less assured than he had at the deposition. Dan also noticed that he was perpetually looking at Sweeney, as if checking for approval.

Despite his age, Ellison seemed alert and articulate, even forthcoming. Slowly, Caldwell took him through his years of experience, both as a police officer and later as a private investigator. Whether you believed him or didn't, there was no question about the fact that he had put in his time.

About ten minutes later, Caldwell got to the night in question, the harrowing shootout at the basketball court where Jack Fisher was killed. Ellison did an excellent job of describing the scene without excessive drama. He didn't need to overdo it. The scene was probably more frightening because he downplayed it. The jury got no sense that he was after sympathy. Instead, they got a just-the-facts recitation from a man who had been through a lot and lived to talk about it.

"Sir," Caldwell said, "let me put the question to you bluntly. Did you see who shot Jack Fisher?"

"I did."

"And who was that?"

"Ethan Pike. The plaintiff's father."

"That was a tumultuous, chaotic scene. Is there any question in your mind about what happened?"

"None whatsoever. I saw Ethan pull the trigger. I saw Jack fall."

"And did you report what you'd seen?"

"First chance I got. I understood why Ethan did it. I didn't like Jack much myself. But he was a fellow officer and we have to put that first. We can never condone murder."

"Of course not. Pass the witness."

Maria moved closer.

"This is not the first time you've been involved in a case with my client, is it?"

"No, ma'am."

"You were both involved in the Ossie Coleman case. Dan represented Ossie in his suit to establish his identity, and then later defended him on a bogus murder charge."

"That is correct."

"What was your involvement?"

"I was hired to investigate the kid."

"And it was the defendant, Conrad Sweeney, who hired you?"

"No, ma'am. You're mistaken. I was hired by the Coleman family."

"At Sweeney's recommendation."

"I believe they may have discussed the matter. They were friends and business partners."

"You've worked for Conrad Sweeney on several occasions."

"True."

"He's been a source of income for you during your retirement years."

"If you're suggesting—"

"I'm not suggesting anything, Mr. Ellison, and I would prefer it if you did not either. We can let the jury draw their own conclusions from the facts."

Ellison clammed up. Score one for Maria.

She continued. "Please describe your interaction with my client during the Coleman case."

"We spoke on one occasion. I knew he was Ethan's son and he knew that my testimony put his daddy away, so you can imagine the tension. But he held his temper in check."

This non-compliment, of course, presumed Dan had a temper he needed to control.

"Did you threaten him?"

"Absolutely not. I warned him against crossing Dr. Sweeney, but that's not a threat. That's just common sense. If the boy had listened to me, we wouldn't be in this courtroom now. Instead, he went looking for trouble and, big surprise, he found some."

"Motion to strike the last non-relevant part of the witness's response," Maria said.

Judge Fernandez nodded. "That will be granted."

"The fact is, you didn't solve the Coleman case, correct? Dan did."

"I would have to agree with that. Of course, he had the benefit of my investigation, which helped him reach the ultimate solution."

"And did his success in that case persuade you that he was a more respectable citizen than your employer Sweeney wants the world to believe?"

Ellison craned his neck. "I'm...not sure I can go that far."

"But you said—"

"I'll give your man credit for cracking the case. I was

impressed. But when I found out about his connections to organized crime and cartels—"

"Objection!"

Caldwell sprang up. "She opened the door, your honor. She asked for the witness's opinion of her client."

"Have to agree with that," the judge said. "The witness may continue."

"When I learned that time after time your client was either involved with or had detailed knowledge of the cartel's activities, I saw things in a different light. It's a lot easier to solve cases when you have inside information. I had to wonder what the large-scale scheme was. Cartels don't let rats talk about their business—unless they have a good reason."

"Again I object," Maria said. She looked worried. Opening this door had been an error and now she was paying for it. "The witness has no personal knowledge of any involvement with cartels."

"I never claimed I did," Ellison insisted. "I just note that, time after time, Daniel Pike seems to have valuable pieces of information about these criminals that no one else has. Not even the police."

The judge nodded. "I'm going to let the witness's testimony stand. Do you have anything else, counselor?"

"Yes, your honor. Mr. Ellison, you mentioned that Jack Fisher was in the car parked beside yours. Was he alone?"

Ellison peered at her for a moment. "I'm not sure I follow."

"You had a partner with you. Ethan Pike had his partner. Who was with Jack?"

It was barely perceptible, but Ellison's eyes darted to the defense table before he answered. "I—I don't remember."

"Seriously? Your memory seems crystal clear on everything else. Like it just happened yesterday. Who was riding shotgun with Jack?"

"I...would assume it was his partner."

"And that would be Gerald Jaquith, right?"

"Uh, yes. That's right."

"Funny thing, though. My client spoke to Officer Jaquith, shortly before his recent death. Jaquith said he wasn't there."

Dan didn't need superpowers to see that Ellison was disturbed. Was he surprised to hear this? Or was it something else?

"Then I guess he wasn't. I knew Gerald. He's a straight-shooter."

"Why wouldn't Jack's partner be with him?"

"I don't know."

"Wouldn't that be standard practice?"

"Yes. Perhaps someone else was assigned that day. Maybe Gerald was sick."

Maria took a step closer, positioning herself between Ellison and Sweeney, blocking his view. "You're going to tell this jury that you have no idea who was in that car with Jack Fisher? Even though you remember everything else imaginable about this traumatic event."

"I do not recall who was in the car with Jack Fisher."

"You don't recall the other officer who you depended upon for your life? For your common defense?"

"I do not."

Dan could see the jurors glancing at one another. No one liked this response. Even the judge bore knitted eyebrows.

"Okaaaaay." Maria was not attempting to hide her disbelief. "One more thing. You told the jury you saw Ethan Pike pull the trigger with your own eyes."

"That is correct."

"Did you see him? Or did you see his reflection in a mirror?"

Ellison tilted his head. "I don't know what you mean."

"At your deposition you testified that you did not directly witness the alleged shooting. You saw it in a mirror. Which raises all kinds of kinds of reliability issues, giving the darkness and the crossfire and—"

"No, that's incorrect."

Maria looked at him as if he had told her one and one was three. "Sir, I was at the deposition. I know what you said."

"I'm afraid this time it's your memory that's failing. I saw this murder—this execution, really—with my own eyes."

Dan grabbed the deposition transcript before Ellison had even finished answering. He flipped through the pages, looking for the relevant passage.

And couldn't find it.

Because it wasn't there.

According to the official record of his testimony, Ellison had turned his head, looked behind him, and seen Ethan shoot Jack in cold blood.

A chill raced down his spine.

Be careful about Marjorie, Shawna had warned Jimmy.

Marjorie. The one sporting a purse most wealthy people couldn't afford.

Sweeney recognized this was a major weakness in Ellison's testimony. So he paid Marjorie to eliminate it.

Maria returned to the table, her arm outstretched. She wanted the transcript to impeach the witness.

Dan shook his head.

He glanced across the room to Sweeney, who covered his mouth with one hand.

But Dan could still detect the smile Sweeney hid.

Maria whirled around. "Mr. Ellison, you have changed your testimony."

"No, ma'am. I have not."

Caldwell rose. "This is easily resolved, your honor. Let's read the relevant passage from the deposition in open court. Let the jury decide."

Which would only make a bad situation worse. "That won't be necessary," Maria said. "Nothing more." She sat down.

She and Dan didn't speak. No words were necessary. They both knew what had just happened. They'd made themselves look like fools.

He should have re-read the transcript before the trial. But instead, he'd been trying to find his sister and—

And now they were paying the price.

CHAPTER THIRTY-ONE

DAN KNEW THAT IN THE WORLD OF RECOVERY, THEY SAID AN addict never gets serious about quitting until he hits rock bottom. The problem with that adage was that there's no rock bottom. There's no limit to the amount of badness this universe is capable of heaping on you.

As this day in court was proving.

"For our final witness," Caldwell announced, "the defendant would like to call Camila Pérez to the stand."

Dan and Maria looked at one another, eyes wide. *What?*

Maria slowly rose. "Objection. Your honor, this witness is not on the list submitted at pretrial by the defendant."

The judge turned to Caldwell. "Is that true?"

"Yes, your honor, I'm afraid it is. But there are extenuating circumstances. We only learned about the availability of this witness recently. And we believe a grave injustice would result if she were not allowed to testify."

The judge waived them forward. "Approach."

Dan followed. He knew he probably shouldn't. He wanted the jury to think of him as a wronged party, not a lawyer. But he needed to hear this for himself.

The judge's lips were pursed. He was obviously unhappy. "Counsel, I have told you before that I have no tolerance for trial by ambush. We submit those witness lists for a reason. All parties should have a fair and equal opportunity to prepare."

"I know, your honor," Drake said, taking the lead, "and I respect that. Believe me, this was not planned. We did reach out to Ms. Pérez earlier, but as you are probably aware, our former mayor is now in prison and she refused to testify. Only last night did we get word that she'd changed her mind."

"That's no excuse," Maria said. "Even if she was only a remote possibility, her name should have been on the list."

"I didn't think there was a remote possibility," Drake replied. "I was wrong. I made a bad call. Penalize me if you must, your honor, but don't penalize my client."

The judge was still frowning. "May I ask what the general nature of the witness's testimony might be?"

"In addition to being involved in at least two major criminal cases with the plaintiff, she also dated him for a significant period of time. He talked about his work. She has first-hand knowledge of his...activities."

"Doesn't sound relevant to me," Maria said. "Sounds like mudslinging. Character assassination."

"But this case is all about the plaintiff's character. He can only suffer from an alleged slander if his reputation has been impacted. And if the statements were untrue. This witness is in a better position than any other person on earth to testify on these subjects."

"She's a convicted criminal," Maria said.

"Just like your client's father," Drake shot back.

"Have you made some kind of deal? Early release in exchange for testimony?"

"Absolutely not," Drake said. "I'm not the district attorney."

"You could offer her money. A job. You might use your influence with the parole board."

"I have done nothing of the kind. She wants to testify."

"So no deal?" the judge asked, looking sternly into Drake's eyes.

"None whatsoever. As I said, last night, she reached out to us."

Dan hated that part worst of all. If Camila wanted to testify, it could only be for one reason. Vengeance.

"I don't like this one bit," Judge Fernandez said. "But I will allow it, with the following provisos. If plaintiff's counsel needs additional time to prepare for cross-examination, I will permit it. If they want to amend their list to add rebuttal witnesses, I will allow it. And if it turns out this woman has nothing relevant to say, I will instruct the jury to disregard it."

"Understood, your honor," Drake said, obviously relieved. He'd just dodged a major bullet and he knew it. "Thank you."

Maria's lips tightened, but she remained silent. Dan understood why. The judge had ruled and nothing she said now would help.

When they returned to their table, Dan scribbled a note.

NO WORRIES. WE'LL SURVIVE.

He just hoped that assessment turned out to be accurate.

A marshal escorted Camila into the courtroom. Dan almost didn't recognize her. Her complexion was pale and bloodless. She'd lost weight—too much. Her gorgeous thick hair had a bad blunt cut. She looked haggard. Her clothes didn't fit well. But her eyes were laser-focused. She wasn't cuffed and she'd obviously had a chance to dress and groom since she left prison, but she still looked shockingly different than she had the last time Dan saw her. His once lovely companion now looked more like one of the Mole People than a former politician with national aspirations.

This was painful. Camila had such potential. Mr. K thought she could be a major political force for good. But she'd squandered it all—and now they witnessed the result.

She briefly made eye contact with Dan as she passed by. She did not avoid his gaze. Her face bore a slight trace of a smile.

That smile was the most frightening thing he'd seen since this trial began.

Camila slid into the witness chair. She stated her name and gave her current address as Lowell Correctional Institution.

"What did you do before your recent incarceration?"

As if the jurors didn't already know. "I was the mayor of this city. I resigned."

"What was the charge lodged against you?"

"Conspiracy to commit homicide. I accepted a plea bargain to a lesser crime. I didn't want to spend the rest of my life in prison. With the deal, I'll probably serve about three years."

"And what was the basis for this allegation?"

"I conveyed information about a hitman."

Caldwell nodded. "We'll come back to that in a moment. I just wanted to be honest with the jury up front so they understand the circumstances. You've been released from prison so you can testify, correct?"

"Yes."

"And have you been offered any kind of deal, promise, or incentive in exchange for your testimony?"

"None whatsoever."

"Thank you. As you know, this is a slander case based upon statements made by Daniel Pike and our client Dr. Conrad Sweeney. Each claims the other made statements damaging to their reputations and earning ability. Do you know either of the parties?"

"I worked with Dr. Sweeney on several occasions when I was mayor." Despite what she'd been through, Camila did not appear to have any problem speaking or collecting her thoughts. "We worked together to build several women's shelters in this city, and numerous other charitable projects."

Dan knew she despised Sweeney just as much as he did. If

she was willing to whitewash that man, he was in serious trouble.

"And did you know the plaintiff, Daniel Pike?"

"Very well."

"What was the nature of your relationship?"

"I first met him when he asked me to testify in a case he handled. After seeing how effective he was in the courtroom, I asked him to represent me. And we started...seeing each other."

"Just for clarification, when you say you were seeing each other..."

"Personally. Intimately."

"You dated?"

"We slept together."

Caldwell paused, making sure the jury kept up. "And when did the intimate relationship begin?"

"Shortly after he began representing me."

Dan sat up straight. That was a lie. Now he understood where this was going...

Caldwell lunged. "Are you saying he had sex with you while you were his client?"

"Absolutely. He seemed to feel it was...important. He was insistent."

"Are you saying he pressured you to have sex with him?"

"I'm saying he made it very clear that if I wanted his services, I was going to have to provide services of another sort."

Dan scribbled furiously. NOT TRUE.

Maria nodded. She knew. But did the jury?

"Would you call this sexual harassment?"

"Objection," Maria said. "Leading. And it calls for a legal conclusion."

Caldwell shrugged. "The witness has been to law school."

The judge nodded. "But it's still leading."

Caldwell rephrased. "Were you comfortable with this relationship?"

"Not at first. I felt like I had no choice. But I didn't want to be locked up for a crime I didn't commit. I felt the only way to stay out of prison was to give him what he wanted. Over and over again."

Dan clenched his teeth. He wanted to scream out what a liar she was, but he knew that wouldn't help. There were seven women on the jury and Sweeney's team was playing to them. They were weaponizing the MeToo movement, creating sexual harassment—plus a violation of the Bar Association's Code of Professional Conduct—where none existed.

He knew Camila was bitter. He had been the one who figured it all out, who unearthed the evidence that put her behind bars. But he had not expected such hatred from a woman who once told him she loved him. Who he had loved. Like no one he had ever loved in his life.

"You said not at first," Caldwell continued. "Did something change?"

"Yes. I guess I got used to it. And I did learn to like him. Even after the case ended, we continued to go out."

Started to go out, in reality. But this testimony had nothing to do with reality.

"Ms. Pérez, as a former lawyer, are you aware of the Bar Association rules pertaining to lawyers having intimate relationships with their clients?"

"I know it is absolutely forbidden," she replied. "I know it is grounds for disbarment. Of course, Dan has been the subject of disbarment proceedings before. More than once."

"Your honor," Caldwell said, "given these new revelations, I respectfully request that the court send a copy of the transcript of this testimony to the Disciplinary Committee of the State Bar Association so it may consider whether to initiate disbarment proceedings against the plaintiff."

Dan tried not to shrug. Been there, done that.

"We'll take that up at a later time, counsel. Proceed."

Caldwell continued. "Have you ever heard the plaintiff mention my client, Conrad Sweeney?"

"Like you wouldn't believe. Constantly. He is absolutely obsessed with the man. Fixated. Crazy."

"Can you give the jury an example?"

"Where to start? In Dan's mind, Dr. Sweeney is the scapegoat for all his problems. Somehow, Sweeney is behind every crime in every case he handles. Somehow, Sweeney is even behind his father's conviction, which happened decades ago. It is truly bizarre."

"Do you have an explanation?"

"Like jealousy? Dr. Sweeney is our most prominent citizen. Given the enormity of Dan's ego, that creates jealousy. Envy. And a huge desire to bring Sweeney down."

"But why?"

"Dan wants what he has. The love and respect of the people. Dan presents himself as a crusading hero, but the truth is, he's as dirty as they come and he knows it. He can never have what Dr. Sweeney earned."

"Is this speculation on your part?"

"Absolutely not. I've heard Dan spout his hatred for Sweeney on many occasions. He sees himself as a sort of modern-day Sherlock Holmes. And every Holmes must have a Moriarty."

Echoing the very words Caldwell had used earlier. And Dan did not believe it was a coincidence.

"You believe he created this supervillain fantasy. In his mind."

"Exactly."

"Objection," Maria said. "This is amateur psychological analysis, not real testimony."

The judge disagreed. "The witness did know the plaintiff well for an extended period of time, and she is highly educated. I'm going to allow it."

"Did you ever see any evidence of Dr. Sweeney being involved in any…nefarious schemes?"

"Absolutely not. I think the man is a hero. He has a heart as big as an ocean. He's used his success and wealth to make this city a better place. He deserves the respect he has."

Dan could feel his fists clenching. He moved them under the table so they wouldn't be visible. But he didn't know how much more of this smear job he could take.

"This case concerns a statement made by my client inidicating that the plaintiff is a criminal and has ties to organized crime," Caldwell said. "Are you aware of any criminal activities by the plaintiff, the man you know so well and intimately?"

"Big time." Camila turned to look at Dan. "Courtroom tricks. Schemes. He's got a black book filled with former clients—gang members and drug pushers, mostly—happy to do his bidding at the drop of a hat. To Dan, the end always justifies the means."

Like when I turned you in? he wondered. Even though it broke my heart into pieces?

"What about organized crime?"

"Dan's connections to organized crime are basically the story of his life. And the secret of his success. That case I mentioned where I testified for him? Sex-trafficking cartel that he suddenly knew more about than anyone. Same thing when he was charged with murder. How'd he get off? Information and testimony stemming from the sex-trafficking cartel. What's the latest? He has the inside skivvy on an organ-smuggling cartel. I mean, c'mon. He's either psychic or he's working with them. And I don't think he's psychic."

"And yet you dated him."

"I looked the other way, I admit it. Until I couldn't any longer. Here's the truth. Dan and his father are basically the same. Apple doesn't fall far from the tree, right? His father did it with a badge and gun and Dan does it with a law degree, but it's the same thing."

Dan winced. This testimony was painful to hear and painful to imagine anyone would believe, but oddly enough, that wasn't the worst of it. The jury appeared to be buying it, and that still wasn't the worst of it.

Sweeney was smiling. Not enough to constitute a gloat. But close.

Which told him he hadn't heard the worst of it yet.

Caldwell paused again, giving her words time to sink in. "Ms. Pérez, you've mentioned that the plaintiff has been involved in criminal activities, but I don't think you've specified a particular criminal act. Can you?"

"Absolutely. I mentioned that I was convicted of helping someone find a hitman."

"Right."

"Guess where I got the info?" She pointed toward the plaintiff's table.

"From the plaintiff?"

"From Daniel Pike. Where else? I didn't know any hitmen. I didn't know anything about the dark web. But he did. I told you about all the contacts he's acquired from years of putting criminals back on the street. He gave me the skinny."

"Why would he do that?"

"To get his ass off the hook." She covered her mouth. "Oh, I'm sorry, your honor."

The judge shook his head. "No worries. Proceed."

"Dan gave me the scoop. I passed it along. And look who ended up in prison. I think he made some kind of deal to save his own skin."

"That's a lie," Dan said, loud enough to be heard. "All of this. A pack of lies."

Maria glared at him. What was he doing? Shut up already.

He didn't know what he was doing. Something just bubbled out and he couldn't hold it back any longer. Bad enough to be lied about. Much worse when it comes from someone you once loved.

The judge banged his gavel. "The plaintiff will be silent. Mr. Pike, you know how to behave in a courtroom."

He bit his lip, glaring at Camila. "I apologize to the court."

The judge turned to the witness stand. "Please continue."

"Speaking as a person versed in the law, do you believe Mr. Pike has been slandered?"

Camila laughed. "I don't think that's possible. You can't slander a criminal by calling him a criminal. That's just stating a fact."

Caldwell nodded. "No more questions."

Maria leapt to her feet. Dan recalled that the judge had offered them additional time to prepare for this cross-ex. Apparently she didn't want it.

"Ms. Pérez, isn't it true that you currently reside in the Lowell Correctional Institution?"

"I already said that."

"Because you were found guilty of a criminal felony."

"I pled guilty."

"Did you mention this nonsense about Dan giving you the hitman info at the time?"

"To whom? There was no trial."

"Amazing that you kept secret something that might help you."

"I don't know that it would've helped me. Where I got the hitman info was not relevant to the charges against me." She paused. "Though it might've led to charges against Dan."

"Then why not tell? Why not bring this arch-criminal to justice?"

"I...suppose I still had...feelings for him."

"You appear to have gotten over that."

"Prison helps you see things more clearly."

Maria took several steps closer. "Ms. Pérez, isn't it a fact that the intimate relationship between you and my client didn't begin until after your case was resolved?"

"You don't know what—"

"In fact, I do know, Ms. Pérez, because I worked on that case. I saw both of you almost every day and I know damn well there was nothing going on between the two of you. Yet."

Judge Fernandez scowled. "Language, counsel."

Maria nodded. "Apologize. You can probably sense my frustration with this...witness."

"I think everyone can sense it," the judge said quietly.

"Ms. Pérez, isn't it true that you actually set my client up to take the fall for a murder? That you knew what really happened but kept quiet—while the two of you were in an intimate relationship?"

"Totally false."

"And isn't it true that when Dan learned the truth about your criminal activities, he turned you in?"

"He ratted me out. But he knew all along—"

"And isn't it true that he ended the relationship when he realized you were a scheming liar willing to throw him to the dogs to save your own political career?"

"Objection," Caldwell said.

Maria ignored her and plowed ahead. "And isn't that why you're here today? Because he told the truth about you, and you're bitter about it and want revenge?"

"*Not true. Not*—"

"Objection!" Caldwell said.

"And isn't it true that you volunteered to testify today, not because you knew anything about the case, but because you wanted to get even with the one man you couldn't fool?"

"Objection!"

The judge banged his gavel. "Ms. Morales. You need to stop talking and let me rule on the pending objection."

"No need. Every word this woman says is a lie. She can go back to prison where she belongs."

"Ms. Morales!"

Maria did not look contrite. "Pass the witness." Pause. "Are we done? Or does the defense have some more lying convicts they'd like to call?"

"Ms. Morales, I'm holding you in contempt."

"Only fair. I hold this witness in contempt." She drew in her breath. "But at least I'm telling the truth."

FATHERS, SONS & SISTERS

CHAPTER THIRTY-TWO

DAN SPENT THE EARLY PART OF THE NIGHT RE-READING EVERY deposition transcript in the case. He didn't find any signs of additional tampering. Garrett was trying to track down Marjorie, but no one seemed to know where she was. Caldwell, who had hired her, said she'd been called back to Manhattan. Dan doubted she had been there in the first place. She'd been hired because she could be bought. Caldwell and Drake, distinguished officers of the court, went along with it.

But Sweeney had engineered it. He'd seen the need from the start, before the depositions began. As always, the grandmaster was three moves ahead of their game. Maybe more.

Dan glanced at his watch. Just before midnight, he started his tour of Walmart parking lots. There were six in the area, and he had no idea which might currently contain Dinah. For all he knew, she might've moved to a Walmart in Oklahoma. But he resolved to start his search and hope for the best.

To his surprise, he found it was not just homeless people sleeping in Walmart parking lots. Many of the people he encountered were simply travelers saving the fees charged by KOA campgrounds. "It's not much to look at," one man with a small RV told him. "But it's free. Park, get some sleep, then move on in the morning."

He'd read that Walmart made a decision at the corporate level to permit this. Perhaps it was a humanitarian gesture. Perhaps they thought it would increase early-morning shopping, as overnight guests came in to use the bathrooms and left with breakfast. Whatever the reason, he soon realized the Walmart crowd was a genuine underground subculture. If the people living in the flood tunnels were Mole People, this was the Concrete Congregation.

At his fourth Walmart he met a man named Floyd who had no RV—but an impressive mustache. Collared but torn shirt. Bolo tie. All Floyd's worldly possessions were in a shopping cart, half full. Floyd had straggly gray hair and an unsightly lesion on his right cheekbone. Dan worried it might be cancerous.

After a few minutes of chitchat, Floyd's tongue loosened. At least this time Dan had committed no apparel faux pas. He wore the most tattered clothes he could find on his boat. He even ripped up his jeans a bit.

"You're a college boy, aren't you?" Floyd asked.

Dan had to admit that he was. "You won't hold that against me?"

"Don't jump to any conclusions. I went to college too."

Dan tried to stifle his surprise.

"I used to be a CPA."

"Then how…?"

"Did I end up homeless and sleeping in the Walmart parking lot? Long story."

"Give me the abridged version."

"Well, there was a girl."

Isn't that how the story always opens? More common than 'Once upon a time.'

"She said she loved me, but she loved booze more. And Oxy.

That habit required money. So she took all mine. I got so messed up I lost my license. Couldn't work. One thing led to another. Lost my house. Kinda fell apart."

"You could pull it back together. You just need a little help. I know a place—"

Floyd held up a hand. "Please don't try to save me. I don't want it and I don't need it." He leaned back, gazing around the parking lot. "This is a good place. Two of the Walmarts in town are no-gos. Don't allow people to sleep in the lot. I don't know why, but this one does, so it's my favorite. I just wish they'd get over the lawn chair rule."

"What's that?"

"Walmart lets us hang here. But there's a certain etiquette involved. You're not supposed to sit in lawn chairs in the lot. I have no idea why."

"Any other rules?"

"There's no parking fee, but they do kinda expect you to buy something. I usually do a little begging till I get enough for one of them Krispy Kremes. Man, I love those donuts."

Dan smiled a bit. "They are tasty." Horrible for you, but tasty. "Do the people here interact much?"

Floyd pulled the last remains of a Hershey bar out of his pocket. Looked like he'd been working on it all day. "Depends on who you're talking about. Not the folks in the RVs. They eat, sleep, spend time with their pets. Some of them even have satellite hook-ups or DVD players so they can watch TV. Can you imagine? Too cheap to pay for a campground, but a satellite dish on their RV."

"You think that's the main motivation? Saving money?"

"I don't know. Sometimes I think some folks just don't know what to do with themselves. They don't know where else to go. After a while, it becomes a habit. Pretty safe, too."

"Really?"

"Sure. Truckers aren't allowed. The parking lot is well lit and on a main road. What can happen? Wind blows a stray shopping cart into your RV? You'll survive."

"Do you like the people? The ones who don't have RVs?"

"They're ok. Migrants, some of them. They hit New England in the fall when it's pretty and not too cold. Come down here in the winter. Maybe crisscross the heartland in the spring. Avoid the tornados and hurricanes. Maybe get to California, where it's always warm. And they have more Walmarts than you could visit in a lifetime."

"I suppose they do at that."

Floyd pulled a weed out of a crack in the pavement. "Mind if I ask you a question for a change?"

"Course not."

"You said you weren't a cop. Why all the questions?"

"I'm looking for someone."

"Why not talk to the folks in the RVs? They're way more respectable-looking than some washed-up homeless CPA."

Dan inched a little closer. "The person I'm looking for was homeless. You're more likely to know her than people who don't come out of their trailers."

"Gotcha. A woman, huh? She do you wrong?"

"No. I've never met her."

"Then why so anxious to find her?"

"She's my sister. Or so people tell me."

Floyd whistled. "And you're just now finding out? Wow. I thought my life was messed up. Why you looking here?"

"I talked to a woman downtown, in the tunnels."

"Mole Person?"

"Yeah. She thought my sister might've gone to a Walmart."

"This sister of yours got a name?"

"Dinah."

The recognition was instantaneous. "Big pretty eyes. Skinny. A chin—" He paused. "Like yours?"

Dan scooted even closer. "I bet that's her."

"Oh man. Oh man."

"What? What is it?"

"That's bad. I'm sorry. But it is. Real bad."

"Have you seen her?"

Floyd nodded, with the saddest expression Dan had ever seen. "I saw her. I saw them take her."

"Who? Who took her?"

"I really don't want to talk about this. Especially not to her brother."

Floyd started to get up, but Dan pushed him down. "Listen to me, Floyd. I don't want to get rough. But—"

"Trust me. You don't want to know."

"I do. And you are going to tell me. One way or the other."

Floyd stuttered. Sweat beaded on his forehead. "I can give you an address. You find out for yourself."

"Fine. Give me the damned address."

Floyd did. And Dan recognized the location.

"Isn't that one of the Sweeney women's shelters?"

"Yeah."

"They've taken her in?"

"Not the way you mean." Floyd rocked back and forth. He looked terrified. "They got lots of women there. But what they're doing..."

"Who is 'they?'"

"You be careful," Floyd said, voice trembling. "They aren't gonna be happy to see you coming over."

"They won't see me coming," Dan muttered. He stood, crushing the paper in his hand. "But they won't forget I was there."

CHAPTER THIRTY-THREE

DAN APPROACHED THE WOMEN'S SHELTER CAUTIOUSLY. According to his phone, it was almost midnight. He doubted they were ever pleased to see angry men arrive here, but even less so late at night.

He could see lights on in the front windows. Someone was in the lobby.

He called Garrett. "Glad you're still awake."

"I never sleep."

"Right, I keep forgetting. Look, can you get online and see what you can learn about this shelter?"

"Sure. Normal web or dark web?"

"Dark. I don't want puff pieces. We all know that women's shelters are a good idea."

"Got it."

"Much appreciated." He didn't expect much to come of it, but it was worth trying. If anyone could find something useful on short notice, it would be Garrett.

No point in delaying this any longer. It was not going to be pleasant, but he would do it, just the same. He took something out of his glove compartment—something Jazlyn had given him long ago—and slid it into his pocket.

If his sister was in there, he wasn't leaving till he found her.

He passed through the front doors, but as soon as the woman at the front desk saw him, she stood and waved toward a security officer—female—on the other side of the room.

"I'm sorry, sir," the woman at the front desk said. Blue jeans. Black Lives Matter T-shirt. Phone in her right hand. "Our visiting hours are over."

"I'm not here to visit anyone."

"We're closed."

"The doors are open."

"We have to leave them open for emergencies. Women in need. You don't appear to qualify."

He saw the security officer cautiously approaching. He raised his hands over his head. "I'm an attorney and I'm investigating a case."

"Do you have a subpoena?"

"No, I haven't had time for that."

"Then I have to ask you to leave."

"I'm looking for my sister."

The woman behind the front desk paused. "If your sister wants to speak to you, I'll be happy to arrange it. Leave your information and I'll contact you after I've spoken to her."

"I don't have that kind of time."

"I'm sorry, but that's how we do it here."

The security officer cut in. She was armed. "Sir, I don't want to evict you forcibly. You can surely see why we have to maintain tight security."

"I do. And I don't want any trouble." But I won't run from it, either. "Can you at least confirm for me that my sister is here?"

The woman at the front desk and the guard exchanged a glance. "What's her name?"

"Dinah."

"Last name?"

"I'm...not sure what name she might use. Maybe Fisher."

The woman glanced down and checked her roster. "We have no one named Dinah, or anything like that."

"Can you call the other Sweeney shelters?"

"Not at this time of night. Look, we only have twelve rooms. Two hallways." She pointed. "You can see for yourself."

"But I really need to talk to my sister. She's not hiding from me. I mean her no harm. I'm trying to help her."

The woman sighed heavily. "Come back tomorrow morning. I'll call around and see if I can find a Dinah."

"Thank you." He nodded toward the guard. "And you." He left the building.

As soon as he reached his car, he pulled out his phone. "Did you get all that?"

Garrett responded. "Heard every word. And I have a problem with it."

"Spill."

"I pulled up the blueprints for that building. They had to be filed at the city planner's office. It's true, they have two corridors and twelve rooms. On the ground level. But that's not the whole story. There's a basement level that woman didn't mention."

"A basement?"

"Just as big as the ground level. And get this—everyone one of these Sweeney shelters has one."

"For what purpose? To shelter more women?"

"I doubt it. All their publicity says there are twelve rooms per building. You can't get to the basement from the ground level. There's no staircase or elevator. There's a door in the back of the building with a single staircase that leads down to the basement. There's no communication between the two floors. I bet the people working in the shelter don't even know it exists."

"Then what's the basement for?"

Garrett sighed. "Much as it pains me to say it, there's only one way you're going to get the answer to that question."

"Roger that. On my way."

"You could call the police."

"Because they love and trust me so?"

"Jake would come."

"Eventually. I'm not waiting. My sister could be in danger."

"At least wait for me to arrive. I can be there in twenty minutes."

"I appreciate the gesture. But no." He disconnected and slid the phone into his pocket.

He didn't know what kind of danger Dinah might be in. He didn't know what kind of danger *he* might be in. But he wasn't going to wait around any longer.

———————

Dan sneaked around the building and found the back door with no trouble. Avoiding the gaze of the guard inside was easy, and there didn't appear to be any additional security on the premises.

At least not outside.

The back door was locked. Fortunately, he knew how to handle that.

His father was not a criminal and neither was he. But his father had been a police officer, and as such, he passed on a few life skills before he was ripped away from his family. Like how to throw a punch. How to throw a baseball.

And how to pick a lock.

As quietly as possible, Dan slid both pieces of the pick into the slot. It didn't take long. There was no deadbolt and the lock was basic. They were not expecting visitors.

Why would they? Who would ever expect anything underhanded in the basement of a women's shelter? The whole concept was so disgusting, so devious—

—that only someone like Sweeney could have conceived it.

The door creaked slightly as he pushed it open. The interior was dark. He cautiously brought out his phone and used the flashlight function.

Damn that thing was bright, at least in here. Did it have a half-bright setting?

A flight of stairs led downward. He cautiously made his way, one careful step at a time, very aware that he was not an invited guest.

Each step seemed to groan. Each squeak made his heart palpitate.

He could feel sweat pouring down the sides of his face. This was not what he went to law school for...

At the foot of the stairs, he found another door. He reached for the doorknob. It was cool to the touch. And not locked.

He opened the door.

The room inside was dimly lit. And humid. Probably not running air conditioning down here. And in Florida this time of year, that could get seriously stifling, even late at night.

The main hallway split into two corridors, but he had a hunch those rooms did not contain women seeking shelter.

Her heard sounds. Music. Bump-and-grind music. Generic soft-rock tracks.

Two rooms down, one of the doors was cracked slightly open. He crept toward it.

Inside, he saw a naked woman. Girl, actually. Dancing.

For a camera.

It was possible she was eighteen, but he didn't think so, and he felt embarrassed even looking long enough to guess. He wasn't going to scrutinize for details.

While he watched she pulled out a dildo and began rubbing

it against herself. She leered into the camera, pressed her fingers to her lips, rocked her hips.

He examined the equipment on the desk. Computers, servers, modems. This was a live sex show going out on the internet.

She bent over and spread her legs. He couldn't stand it any longer. He cleared his throat and asked, "Are you Dinah?"

The woman jumped. She had dark circles around her eyes and looked as if she hadn't eaten in far too long. "Who the hell are you?"

"Daniel Pike. I'm looking for my sister, Dinah."

"Get the hell out of here before I call—"

"Where's Dinah?" He realized, sadly, he might not be able to identify his sister on sight. He needed directions. "You must know. Where's Dinah?"

"She's across the hall in—"

Someone shoved Dan hard from behind. He tumbled forward, crashing into the equipment table. The young woman screamed.

A huge, musclebound brute glared at him. "You make big mistake, mister." He spoke with a Spanish, probably a South American, accent.

Dan scrambled to his feet and held up his hands. The woman raced out of the room. "I don't want any violence."

"Then you should have stayed home."

"There's no reason for us to fight."

The man grinned. "No worries. I don't think fight will last long." He reared back his ham-sized fist.

Dan pulled a taser out of his jacket and shoved it into the man's gut.

The huge man froze, shook for a few moments, then tumbled to the floor. A moment later, he looked as if he might get up. Dan jammed the taser back into his side.

The man shuddered violently. Dan held the taser in place for several seconds, till he appeared to have completely lost control of his body.

Sweeney's people had tried to run him over with a car, beat him so badly he ended up in the hospital, and shot at him. He wasn't taking any more chances with these bastards.

Once it was clear the man wasn't getting up any time soon, he ran into the hallway and shouted. "Listen up. This is a raid. Dinah? I'm looking for you, Dinah!"

Panic followed. Doors flew open. Each room looked like the one he had already seen—television cameras, servers, and naked women.

"This is a raid. Leave now and you won't be arrested. *Dinah?*"

One of the girls pointed toward a closed door.

Dan flung the door open.

The second he saw her, he knew she was the one. Thin. Too thin. Tousled brown hair. Tracks on her arms. Big eyes.

His mother's eyes.

He tore off his jacket and tossed it to her. "Here, put this on."

She looked completely confused. "I…have clothes."

"Good. Put on some pants. We need to hurry." He didn't know for sure, but it was possible that the man on the floor in the other room was not the only guard on the premises. Or that he might recover and this time be smart enough to stay away from the taser.

Thank God, Dinah did as she was told.

"Who…are you?" she asked as she pulled on a fringe-heavy pair of jeans.

"My name is Daniel Pike."

She turned her head.

"Yes, that's right, Pike. You may have heard that before. It was our mother's name after her second marriage." He paused. "I'm your brother. Half-brother. Same mom, different daddy."

She stared at him. Her face was red and blemished and her

arms suggested a drug habit, as did the fuzziness in her eyes and her slow responses. "No way."

"Yes way."

"I don't have a brother. I don't have any family."

"I thought the same thing once. Turns out we were both wrong."

"But—"

"Can you trust me? I know you don't know me, but I just want to help you."

She hesitated.

"We have to get out of here before someone sends reinforcements."

She looked down at the floor. "I...need this job."

"This is not a job. This is a criminal enterprise. And an affront against humanity."

"I still need the money. I got...expenses."

"How long have you been doing this?"

"I don't know. A year maybe?" She paused. "Hard to remember. The junk. The men. They take what they want and tell me what to do and—and—"

She started to cry.

All at once, he lost it. It boiled up and Dan couldn't keep it bottled inside any longer. He grabbed the camera and smashed it against the wall, letting out something between a growl and a battle cry. He picked up the computer CPU and smashed it on the ground, stomping on it. Then he picked it up and smashed it again. Then jumped up and down on it. Then threw the server across the room.

Dinah cried. "I need that stuff!"

"You don't," Dan said breathlessly.

"I—I got nothing else. They pay me forty dollars a night."

Probably not one percent of what her bosses made off this disgusting porn. "Good news, Dinah. Your newfound brother has plenty of money, and if necessary, he'll spend every damn penny of it making sure you get off drugs and find a better way to fill your days. Your life is about to change." He glanced at the door. "Assuming we get out of here alive. Come on."

He didn't know if she believed him or was just too weak to resist, but she followed him out the door, out of the darkness, into the light.

CHAPTER THIRTY-FOUR

DAN SAT IN ONE OF THE COMFORTABLE BLACK CHAIRS IN JUDGE Fernandez' chambers, amazed. At long last, Caldwell had dropped her Vulcan façade and displayed something resembling normal human emotion.

"Your honor, this is an outrage! Daniel Pike is a criminal!"

"Yes," the judge said, his fingers drumming his desktop. "That's what you've been saying all along."

"But now there's absolutely no doubt. The man broke into a women's shelter, after being told by the guard to leave the premises, and completely trashed a video center."

"Can you prove that?"

"He's not denying it!" She was practically shouting. And she had enough experience to know that was not the best way to persuade a judge of anything. She was losing her grip and her common sense at the same time. Drake kept leaning in, trying to quiet her, but it was not working, mostly because she never took a breath long enough to give him a chance to speak.

Fernandez turned his head toward Dan. "That true?"

"Yup. Did she mention that the so-called video center was live-casting sexually explicit porn over the internet, some of it

involving minors, and all of it involving women so drugged up
they didn't know what they were doing?"

Fernandez pressed his hand against his temples. "No, she
didn't." He turned back to Caldwell. "Did you bury the lede?"

Drake cut in. "The police are still investigating. But that
floor was equipped for video and computer training. Trying to
help battered women learn marketable skills so they can live
independently."

Maria made a snorting noise. "That's a load of crap. The
police have yet to find a woman who received any training in
that basement. The women running the shelter didn't even
know it existed."

"That doesn't prove—"

"It does to me."

"The jury has a right—"

"You've already polluted their minds—"

"Stop!" This time, it was the judge's turn to shout. "I will not
have this bickering in chambers. None of you are doing your
clients a bit of good."

A chorus of softly murmured apologies followed.

"Have I mentioned that I hate this case?" the judge continued. "Maybe I shouldn't. Maybe this will get me recused. Of
course, that would be a blessing. I have hated this case since the
day it was filed. And I still do."

"But—"

Fernandez raised a finger. "We will take turns. We will use
our indoor voices. We will present our arguments without
invective or insult. Do you understand?"

All four attorneys nodded.

At Maria's request, the judge had granted a three-day
continuance. After Dan found Dinah, he immediately took her
to St. Petersburg General where she was treated for malnutri-
tion and heroin abuse. After a few hours, she started going into
withdrawal, but the doctors were able to treat her with

methadone. Of course she didn't have health insurance, but Dan put down a sizable deposit and agreed to cover all costs, a package of treatment and pharmaceuticals that, given the current state of the American health care system, was likely to be astronomical. But he did it without hesitation.

It was almost two days before she was able to speak coherently. But once she trusted Dan enough to tell her story, what she had to say was shocking. And keenly relevant to this case.

Judge Fernandez drew in his breath. "Ok, Ms. Caldwell, you called this party. What's your beef?"

"I want to reopen our defense case."

"I thought you were done. I thought it was rebuttal witness time."

"I was done. But this is newly discovered evidence."

"Again?" Maria said, arching an eyebrow.

"And it's relevant?" the judge asked.

"The plaintiff is suing because my client called him a criminal. And three nights ago, he broke and entered private property and smashed up the joint. I would have to say it's relevant."

"And I would normally be receptive to newly discovered evidence. But not after you've rested your case. If I started allowing people to do that, no case would ever end."

"But this is unquestionably a crime!"

"But the issue is whether your client's statements were true at the time he made them, not months later. Have the police pressed charges?"

No response.

"Funny that. Unquestionably a crime, Pike admits doing it, but no one presses charges. Makes me think there's more to this than you're letting on."

"There is," Dan said quietly.

The judge raised his finger. "Not your turn yet."

"Sorry."

Caldwell and Drake did not speak.

"Ok," the judge said, "defendant's motion denied. Ms. Morales, I believe you had an issue you wanted to raise?"

"Yes. We would like to call a rebuttal witness. It's a direct response to the defendant's case, and specifically to the defendant's counterclaims."

"You are entitled to do so."

"The witness is not on their list," Caldwell growled.

"I can still allow it, if the plaintiff heard something unexpected during your presentation and needs a new witness to respond. Is that the situation, Ms. Morales?"

It would simplify matters if she said yes, but Dan knew Maria would never lie. "Not really, your honor. But we didn't know where this woman was until three days ago. And we couldn't talk to her until yesterday. She was being exploited by an illegal pornography operation operating in the bowels of Sweeney's women's shelters. He built a façade of shelters supposedly to help women, when in reality he was exploiting them in the basest possible way."

Drake leaned in. "There's no proof of force or—"

"All pornography degrades women, by definition. Your client is a disgusting—"

Judge Fernandez raised his finger again. "Counsel. No invective."

She sucked it in. "I apologize. To your honor. Not to Sweeney."

"Your honor," Drake said, "Dr. Sweeney is one of the city's most distinguished citizens."

"So you keep saying. I'm beginning to wonder if he doth protest too much."

"Plus, he's a billionaire."

"Was," Maria added.

"Why would a man of his position and means be involved in some disgusting penny-ante porn operation?"

"Except it isn't penny-ante at all," Dan said. Garrett had done the research and filled his head with the relevant info. "Sexually explicit photos and videos are huge moneymakers. Some teens sell their own pics on social media sites to get extra cash. The net is full of places like Nudes4Sale and OnlyFans.com. Estimates indicate that perhaps a third of the women—girls, really—performing on them are underage. Sometimes as young as fourteen. The sites can charge more money for underage girls. Most sell subscriptions at a huge price, and in exchange, they offer live-streamed shows like the ones coming out of the basements of the Sweeney shelters."

"You sure know a lot about porn," Drake said, smirking.

"I come to court prepared. You should try it sometime." Dan plowed ahead before the judge had a chance to reprimand him. "The performers—the women—are often runaways or homeless or drug addicts or all of the above. They work for very little, making the operations even more profitable. It's a billion-dollar business. Exactly the sort of thing a former billionaire with massive debt and cash-flow problems might try." Pause. "If he was completely without conscience or morals."

Drake cut in. "The truth is, your honor, this investigation is just beginning and we don't know all the details. But Dr. Sweeney disavows any knowledge of what was taking place beneath these buildings—"

Maria made a snorting noise.

Drake threw back his shoulders. "I deeply resent that."

"You're claiming Sweeney didn't know all the buildings he built had basements?"

"Those were designed for training purposes."

"With a separate secret entrance only accessible from the rear of the building? That no one working in the shelters even knew about?"

Drake turned to the judge. "Are we going to argue this in chambers?"

"No," the judge said firmly, "we are not. And I have to warn you, Ms. Morales, that if you make any of these charges during your rebuttal case, you will be opening a dangerous door. I will have no choice but to allow the defendant to respond in kind."

"Understood, your honor. We won't go there." Dan could feel the regret in her voice. She would love to go there.

The judge nodded. "I will allow you to call your rebuttal witness."

Caldwell sat up. "Your honor, may I lodge my formal—"

"Wasn't it just a few days ago that you wanted to add a witness who wasn't on your list?"

"That was completely different—"

"Yeah, it always is. I let you call your witness and I will let them call theirs. You people want trial by ambush, fine. Live with it." He rose. "Will there be anything else? Because I would really like to get this case over with."

No one spoke.

"Ms. Morales, is your rebuttal witness ready to testify?"

"She's very shaky, your honor. And nervous."

"Witnesses always are."

"She was just released from the hospital. She's in a weakened state. But she is prepared to testify. In fact...she wants to testify."

The judge nodded. "Let's give her that opportunity, shall we?"

DAN AND MARIA LEFT THE JUDGE'S CHAMBERS THROUGH THE connecting door to the courtroom. As they passed by the defendant's table, Sweeney sprang up and shoved Dan in the chest with the flat of his hand.

"What the hell?" Dan recovered his footing. "Keep your hands off me, you acid-spitting toad."

"Have you completely lost your mind?" Sweeney bellowed.

Out the corner of his eye, Dan saw the sheriff moving forward. He raised a hand to stop him. "I don't know what you mean, Sweeney, but I'm pretty sure your lawyers don't want us to be talking."

"That's right," Drake said, coming up behind them. He tried to push forward, but Sweeney shoved him back, and since he outweighed Drake by about a hundred pounds, Drake couldn't get past him.

Sweeney turned back to Dan, growling. "You are going to get yourself killed."

Dan tried to stay calm, even though his heart was racing. "Is that a threat?"

"It's not a threat, you imbecile. It's a warning. You have no idea what you're messing with. You never have and you still don't."

"Please enlighten me."

"Do you not see how you've been led by the nose?"

"No one led me to your disgusting underground—"

"Why do you think The Captain told you about your sister in the first place? Just to be nice?"

That stopped him cold.

"If you don't stop being such a blithering idiot, you're going to be a blithering corpse."

Dan rediscovered his tongue. "That still sounds like a threat. Gonna hire another sniper to take potshots at me?"

Caldwell grabbed Sweeney's arm, trying unsuccessfully to move the unmovable object. "This conversation ends now."

Sweeney completely ignored her. "Listen to me, you infant. This business at the shelter is the last straw. You have interfered far too many times. It's just dumb luck you're still up and around. But this latest stunt will guarantee your demise."

"You're not scaring me."

Sweeney stepped closer. "These people will not stop until you're dead. You, and that little Mexican spitfire representing you, and your queer partner, and your mysterious boss—" He drew in his breath. "And your sister. This will not end until everyone you know is dead."

Dan stared at him, transfixed. He wanted to look as if this diatribe hadn't shaken him. But it had.

Caldwell finally managed to pull Sweeney away and get him into his chair.

Maria did the same with Dan. "Don't let that man get to you. We have a plan. We're going to go through with the plan."

"Maybe Garrett was right. Maybe I am being selfish, stirring up trouble for no good reason. Maybe I am being irresponsible."

"You know what? Maybe you are." Maria glared at him with almost the same expression Sweeney had given him moments before. "But whether we like it or not, you did file this suit, and we are stuck in this courtroom, and I do not plan to go down in flames. Furthermore, your sister is waiting outside with Jimmy and she's counting on you too. So pull it together and let's finish this trial."

"Gee whiz," he muttered. "Tell me how you really feel."

She almost smiled. "Stop sulking and shut up. I've got a trial to win."

CHAPTER THIRTY-FIVE

DAN HAD ONLY KNOWN HIS SISTER FOR A FEW DAYS, BUT EVEN though he knew it was sentimental and irrational, he felt as if he had known her for much longer. And he couldn't care more about her if he known her forever. Even though she had obviously made some mistakes, he couldn't help but admire how much strength she had shown these past few days in the face of physical pain and great adversity, battling feelings of helplessness and despair and trying to pull herself together.

The last morning she was in the hospital, finally clear-headed, he and Maria were both in her room. She blinked several times, then said, "Are you really my brother?"

"I really am."

She shook her head. "Far out."

Maria found her some clothes to wear in court. She didn't appear to have any worldly possessions. He didn't know how she had survived all these years and thought it was best he didn't. The doctors said she had no debilitating conditions and that a month of healthy living should put her back in good shape. Might hold off on the kitesurfing lessons, but bottom line—she would recover.

Dan had a sister.

"Would you please state your name for the jury?"

"Dinah Pleasance Fisher."

"What is your occupation?"

"I…don't have one. I've been living on the streets for years. Homeless."

"Are you related to anyone in this courtroom?"

She hesitated a moment. "I've been told that I'm Dan Pike's big sister."

The reaction from the jury was evident and immediate. Dan wasn't sure what surprised them more—that he had a sister, or that she had to be told about it.

"Perhaps it would be simpler if you explained your background to the jury. Your family history."

Dinah nodded. "My father was Jack Fisher. He was killed and I think the jury already knows about that. But long before he was dead, my mother divorced him and married Dan's father. After that marriage, Dan was born. That's why he's my brother."

Dinah was speaking slowly but deliberately. Probably just as well. This was a lot for the jury to drink in.

"My father was a police officer," Dinah continued. "Like Dan's dad. But my dad was horrible to my mother. Our mother. Abusive. Beat her. Called her—"

"Objection," Caldwell said. "Hearsay. She was a child. She can't possibly remember—"

"You're wrong," Dinah said. "I do remember. I saw it with my own eyes."

"Overruled," the judge said quietly. "Please continue."

"Well, he called her ugly names. Disgusting names. My mother was a wonderful woman, but she didn't know what to do about him. You can't go to the cops when it's a cop beating you up. Cops stick together. I think people are just starting to learn how toxic that cop community can be. He carried a gun, you know. I remember being scared of that thing. I know my mother was. She was afraid he'd get mad one night and shoot her and then me and the cops would make it look like a suicide or something. My mother cried every night. I cried most nights too."

Dinah took a deep breath. "She put me up for adoption when I was still very young. My dad never wanted kids and complained about me constantly, so she gave me to a childless couple this doctor knew. And later divorced my dad, but that happened long after I was gone, so if you want to call that hearsay, fine. It's true. You can look it up."

Dan smiled. She was definitely related to him.

"The adoption didn't work out. I tried, but that couple had problems of their own and the dad was creepy. Snorted cocaine, kept touching me all the time. I ran away from home. Cops hauled me back. I ran away again. You get the picture." She paused. "I was getting ready to run again when my father reappeared. He'd been to court and somehow gotten custody. I didn't want to go with him. But I had no choice."

"How long did you live with him?"

"About a year."

"Let's come back to that in a minute. What did you do after your father died?"

"Anything I could. I lived on the streets."

"Why didn't you return to your birth mother?"

"I didn't think she'd want me. She gave me up once before. I suppose I was angry."

"Where did you go?"

"To be honest, I don't remember a whole lot about the next several years. Too much horse in the bloodstream. I was doing like a bundle of heroin a day. That's ten bags, each bag about a tenth of a gram."

"Is that a lot?"

"That's enough to kill you. Especially if it's cut with fentanyl.

Miracle I didn't totally lose my mind. My main dealer lost all his teeth to crack, but somehow, I never got the message. I loved loading up the syringe, finding a vein, feeling it ooze like a warm blanket through my body. One night I went psychotic and threatened some people I didn't know. Someone found me and the state paid for a stay at a rehab. I was in withdrawal from heroin and benzos, so you can imagine how pleasant I was to be around. I had seizures. Scary stuff."

"Did it get better?"

"Eventually. But I was lonely and...filled with hate. Mostly for myself. Nothing made me happy. They tried to teach me how to live healthy. Eat right. Exercise. Yoga. Meditate. When it was time for me to go, I was sad. But I finally felt good about myself."

"What happened next?"

"I'd made a few friends in rehab, but it didn't last once we were out. We split up. Everyone had their own lives to get back to. Everyone but me. I got a crap job at a restaurant. I tried to stay clean, but it was so hard. I wanted to quit, but I couldn't make myself do it. I know, it makes no sense. Curiouser and curiouser. Some nights I was so lonely. I started to repeat this endless cycle. Relapse, recovery. Relapse, recovery. Got put in another rehab, inpatient. Then sober living. I was trying, really. But I could never quit the junk. Not for long. Said the Serenity Prayer every day. Didn't help. Worked the Twelve Steps enough times to add up to about a hundred and forty steps. Didn't take."

"What did you do next?"

"I went into what they call the Florida Model, cheaper than rehabs. We lived in recovery residences or sober homes, usually with a lot of roomies. I had to go to outpatient therapy and talk about myself. Did a lot of group grope. It's like a whole industry now, all the rehabs and clinics and stuff. Some people told me that South Florida's addiction-treatment business rivaled its tourism business. Some people call it the Florida Shuffle. Run an expensive rehab, get lots of money—because most of your patients shuffle back again later. More money for the rehabs. Even the guys who test urine get rich. But the patients don't get better. It's like the efforts to treat the disease only make it worse."

"How long did you...cycle through these programs?"

"Almost twenty years."

The jurors audibly gasped.

"I didn't blame anyone but myself. The main reason for the Florida Shuffle, if you ask me, is that when you get out of these programs—you got nowhere to go. Nothing you want to do. Some ex-addicts work in treatment centers. It's the only thing they know. But most just shuffle along till they relapse again.

"After that, I gave up. I knew I was never gonna be able to quit. The rehabs were sick of me and no one would hire me. I was a Mole Person for a while. Lived in the flood tunnels downtown. Not as bad as it sounds, actually. At least most of the people were nice. Then this cop started coming around, hassling me. Pawing on me. I don't know why he targeted me. Maybe I overreacted because he wore a badge and a gun and he reminded me of my father. But he was trying to get close and I didn't want any part of that. So I ran."

"Where did you go?"

"Walmart." She grinned. "Not to shop. To live. I slept in the parking lot, under a car or maybe on a blanket or inflatable mattress if I was lucky. Then these guys with funny accents started coming around. Tellin' me how pretty I was and how I could make lots of money posing for pictures. Well, what was I gonna do? Not like I had a ton of options."

Dan clenched his eyes shut. *I should have been there. I should have been there.*

"It wasn't hard work," Dinah continued. "It was just...dirty. They put me in a room and told me what to do. I knew the camera was on, but I pretended I was alone, just being silly.

They changed it up from time to time. Didn't want the audience to get bored, I guess. I danced naked. Jiggled. Touched myself. Used sex toys. Pretended like I was turning myself on. Faked orgasms. That kind of stuff. I don't remember all the details. They kept me junked up and that made everything easy. Also made it easy to forget."

"How long did you do this?"

"Something like a year. They moved me around. Just a few months ago moved me to the new building, but what did it matter? They were all the same."

"You were doing these livestream sex shows until..."

"Until four nights ago. When my brother Dan found me. And saved me."

Dan felt a clutching in his stomach. Don't cry, he told himself. Do not cry.

"Thank you," Maria said. "I'm sure that was difficult and unpleasant, and we very much appreciate your honesty. Now I'm going to ask you to return to the part of your childhood that we skipped. Because I think the jury will now be able to understand why it's important to this case."

Dinah nodded. "About the time I was ten, my father came looking for me. He hadn't been happy about the adoption, and my mom had dumped him, married someone else—Dan's dad—and he was pissed about it. I guess the best way he could think of to get revenge on Mom was to track me down."

"What exactly happened?"

"He had some kind of court order, so my adoptive parents had no say in it—and they didn't fight too hard. I was a handful."

"What happened when you lived with your father?"

Her head sagged. "He was cruel, just like he'd been to my mother. Mean. Hit me. Hard. And..." She drew in her breath. "And he abused me."

Maria bit down on her lip. "When you say he abused you..."

"I'm talking about sex. He had sex with me. His own daughter. I didn't like it but what could I do? I depended on him. He outweighed me and he had a gun. And—And—" Her voice choked. "He was my daddy."

"How long did this continue?"

"Months. I was helpless. Then one day we were getting groceries and my mom spotted me. She didn't know my father had yanked me away from my adoptive parents. She tried to take me from him, but she couldn't. So she sent her husband over."

"Dan's father."

"Right. Boy, do I remember that night. Like it was happening right now. I was cowering upstairs but I heard every word. Dan's dad knew about the incest. I don't know how. Probably wasn't hard to figure out if you knew my father. He offered to take custody, but my dad refused. He laughed at him. Threatened him. They were both cops, so who were they going to call for help? It was bad."

"What happened next?"

"My mom showed up. With a gun. She took a shot at my dad. Barely creased him. He took the gun away and laughed at her. 'Now there's nothing you can do,' he said. 'Neither one of you. Come after me and I tell the cops your wife tried to kill me. She goes to prison. I keep your daughter forever.' And he hit my mom. Real hard."

Maria swallowed. "What happened next?"

"Dan's father rushed him. Started pounding on him. Jack screamed. 'One more punch and your wife goes away for attempted murder.' So Dan's dad stopped. I could tell he didn't want to, but he did."

"And then?"

"Jack laughed. Said he'd be dropping by for more of the same, to slap her around whenever he felt like it. 'You can't be with her every second,' he told Dan's dad. I remember his words so well. He said, 'Sweet. Got my sex bag and my punching bag. Perfect.' My mother tried to get the gun away from him, but Dan's father held her back. I remember what he said too."

"Which was?"

"He said, 'Not now. Not like that.'"

Dan could barely contain himself. He breathed fast and hard, trying to keep it all locked inside. But the tears trickled out just the same. He'd figured it all out days ago, but hearing it spoken aloud in open court was entirely different.

Now he realized the truth. His father *had* shot Jack Fisher. And for a damn good reason. There was no other way to stop him.

Maria was visibly shaken, but she continued. "Do you know what happened after that?"

"To my dad? No. As soon as he left for work the next morning, I took all the money I could find in the house, ran away and never came back. I didn't care if I starved. I wasn't living with that man any longer. What I didn't know was—apparently my dad wasn't coming home either."

Because that was the night of the fatal shootout. Dan's father saw an opportunity to eliminate this odious man. He had no way of knowing Ellison could see him in the mirror. But even when Ellison fingered him, he never lied. He said he wasn't guilty, because in his mind, he wasn't. He did the right thing. He protected his family. He sacrificed himself, but his wife would be safe. Dinah would be safe.

And his little boy would survive.

Which he did.

His father became judge and jury. And executioner.

And he was not about to question his father's decision. He—

Wait a minute.

Dan felt a tingling inside his brain. He closed his eyes to focus.

Sweeney. Shelters. Children.

Something was tugging at the right hemisphere of his brain, trying to get his attention.

Partners. Off-duty. Cartel.

Getting closer. But what was it?

Tattoos. Jaquith. Kramer.

He closed his eyes. He didn't want to miss the testimony, but he had to connect the dots.

Mirror. Gunfire. Certainty. I am completely certain.

His eyes popped open. He could see it all now. For the first time in his entire life, it all started to make sense.

There will still be a reckoning, Dad. Once I know everyone is safe.

"Your honor," Caldwell said, "I object to this entire line of testimony. This is a pathetic effort by the plaintiff to garner sympathy by transforming a convicted criminal into—"

"Overruled," the judge said quietly.

"I haven't even finished."

"Overruled."

"Your honor, this isn't—"

Fernandez' face tightened. "Counsel, you have been over-ruled. If you speak again, I will hold you in contempt of court."

Caldwell took her seat.

Maria resumed. "Anything else, Dinah?"

Her voice waivered. "I think I was suffering from some kind of PTSD. That's what the rehab therapists told me. I was poor and unguided and stupid. A prime candidate for the worst people."

Maria nodded. "I'm so sorry you had to experience that. We like to think of ourselves as a progressive, caring society. But it's obvious that some people still slip through the cracks."

Dinah lifted her chin. "Don't worry about me. I'm gonna be okay now. I'm determined to stay clean. And for the first time in forever, I'm not alone." Her head turned and her eyes filled with tears. "I got a brother to look after me now."

There was no cross-examination.

CHAPTER THIRTY-SIX

DAN TOLD HIMSELF NOT TO WORRY. THEY HAD DONE EVERYTHING they could do to win this case and to rehabilitate his father's name. Even if they didn't prevail—he had learned what truly happened to his father and why Jack Fisher died.

More importantly, he had a sister he never knew about before. She'd had a hellish life, but all that was about to change. He would make certain of it. His father had given everything to protect Dinah. He would continue his father's work.

Since she represented the plaintiff, Maria was the first to close.

"Well, this has been a wild ride, hasn't it?" She allowed herself a small smile. Dan knew she didn't want to appear to trivialize all that had transpired. But a brief recognition that this was not your typical slander trial was probably permissible. "This case initially was about whether Conrad Sweeney's remarks constituted actionable slander toward Daniel Pike— but it ended up being about much more. It ended up being about finding the truth, finding justice, and righting wrongs festering for far too long."

She paused a moment, allowing the jury to reflect on what she said. "Maybe it's just me, but I think the slander part of this case is relatively easy. Sweeney said my client was a criminal, that his father was a criminal, and that they both were associated with organized crime. I know Sweeney wants to mince words and quibble, but that's what he said and we all heard it. Dan has never committed a criminal offense and has never been in league with organized crime. In fact, he's helped stop a major cartel. Therefore, Sweeney's statements are false, and the only question for this jury to determine is what a fair amount would be to compensate Dan for the obvious damage to his reputation."

She stood on one side of the jury box, which Dan noticed allowed the jury a clear view of him. Probably good strategy, but it kept him in focus. He had to sit up straight, try to look respectable, and not react to anything she said.

"Let's start with Dan's father. He was convicted of murder. True. But we have new insight on that case now, don't we? Although my opponents will undoubtedly attempt to throw shade on Dan's sister, let me remind you that her testimony is completely undisputed. Did Dan's father fire that gun? Looks that way. Was he a criminal or a crusader?" She drew in her breath. "You decide."

Another pause for reflection. "The issue for you jurors is whether the defendant slandered my client. Have they introduced any evidence that Dan is a criminal? None whatsoever. Lots of mudslinging, but no proof. Has Dan ever been accused? Sure. And he's been exonerated each and every time. Has he helped clients gain acquittal? Yes—because the prosecution couldn't prove their case. His only association with organized crime led to shutting down a major smuggling ring. And they want to call this man a criminal? I wish we had more like him. The world would be a much safer place."

She leaned against the rail, her head looking down reflectively. "I must make some brief mention of the testimony of Camila Pérez. I think you already know what I'm going to say. This is the testimony of an ex-girlfriend, one who pled guilty to a heinous crime. She's angry and she wants vengeance, but that's no reason to believe a word she says. Why would Dan give her information about a hitman? Dan was the one who turned her in. If he'd been involved, that act would've incriminated him. But it didn't, and this is important, because at the time of her arrest and while her case was pending, never once did Camila suggest that she got any information from Dan. That allegation arose for the first time in this courtroom. The bitter lies of an angry woman scorned."

She smiled a bit. "Speaking of vengeance, I should mention Sweeney's counterclaims against Dan, his attempts to punish Dan for defending the truth. What did Dan say that wasn't true?"

She was forbidden from mentioning the porn-streaming sites the police had found in the basements of the Sweeney women's shelters, but it had been plastered all over the news and she felt certain at least a few of the jurors knew about it. They had been instructed to avoid coverage of this case, but that didn't mean they ignored all news. Sweeney's reputation had been seriously tarnished, despite his disavowals.

"Let me add one last thing," Maria said, "and I'll leave it at that. It is impossible to impugn the dignity of a man who has none. It is impossible to besmirch the reputation of a man who deserves none. Of a man who hides behind a veneer of charity while profiteering in the most disgusting ways imaginable. Calling out a man like that is not slander. It's public service."

She took a few steps back. "I know you have much to think about, so I'll let you get to it. But please remember this one thing. There is a reason why civil suits exist. It is not for retribution, or rehabilitation, or so people can have the nonexistent pleasure of duking it out in public. Civil courts exist for the same reason as criminal courts. To see that justice is done. So that's all I ask of you. Let justice be done."

Maria retook her seat, and barely a second later Drake was on his feet doing his best to shatter the mood. "I'll be honest with you. I can't believe we're still here. This case should have been dismissed a long time ago. Because there is no doubt about anything. There are barely any disputed facts. This is the clearest case of slander I've seen in my professional life, and I've seen a lot. I'm not just saying that. I mean it."

Drake took a breath, visibly trying to chill. "Did Daniel Pike slander Conrad Sweeney? Unquestionably. You heard what he said. How could that not be slander? Was there any basis in fact? Did they prove my client is involved in any criminal activity? No. Did they prove Pike's father wasn't a criminal? No. They pulled a rabbit out of a hat, producing an alleged sister no one has ever heard of, a woman who lived on the streets, sold her body for money, and addled her brain with so many drugs that she is...probably very susceptible to suggestion. Can you trust anything she said?" Drake shook his head. "I wouldn't. You have an eyewitness who saw Pike's father execute another officer. Case closed. There is no excuse for murder. Leave it at that.

"I notice opposing counsel skirted over the details of her client's involvement with criminal activities. He has repeatedly represented and set free dangerous criminals. He has repeatedly had inside information about cartel activities. Isn't it ironic that they accuse my blameless client of the same thing? Dr. Sweeney has a history of public service going back decades. That's not a façade, that's a fact. Pike was involved in one raid—which ultimately resulted in a violent courtroom execution—and we're supposed to forget about his decades of criminal associations? I don't think so. My opponent wants you to ignore the testimony of our former mayor, but why would you? She's the only person in a position to know what occurred between them. Think about this logically—who is more likely to have information about paid assassins? The mayor? Or a man who has spent his entire adult life protecting murderers and gang leaders?"

Drake took a step closer, leaning into the rail. "Let me leave you with one final thought. Conrad Sweeney has not only been slandered—he has been damaged. He has suffered injury to his reputation which has affected his business. Even if you somehow thought Pike had been slandered, what has he lost? What damage can you do to the reputation of a career criminal confederate? None. But my client has lost millions in the wake of Daniel Pike's remarks, a public confrontation Pike sought and staged for the express purpose of causing harm."

He pressed his hands together. "Let me make this easy for you. Dr. Sweeney has been slandered. Dr. Sweeney has lost millions because of it. And Daniel Pike has the means to make him whole again. They want justice? Good. Let's have justice. Let's have justice for the most prominent, most beloved philanthropist in the city of St. Petersburg."

DAN AND MARIA SAT IN THE HALLWAY OUTSIDE THE COURTROOM while they waited for the jury to return. Jimmy arrived with sandwiches—grilled cheese for Maria, ham and cheese for the rest. Garrett conferenced with Jake Kakazu and brought back the latest information.

"It's official—the police have found video-porn operations like the one Dan trashed in the basement of every single one of the Sweeney shelters. And get this—in some cases, the women performing for the cameras first arrived seeking shelter from an abusive partner or parent."

Jimmy laid down his sandwich. "Okay, now I'm not hungry."

"That's disgusting," Maria said. "Do you think they'll bring charges?"

"Eventually," Garrett said. "The question is—against whom? Sweeney claims he knew nothing about it."

"He built those buildings!"

"But he doesn't actually own them. He just helped raise the funds."

"And now we know why," Dan muttered.

"Someone had to know," Maria said.

"Agreed. But proving who did and who didn't is going to be tricky. Jake is determined to bring charges. He just needs more evidence."

"It had to be Sweeney," Dan said. "He authorized the blueprints. He needed the money."

"But Sweeney always uses minions to do his dirty work," Garrett replied. "Even if he was behind it, they might never be able to trace anything back to him."

"So he just gets away with it? Again?" Dan clenched his fists. "I don't think I can stand it."

Jimmy changed the subject. "On a happier note, Dan, while you were in court today, I tricked out the empty office upstairs and turned it into a cozy little bedroom. Dinah chose the linens. I think she likes it."

Dan tried to calm down. "I offered to let her stay with me."

"On your boat? Give me a break. You don't have room for a hamster, much less an adult female."

"I suppose." He paused a moment. "You really think she liked it?"

"I know she did. She bought towels with a beach pattern. A bedspread that has waves crashing against the shore."

Dan felt his eyes twitching. "She...likes the water?"

Jimmy smiled. "Of course she does. She's your sister. I got

her a swimsuit." He coughed. "She says she's never had one before."

Dan turned so no one could see his face. "Probably be a damn fine kitesurfer."

Maria laid her hand on his shoulder. "No doubt about it."

Jimmy checked his watch. "Anyone care to guess how much longer the jury will take?"

Maria shook her head. "I bet it happens tonight. Judge Fernandez says he's keeping the jury here till they decide. He's so sick of this case it's palpable. Even if there's a holdout on the jury, they'll cave eventually. They get hungry. They want to get home to watch their favorite show. They join the majority."

"And what do you think that majority vote will be?"

"Only fools make predictions about juries. And my daddy didn't raise any fools."

Jimmy nodded. "By the way, I thought your closing was dynamite. Dead on. Perfect."

"Thanks. But Drake's closing was smart. Deceptive. But smart. Sweeney *has* lost millions. If the jury finds in his favor…"

Dan finished the sentence. "They could render a judgment against me in the millions. I could be bankrupted—just when I have a sister who needs my help. He could try to collect from all of you, since you're my partners. It could wipe out our entire firm. Even Mr. K." He looked up. "You were right, Garrett. In my quest for truth, I may have doomed everyone I know." He paused. "And love."

Jimmy took a deep breath, then shrugged. "I'm ok with that."

Dan blinked. "What?"

"Me too," Garrett echoed.

"What are you saying?"

"What we're saying," Maria explained, "is that we're a team, and we stand with you, no matter what." She smiled. "Hell, it was worth it just to see the expression on Sweeney's face when you called him an acid-spitting toad."

"That was good," Garrett agreed. They all laughed. Then fell silent.

"Of course," Jimmy said, "given my choice, I'd probably rather not be penniless."

The ensuing combination of laughter and tears bordered on the hysterical.

CHAPTER THIRTY-SEVEN

DAN'S PHONE TOLD HIM IT WAS ALMOST TEN WHEN HE FINALLY got the text. The jury was returning.

"Last chance to make predictions," he murmured to Maria as they took their seats at the plaintiff's table.

"No fools, remember?"

"Maybe a sporting proposition?"

"Let's wait and see if we have any money when this is over."

The opposing parties filed into the courtroom. Sweeney was still present, surprisingly. Dan expected him to leave as soon as the jury was dismissed, but he re-entered wearing a smug, confident grin that begged to be slapped off.

The judge called the court back into session. A few moments later, the bailiff brought the jury back.

There was no grinning or winking. Of course, there could be many explanations for the poker faces. Everyone liked having a secret, and right now, for at least a few more moments, they had a good one.

"Have you reached a verdict?"

A middle-aged stout woman in the back row rose. "We have, your honor." She held up the verdict form.

The bailiff took it and carried it to the judge. The judge looked it over, presumably checking for technical deficiencies. As far as Dan was concerned, it was a power play. The judge wanted to know before anyone else did. And damned if the man didn't maintain the same inscrutable poker face.

Judge Fernandez passed the form back to the bailiff, who carried it to the forewoman, who would announce the verdict.

"On the plaintiff's claim against the defendant for slander in violation of the laws of the State of Florida, we find for the defendant."

Dan felt his stomach drop. They found for Sweeney? *Sweeney?*

He felt Maria's hand cover his. Stay calm, she was saying. Stay calm.

Did she think he would explode? More likely he would cry. This was his fault. He hadn't proved his case. He didn't prove damages and the jury probably didn't think Sweeney's comments were bad enough to complain about. In some cynical minds, the difference between a criminal lawyer and a criminal wasn't that great.

Sweeney was grinning, and it had spread to his two lawyers.

"And on the defendant's counterclaim?" the judge asked.

The forewoman nodded. "On the defendant's counterclaim against the plaintiff for slander in violation of the laws of the State of Florida, we find in favor of the defendant."

Oh my God. Oh my God. It was actually happening. His worst nightmare. Sweeney won. They bought his bull. They were going to give him everything he wanted.

He had taken on the most powerful man in the city and come up short. Not only would he pay, but his sister, his firm, and everyone he cared about in the entire world would pay too.

At the other table, Sweeney was sneering. That's what you get when you take me on, he was saying without words.

The judge cleared his throat. "Did the jury make a determination on the subject of damages to be awarded to the defendant?"

"We did, your honor." The forewoman glanced down at her paper. "On the counterclaim for slander, the jury finds that the defendant should be awarded the amount of...one cent."

Dan's lips parted. Did he hear that right?

"Is there anything further?"

The forewoman shook her head.

"Very well. I want to thank the jury for its service during this long and complex trial. You have performed your civic duty..."

The judge continued to talk, but Dan didn't hear much of it.

One cent? A penny?

In other words, the jury was saying that, yes, technically Dan had slandered Sweeney. He had picked a fight that didn't need to be fought. But they didn't much care. And they thought the damage to Sweeney's reputation amounted to...one cent.

When the judge dismissed the court, Dan and Maria rose.

"I consider this a win," Maria said.

"I don't," Dan replied. "But I'm grateful that I haven't destroyed everyone I know."

The party at the other table packed their belongings. Caldwell and Drake didn't look happy. They had probably run up two or three hundred thousand bucks in legal fees—and managed to recover one cent.

Dan crossed to their table.

Caldwell cut him off before he could speak. "Don't gloat. It's so tasteless."

He shook his head, then leaned toward Sweeney.

"And," Caldwell added, "don't initiate another lawsuit."

Dan ignored her. "We're not done, Sweeney. Once this verdict hits the news, your reputation will be finished. Once the police end their investigation of your sleazy porn operation, you'll be in prison."

Sweeney chuckled. "You are so naïve. Do you think I don't

know about Detective Kakazu's investigation? He can't hurt me. I have more friends in the police department than he does."

"This is too big to be swept under the rug. The public will insist the D.A presses charges."

"Oh, I agree with that." Sweeney said. "But who exactly will be charged? You were on the premises, not me. You trashed the place like a crazy man. We have video from a security camera. You entered like you owned the place, treated the equipment like it was your own, and addressed one of the women by her first name. Seems like you knew all about it."

"You'll never make that stick. This is the moment when everything changes."

"I know one thing that will never change." Sweeney's mouth widened, baring his teeth. "Your father was a murderer. He died in prison, a murderer."

"My father was a hero," Dan spat back. "He opposed you and your cartel, way back then. That's why you were in the cop car with Fisher the night of the shootout, isn't it?"

Drake and Caldwell looked horrified. Sweeney said nothing.

But his eyes told Dan everything he needed to know.

"Fisher was a loose cannon and he threatened the empire you and your evil friends were building," Dan continued. "You were going to take him out. You probably engineered the shootout to provide cover. But my father beat you to the punch. My father, though, was motivated by love. And you, as always, were motivated by greed."

Sweeney stared at him, his eyes steely gray. "Anything else, little boy?"

"Yes. I'm going to finish what my father started. You just wait and see."

CHAPTER THIRTY-EIGHT

SWEENEY PICKED UP THE PAINTING AND RAISED IT OVER HIS HEAD, his eyes red, his face flush with anger.

"This cannot continue!" he bellowed.

Prudence rushed in to stop him from damaging the multi-million-dollar Basquiat. "Please stay calm, Dr. Sweeney. You paid millions for that."

"It's mine and I can do with it what I will!"

Prudence tightened her grip. "You may need it, sir. We must remedy our cash-flow problems."

"I swore I would never sell a painting."

Prudence's voice dropped so low it was barely audible. "Your creditors may not leave you any choice."

Sweeney let her take the painting, but pounded his fists on his desk. With a deafening cry he swept everything on top of it onto the floor.

After a few more moments of bellowing, he collapsed into the black padded desk chair. The moonlight came through the ceiling-high windows on the east side, affording a gorgeous view of St. Petersburg at night. He barely glanced at it. He had to get a grip on himself. He had to rein it in. If he let that pipsqueak lawyer get the best of him, he was lost.

He had assembled a group of cohorts in his office, and he knew none of them had ever seen him behave this way. Ellison clearly wanted to leave. Bastard. After all he had done for that man. But that showed how badly his power had eroded. No one saw him as invincible anymore. They saw him as a once-great man headed toward his doom. Shawna had made it clear she wanted to sever her ties to him. A black-market kidney was the only thing keeping her here. Even Marjorie, the crooked court reporter, looked as if she was sorry she ever got involved with him. His contact at the police station was visibly trembling.

And then there was Fabian Fuentes. The Captain's replacement. He hadn't even been invited. But here he was. That couldn't possibly be good. The cartel thrived on strength. As soon as they perceived a weak link, they cut it loose. It was a survival instinct.

He inhaled deeply, micro-meditating to pull himself together. He needed to regain his calm. He needed to be the cool, in-control power broker they were accustomed to seeing in this penthouse office.

"Let's get down to why I called you here," Sweeney said. "It is clear that I have erred. I let my sympathies overcome my business instincts. I gave Pike too much rope. I felt sorry for the poor fatherless imbecile. I knew his father, I knew what happened, and I let that interfere with my judgment. I dealt with Jaquith and I should have dealt with Pike at the same time. Fully and finally. But now the kid gloves are coming off. Now I'm out for blood. Now—"

Fuentes interrupted. "Now you cannot."

Sweeney paused. He did not like being interrupted. But of course, Fuentes knew that. "I assure you that I can arrange—"

"It is not a matter of what you can arrange. It is simple common sense. You have waited too long and allowed the dispute between you and Pike to become too well known. Too high-profile. If anything happens to him now, you will be the first person the police suspect. You do not need to be in more trouble than you already are."

Sweeney continued taking deep breaths, trying to rein in his anger. "For a time, my friend, I thought that you and your... associates were going to deal with Mr. Pike."

Fuentes steepled his fingers before his face—the same power gesture Sweeney himself had employed on many occasions. "You misunderstood our motivations. Perhaps you have always misunderstood. So much."

Sweeney would not let the roiling in his stomach show. "What is that supposed to mean?"

Fuentes rose. "Are you truly so foolish?" Now he was the one to chuckle. At him! "You, who fancy yourself so smart. But your ego blinds you."

Sweeney did not like this at all. He knew no one would speak to him like this—if he had any intention of working with him in the future.

Fuentes continued. "Do you know why The Captain told Pike about his sister? To use an American phrase, it was a honey trap. We knew about Pike. Knew more than you, apparently. About his family. We knew if he discovered he had a sister, he would hunt for her relentlessly, just as he sought the truth about his father. And where would that investigation inevitably lead?"

Sweeney felt a cold chill spread across his body.

"To your little porno booths. A major new enterprise which you failed to mention to your business partners." Fuentes stepped even closer. "This cartel made you what you are. But you didn't mention this income stream to us. Didn't offer us a cut."

"It was a completely separate operation. An independent income stream."

"Yes, one that potentially threatened all the others. And us.

Your clumsiness put us at risk. So we hastened the inevitable discovery." He placed his hands on the edge of the desk and leaned forward. "To get you out of the way."

Sweeney's eyes narrowed. "What are you saying?"

"We are cutting you loose, Sweeney. You have done too much damage. You had your day, but now your incompetence has closed our primary operations and reduced us to shark-fin smuggling. As soon as I return to my office, we will cause certain records to be released. Records that will guarantee state and federal officials file criminal charges against you. You are going down."

Sweeney's jaw trembled. "If you do that, I'll turn state's evidence. I'll tell them everything."

"They won't make a deal with you. You're the big fish. They will make a deal with everyone here so they can nail you."

"I'll tell them about the cartel."

"They already know about the cartel. At least as it existed in the past. That is why we are making changes. Moving our operations elsewhere." He laughed again, right in Sweeney's face. "I predict you will die in prison before your case comes to trial."

Sweeney grabbed Fuentes' head and smashed it down on the desktop.

Fuentes was startled, but he reacted quickly. After a brief stagger, he leapt onto the desk and swung out with his left foot, trying to kick Sweeney in the jaw. He missed by inches.

Sweeney grabbed his leg and yanked hard, pulling Fuentes off the desk and onto the floor in a butt-first crash. For such a large man, Sweeney moved with surprising speed and strength. As soon as Fuentes hit the floor, Sweeney kicked him hard in the ribs.

Fuentes cried out, clutching his side. He rolled, just barely avoiding a follow-up kick. He managed to get onto his feet, but Sweeney pounced, throwing his arms around Fuentes and knocking the man back down to the ground. He shoved Fuentes flat and wrapped a stranglehold around his neck.

Sweeney looked up to see everyone else in the office staring at them, stunned, immobilized. They didn't know whether they should interfere, help, hurt, or run.

They were not going to be of any use.

He pulled hard on Fuentes' neck, hoping to snap it or strangle him, whichever happened first. Fuentes managed to jab an elbow backward into Sweeney's side. He loosened his grip and Fuentes made the most of it. He shook Sweeney off and crawled away, kicking Sweeney's grasping hands behind him.

"You tried to have me killed," Fuentes growled.

"This time I'll finish the job."

"And you killed Roberto. For no reason. You are a complete bastard. And a traitor."

Both men circled one another, poised like sumo wrestlers waiting for the fight to begin.

"You are history," Fuentes said, wiping the blood from his lips. "You might as well throw yourself out that window. It would be quicker."

"I had a different plan in mind."

Sweeney raced at him, hitting him hard and shoving him toward the floor-to-ceiling window. Sweeney knew they were composed of thick reinforced glass and, unlike what you saw in the movies, would not shatter easily.

Nonetheless, he felt certain he could muster the strength to do the job.

He pushed Fuentes as hard as he could, but somehow the man got a leg between his. He stumbled, fell off balance. That was all the advantage Fuentes needed.

He raised the flat of his hand and smashed it into Sweeney's face. Blood spurted everywhere. He could feel the pain. The man had damaged his nose, probably broken it.

Before Fuentes could retract his arm, Sweeney grabbed it

and wrenched it backward. Fuentes tumbled sideways, screaming.

Sweeney lifted the man's arm to his face and bit it. Hard.

Fuentes screamed even louder. He pulled his arm free, then hit Sweeney with a full-body tackle. He used Sweeney's weight against him, propelling him backward.

Sweeney hit the window hard, face first.

He felt the window crack under the strain. He could see the glass splinter.

Then he felt Fuentes' boot pressing against the small of his back.

"You are a little man," Fuentes growled. "And in a moment, you will be no man at all."

Sweeney clenched his eyes shut, waiting for the inevitable.

He heard a hollow thud followed by a grunting noise.

But he was still standing, still pressed against the window.

Then he heard a gunshot. Followed by a crash that shattered his ears.

He pushed backward, away from the shattered glass, trying to avoid being caught in the sudden suction.

Fuentes' bloody face stared at him and he plunged into the abyss, screaming.

Sweeney turned slowly. What had happened?

Prudence stood behind him, a blood-caked lamp in one hand, a pistol in the other.

Sweeney eventually found his tongue. "Thank you."

"No need," Prudence said. "Just doing my job. Are you hurt, sir?"

"Not seriously." He took out a handkerchief and wiped his bloody nose, then peered at the broken window. "But I think we're going to need to do some damage control..."

CHAPTER THIRTY-NINE

DAN PUT THE FINISHING SEASONING ON HIS FIVE-CHEESE tortellini. He wasn't sure how well Dinah tolerated spicy foods, so he went easy on the red chili flakes. The mushroom sauce, which involved sour cream and cream cheese and several other ingredients, would probably be sufficient to give it a robust flavor.

He smiled as he scooped helpings into bowls. He felt happy. He was happy.

And it had been a long time since that was true.

"Does he always cook like this?" Dinah asked Maria. The two women sat at the kitchen bar watching.

"Nope. Just when he's in a good mood."

"So that means...?"

Maria nodded. "Very."

Jimmy and Garrett joined them, grabbing bowls. They all took them into the living room to eat. Garrett pushed a few buttons and soon Mr. K was audible from the television monitor above the hearth.

"How's my team doing?" K asked. The happiness must be

infectious, Dan thought, because K sounded just as jubilant as he felt.

A chorus of positive responses answered.

"And how are you, Dinah?" Mr. K asked. "Are you finding the room upstairs satisfactory?"

"Compared to what I've had in the past, it's the Taj Mahal."

"I'm glad you're pleased."

Dinah looked from side to side. "Am I the only one who thinks it's weird to talk..."

"...to a disembodied voice?" Dan shrugged. "You get used to it."

"But...I don't know where to look when I talk to him."

"And the wonderful thing is—it doesn't matter."

"Fine. Mr. K, I'm really grateful. But I don't want to be a burden."

"Dinah, you stay as long as you like. We have plenty of room."

"You don't need the space?"

"Not unless we hire another lawyer. And we don't need another lawyer." He hesitated. "Though it occurred to me that a paralegal might be useful. Someone to help with the discovery and the paperwork. And you know, certification only takes six months."

Dinah turned toward her brother. "Is he telling me this for a reason?"

"Everything K does is for a reason."

She nodded. "I'll bear that in mind."

"By the way," K continued, "I made that contribution you requested, Dan."

"Thanks. You can take it out of my salary."

"No need. It's a good cause and I can use the tax deduction. But the point is...I think they'll be amenable to any suggestion you make."

Jimmy appeared clueless. "Am I supposed to understand this?"

"No," Dan replied.

"That's good."

K continued. "What happens next, team?"

"Well," Dinah said, "Dan says he's going to teach me to kite-surf."

"Are you excited about that?"

"Honestly? I don't even know what it means."

Maria placed a comforting hand on her shoulder. "It will be okay, dear. We've all done it. It's like a rite of passage here."

"That and playing Gloomhaven," Jimmy said, "which is far more fun. I see you as a warrior princess, Dinah."

She grinned. "I like the sound of that. Do I get to carry a sword?"

"And shield."

"And beat up bad guys?"

"In the game. Mostly orcs and ogres."

"Deal me in."

"What about you, Dan?" K said. "Other than kitesurfing. Any plans?"

"Yes." He stood, pulled Maria up, lifted her into the air, and kissed her as hard as he possibly could.

The kiss went on and on.

"Geez," Jimmy muttered. "Stop already. It's like watching Mom and Dad make out. Ick."

Dinah giggled. "Do they do that a lot?"

"No, thank God. Let's hope they don't start."

Maria pulled away, though she was still up in the air. "Okay, Casanova, stop."

"What? You didn't like it?"

A slow smile crept across her face. "I did. But...you know. Not in front of your sister."

"Of course."

"You know," Mr. K said, "for possibly the first time ever, I wish I were there to see what's going on."

"I'll send you a video," Jimmy answered, putting away his phone.

Maria whirled. "You made a video?"

"Just a little something for social media."

"Jimmy! Destroy that immediately."

"What's in it for me?"

"Dessert."

"Okay. Deleted."

"This has turned out very well," Mr. K said. "Very well indeed."

"Thanks to Dan," Garrett said.

Dan didn't know what to say. This—from Garrett? "I had lots of help."

"Don't minimize it," Garrett replied. "I know I've criticized you and the way you do things. But you've performed a great public service. You've made this town a better place to live."

"I was just...doing my job."

Garrett placed his hand on Dan's shoulder. "You've done much more than your job. You've done more than I would've imagined possible." He paused, drew in his breath, then spoke again. "Your father would be very proud of you."

DAN HAD THREE STOPS TO MAKE BEFORE THE DAY WAS DONE. Happily, Dinah agreed to accompany him.

First stop, the children's museum. It only took a few minutes to track down Beth Kramer. She was teaching some schoolkids about fungi. When she finished, they talked.

"Beth, you mentioned that you needed volunteers. I've brought you one. This is my sister, Dinah."

Beth's eyes widened. "Your sister? There are more like you?"

"As it turns out."

"Good. That will keep the city in line. Until you get around to having your kids."

"Wait a minute—"

Beth looked at Dinah. "Does he at least have a girlfriend?"

"Does he ever. Super-smoochies."

"That's a good start." She took Dinah's hand. "Glad to meet you. Do you like children?"

Dinah looked unsure. "I guess we're about to find out."

Beth laughed. "Fair enough."

"Dinah is thinking about taking some classes in the fall," Dan explained. "But I thought she'd like to have something to do till then. I can't think of anyone better to work with."

"You flatterer. And you're going to teach a cooking class this weekend, right?"

Dan tilted his head. "If you insist."

"I do. But bring Dinah. She looks like she could be a big help around her. And nothing personal, but she's way cuter than you."

Dinah blushed.

THE TRIP TO THE RESCUE POUND TOOK NO TIME AT ALL. PetSmart took even less. But it did take him a while to locate Mandy. Navigating the tunnels was more complicated than he remembered.

He found her nestled behind the unattached door in the tiny nook she called home.

He'd wanted this to be a surprise, but the animal started announcing himself the moment Dan knocked on the door.

Mandy pushed the door to the side, saw the puppy, and clapped her hands together. "You brought me a puppy?"

Dan handed the tiny chihuahua mix to her. "Rescue dog. He needs a home." And you need a friend.

She took the dog and cradled it close. "Aw. You remind me of my Bustopher."

"I know you can't replace someone you've lost but...I don't know. I hated to think of you living out here alone."

"It's not so bad. Storm didn't come." She lifted the puppy up and he licked her face. "Aww. We're going to be good friends."

"I'm certain of it. He's seen the vet, gotten his shots and whatnot. I brought you some food and water and doggie dishes. I'll check back with you to see how...you're both doing. And when you're ready to move, I know a place you could go."

"I don't want no charity." She pressed her nose against the puppy's. "I think we're going to be fine right here."

He hoped she would change her mind later. But maybe having someone to take care of would be the first step in her recovery. The next could be an indoor apartment.

"Did you find your sister?" Mandy asked.

"Sure did. I can never thank you enough for your help."

"You've done plenty. Does the dog have a name?"

"Nope. That's your job."

"Then I'm going to call him Dan. Is it all right with you?"

He twisted his neck. "Eeeh...if that's what you want."

"It is." Mandy's eyes sparkled. "This is the best thing you could possibly have done for me."

EPILOGUE

DAN MADE IT TO THE SENIOR-CARE CENTER JUST BEFORE FIVE. HE had hoped to bring Dinah, but she was still training at the children's museum, and this place would close to visitors at six. He would bring her next time.

Once he was in the room, he took a chair and stared at the resident. She looked much older than she was. She wore a comfortable dress that was basically a nightgown. Or hospital gown. Or pajamas. She was gray-haired and wrinkled, especially around the eyes.

And how well he knew those eyes.

She did not appear to recognize him. "What brings you here, mister?"

"It's Tuesday. I come every Tuesday."

"Well, that's fine then. I don't get many visitors." She had some crocheting in her lap but did not appear to have made much progress.

"Have you been outside? Lovely day. Not too hot, but warm enough."

"Mister, I live in Florida. Every day is a nice day."

Bit of an exaggeration, but he wasn't going to argue. He spotted a puzzle book at her feet. "Been doing the crossword?"

"Not so much," the woman said. "Anymore I find it hard to focus. I don't know why. Curiouser and curiouser. Used to love solving puzzles."

"Runs in the family. You get out of this room much?"

"Some. They have activities. I don't like the dancing. They play the music too loud. And I can't stand the Bingo. Stupidest game ever. Pure luck. Nothing to it."

Almost everything about her had changed...but some things would always remain the same. He leaned forward and took her hand.

"You're being a bit forward, mister."

"I know you don't remember this. But you're my mother. I'm your son."

"Nonsense. I have a son. But he never comes to see me."

"He does. You just don't remember."

"He got mad at me. Long time ago. They took my husband away, you know. Took him and locked him up and we had to find some way to survive without him. My son blamed me."

Dan's chin lowered. "I know I did."

"I didn't want my husband to do that. I was going to take care of it."

"You were going to get yourself thrown in prison." Dan paused. "He took care of you."

"I don't really remember it all. It's hard to remember anything these days."

He squeezed her hand tighter. "I know, Mom. But I'm going to keep visiting you, just the same. I want you to know—I'm sorry I was so bad to you when I was a stupid ignorant kid. I know you did the best you could."

"I tried to make it better," she said. "But sometimes your mistakes haunt you. Sometimes they just plain tear you apart."

"I know exactly what you mean." He scooted even closer and lowered his voice. "Mom, you can stop worrying about Dinah. I found her. She's safe. No one is ever going to mistreat Dinah again."

"Dinah. I love that name. Isn't that a pretty name?"

"It is. And let me tell you something else, Mom. Your husband loved you. More than you could ever know. He would've done anything for you. In fact—he gave up everything for you."

"I had a husband," she said. Her eyes seemed to retract. "He was a good man. I loved him."

"I know you did." He wrapped his arms around her and hugged her tight. "He loved you too, Mom. And so do I."

DAN'S RECIPES

Need a great Relationship Dish? Try Dan's Flatbread Not-Pizza. Only takes about 30 minutes to make.

Ingredients (for two servings):
   Flatbread (2)
   Zucchini (1)
   Grape or cherry tomatoes (4-6 oz.)
   Ricotta cheese (4 oz.)
   Lemon (1)
   Garlic (2-4 cloves)
   Honey
   Basil (fresh is always best)
   Chili flakes (or chili pepper)

Instructions:
   1) Preheat oven to 450 degrees. Halve the zucchini lengthwise, then slice into thin half moons. Halve the tomatoes. Mince the garlic. Zest the lemon, then quarter it.
   2) Heat a little olive oil in a large pan on medium-high heat.

When hot, add the zucchini and cook, stirring, for 5-6 minutes. Season to taste with kosher salt and pepper.

3) In a separate bowl, mix the tomatoes, garlic, and a little olive oil. Season to taste with salt and pepper.

4) In another small bowl, mix the ricotta, lemon juice, a little olive oil, and half your zest. Season to taste with salt and pepper.

5) Oil a baking sheet, then place the flatbreads on it. Spread with the ricotta. Top with zucchini and tomoatoes (cut sides up). Bake until golden brown, about 10 minutes.

6) Remove the flatbread from the oven and sprinkle with basil, the remaining zest, and chili flakes to taste. Drizzle with honey. Garnish with the lemon.

ABOUT THE AUTHOR

William Bernhardt is the author of over fifty books, including *The Last Chance Lawyer* (#1 National Bestseller), the historical novels *Challengers of the Dust* and *Nemesis*, two books of poetry, and the Red Sneaker books on writing. In addition, Bernhardt founded the Red Sneaker Writers Center to mentor aspiring authors. The Center hosts an annual conference (WriterCon), small-group seminars, a newsletter, and a bi-weekly podcast. He is also the owner of Balkan Press, which publishes poetry and fiction as well as the literary journal *Conclave*.

Bernhardt has received the Southern Writers Guild's Gold Medal Award, the Royden B. Davis Distinguished Author Award (University of Pennsylvania) and the H. Louise Cobb Distinguished Author Award (Oklahoma State), which is given "in recognition of an outstanding body of work that has profoundly influenced the way in which we understand ourselves and American society at large." In 2019, he received the Arrell Gibson Lifetime Achievement Award from the Oklahoma Center for the Book.

In addition Bernhardt has written plays, a musical (book and score), humor, children stories, biography, and puzzles. He has edited two anthologies (*Legal Briefs* and *Natural Suspect*) as fundraisers for The Nature Conservancy and the Children's Legal Defense Fund. In his spare time, he has enjoyed surfing, digging for dinosaurs, trekking through the Himalayas, paragliding, scuba diving, caving, zip-lining over the canopy of the Costa Rican rain forest, and jumping out of an airplane at 10,000 feet.

In 2017, when Bernhardt delivered the keynote address at the San Francisco Writers Conference, chairman Michael Larsen noted that in addition to penning novels, Bernhardt can "write a sonnet, play a sonata, plant a garden, try a lawsuit, teach a class, cook a gourmet meal, beat you at Scrabble, and work the *New York Times* crossword in under five minutes."

ALSO BY WILLIAM BERNHARDT

The Daniel Pike Novels

The Last Chance Lawyer

Court of Killers

Trial by Blood

Twisted Justice

Judge and Jury

Final Verdict

The Ben Kincaid Novels

Primary Justice

Blind Justice

Deadly Justice

Perfect Justice

Cruel Justice

Naked Justice

Extreme Justice

Dark Justice

Silent Justice

Murder One

Criminal Intent

Death Row

Hate Crime

Capitol Murder

Capitol Threat

Capitol Conspiracy

Capitol Offense

Capitol Betrayal

Justice Returns

Other Novels

Challengers of the Dust

The Game Master

Nemesis: The Final Case of Eliot Ness

Dark Eye

Strip Search

Double Jeopardy

The Midnight Before Christmas

Final Round

The Code of Buddyhood

The Red Sneaker Series on Writing

Story Structure: The Key to Successful Fiction

Creating Character: Bringing Your Story to Life

Perfecting Plot: Charting the Hero's Journey

Dynamic Dialogue: Letting Your Story Speak

Sizzling Style: Every Word Matters

Powerful Premise: Writing the Irresistible

Excellent Editing: The Writing Process

Thinking Theme: The Heart of the Matter

What Writers Need to Know: Essential Topics

Dazzling Description: Painting the Perfect Picture

The Fundamentals of Fiction (video series)

Poetry

The White Bird

The Ocean's Edge

For Young Readers

Shine

Princess Alice and the Dreadful Dragon

Equal Justice: The Courage of Ada Sipuel

The Black Sentry

Edited by William Bernhardt

Legal Briefs: Short Stories by Today's Best Thriller Writers

Natural Suspect: A Collaborative Novel of Suspense